The Truth About Irene

Also by Suzie Peace Pybus

When All The Birds Sing
Paint the Walls Red

The Truth About Irene

SUZIE PEACE PYBUS

Echidna Ink

I acknowledge and pay my respects to
the Moomairremener people of Unghanyenna country
on whose unceded land this book was written.

Editing by Lynne Lloyd: lloydmosspublishing.com

Cover design, title pages and butterfly illustration by Jennifer Magno: jennifermagno.com

ISBN: 978-1-7636992-2-9 (print)
ISBN: 978-1-7636992-3-6 (ebook)

For Mum and Dad
for being my loudest cheer squad

There are more things in heaven and earth, Horatio,
Than are dreamt of in your philosophy.
—Shakespeare, Hamlet, Act 1 Scene 5

PART ONE

IRENE 2014

The trousers go first, all twenty-eight pairs. Irene folds them—jeans, Country Road casuals, overalls, dress pants and a dozen pairs of shorts. She even re-irons the dress pants (never let it be whispered that Irene Blackford's husband's trousers are crinkled). She packs them into two cardboard boxes which she sets on the front seat of the ute. She swings herself in, tucks her skirt neatly under her backside and drives to the local op shop.

Irene carries one box to the door, balancing it carefully with one arm while fumbling the door handle with the other. She pushes the door open with her hip and steps inside. Seeing no one, she weaves her way around the racks of clothes and sets the box on top of the crowded counter, shifting a basket of dusty knick-knacks to make room.

Irene is heading back to the door when she spies a flash of orange from the corner of her eye. She turns briefly to see Bea clipping towards her from the other end of the shop, one hand holding onto her hennaed up-do as if it might fall off.

'Some of Bill's things,' Irene calls, gesturing at the counter. She strides back out the door, stopping to click the locking gear in place so it will stay open.

By the time Irene re-enters the shop carrying the other box, Bea has disappeared, evidently unaware Irene is coming back. Irene is about to make her way to the counter when voices float over a perforated hard-board stand displaying headscarves and tarnished costume jewellery.

'...and the dirt barely settled on his grave.'

'I s'pose everyone grieves in their own way.'

Irene spins around and marches back out the door. She returns the box to the front seat of the ute, throws herself in, turns on the engine and reverses, skidding the tyres in the gravel.

'Stuff you,' she mutters as she drives out of the parking area. 'And stuff you too, Freda,' she says as she drives down the main road.

Other words are jostling about in Irene's head. Words she's never said in her life. Irene wants to say them. In fact, they're simply itching to be said.

'Stuff it,' she growls as she turns in through the farm gate, forcing the other more ugly words back down her throat.

She drives over the cattle grid and pulls up outside the house on the edge of the property, leaving the box on the seat of the ute. Next week, she'll take it into Hobart when she goes in for her appointments. The city people can have Bill's clothes.

She unlocks the front door, checks the security keys and goes into the kitchen to put the kettle on. While it heats up, she slumps into a seat at the dining table and wonders what to have for dinner. Probably toast as anything else feels too hard. The oven clock is flashing, indi-cating a recent power failure. The power is always going off.

'Stuff you too,' she says wearily to the oven clock, and presses her face in her hands.

It was Helen's idea.

'Start sorting Dad's stuff out, Mum. It'll make you feel better,' Helen had said, standing there in Irene's kitchen in her sensible shoes. Helen was altogether sensible. Practical skirt. Pursed lips. Dark hair cut perfectly straight at the shoulders. Sometimes Irene feels like a child around Helen.

Irene had started sorting and Helen was right, she did feel better. Accomplished, even. Like in the days before the big house with the fancy kitchen.

Irene takes her tea into the living room and stands at the long wall of windows, looking across the cow paddocks and up into the hills. It's a grand view. Their own little paradise in a remote part of Tasmania, away from the city bustle. Well, just hers now that Bill is gone.

Just over the hill lies Crayfish Cove, the fishing and farming village that has been Irene's hometown for most of her life. From her vantage point, she can see a tiny patch of the sea—sometimes blue, sometimes grey-green or white with froth, depending on the weather.

The house faces away from the main industry of the dairy farm, but from the corner window the glinting metal roofs of the milking sheds can be seen. In the middle distance, the roof of the original farmhouse juts up from behind a hillock, smoke pouring from its chimney. Sing will be in the old kitchen now, preparing dinner, waiting for Irene's son to come in from the milking. Irene pictures her daughter-in-law—small-boned and fragile as a child. Caleb broad-shouldered and tough like his father. Another worry for Irene.

Breathe in for four, hold for eight, let it out slowly. Repeat.

Irene sets her empty cup on its saucer and watches a magpie pulling a worm from the grass beside the verandah. Its baby peeps behind it, mouth open, impatient.

Well. She has started, she may as well keep going.

Irene returns to the huge bedroom with the plush rose-pink carpet and another wall of windows, and opens the walk-in wardrobe. Light filters in through a skylight, illuminating the neatly hanging clothes. She lifts one of Bill's shirts by its hanger—white with fine blue stripes—and runs her fingers down the brushed cotton. It's one of her favourites. She holds it against herself and looks into the mirror hanging on the back of the wardrobe door.

Ugh, what has happened to her? She re-hangs the shirt and takes another look in the mirror. Her long, chestnut-auburn hair could do with a wash. She bends her head to inspect the roots where her hair parts. Huh, barely sixty and already white. Not salt-and-pepper either but actual blaring marshmallow-white. Time to make an appointment with Zola.

Irene lifts her heavy hair in both hands, twists it behind her head and holds it there. Her chestnut mane, Bill had called it, which always made Irene think of a horse. Mischief stirs in her abdomen.

In a drawer in the main bathroom, Irene finds her trimming scissors. She stands in front of the mirror, takes a length of her hair and snips. She takes another lock and snips again. And again. Snip...snip...snip... Irene drops each handful of hair into the bathroom sink. The left side is shorter than the right now. Snip...snip...snip...

Something happens inside Irene. A boundary has been crossed. Her grandmother's words come back to her—*May as well be hung for a sheep as a lamb.* Irene keeps snipping.

The sink overflows with a cloud of auburn hair and Irene's head is... Well, it's light. *Irene* is light. As if she's lost a few kilos or grown wings that lift her off the ground a teensy bit.

She turns her head this way and that, inspecting her handiwork in the mirror. A bit more off here... an adjustment there... She chuckles. Definitely an Annie Lennox thing happening here.

The new look doesn't go with the plaid skirt though. Irene returns to the wardrobe, strips down to her underwear and pulls on a pair of black jeans. She takes down Bill's white shirt with the fine stripes and puts it on. Searches for a jacket. Bill's black suit jacket with the narrow lapels is perfect. All she needs now is some music.

Irene slips a Eurythmics CD into the player in the living room and turns up the volume. The music (somehow) jumps from the CD player to a small speaker sitting on a shelf in her bedroom. Something Helen set up.

Annie Lennox's voice fills the room. Irene stands in front of the floor-to-ceiling mirror attached to the bedroom wall. She joins her voice with Annie's and belts out *Sweet Dreams (Are Made Of This)*, moving her body with the beat.

Walk forward, tilt the shoulders, a twirl of the hands, little shimmy to the right. Who is the mysterious woman in the mirror with the white pixie cut and perky auburn tips? She leans forward and pouts, turns her head seductively to lock eyes with her reflection.

Irene sings, twirls, shimmies, throws her arms into the air...

'Mum!'

Irene turns.

Helen stands in the doorway, mouth frozen open in shock.

Irene's arms fall to her sides.

Helen shoots forward, staring at Irene's head. 'What have you done?'

Irene looks in the mirror. What *has* she done?

Helen lifts Bill's jacket from Irene's shoulders and slips it off. 'Are you alright? Your hair! And that's Dad's jacket.'

'Of course I'm alright.' Irene keeps staring into the mirror. Is she alright? There's an old, dishevelled woman in the glass, staring back. Shaggy hair, over-sized man's shirt hanging limp from her shoulders. She looks like she might be homeless.

As Helen stands there, holding Bill's jacket and gaping at her, the song on the CD ends and another begins. Helen clicks her tongue, lays the jacket on a chair and goes out to turn the music off.

'Are you sure you're okay, Mum?' she asks when she returns. 'I mean, why would you cut off your hair?'

'It got heavy, that's all.' Irene puts her hand to her head and feels her scalp through the little hair she has left.

'I'll make an appointment with Zola for you.' Helen slumps down on the edge of Irene's bed and pulls her mobile phone from her cardigan pocket.

'I can do that,' Irene says.

'Are you sure?'

Irene folds her arms. 'I'm not an invalid, Helen.'

'Fine.' Helen rises from the bed and gives Irene a look. 'I brought you some soup. I'll go and put it in the fridge. You just—I don't know—get dressed.'

Light flicks in through the windows as the clouds shift away from the sun. Irene looks out as it drapes itself across the paddocks.

'Look at that,' she says.

Helen barely stifles a sigh behind her. 'What?'

'The sun on the grass. Can you see that? It's like a blanket of sequins. And look—the paddocks, the hills, the lovely gum trees.' Irene moves closer to the glass. 'It's beautiful. Why didn't he put a door here somewhere? A sliding one, or French windows or something. Have you ever wondered that?'

'It's a bedroom, Mum. Look, I have to pick Poppy up from school soon, so—'

'Yes, alright.' Irene turns to smile at her daughter. 'Thanks for bringing the soup, it was very kind.'

As Helen leaves, Irene turns back to the window. Bill had insisted on bare windows with no dressings. No need, he said, out here with just the cows and not another house for miles (besides the original farmhouse). But Irene feels exposed at night as if there are eyes out there peering in at her. And in the daytime, there's the tantalising view through the windows and no door to access it.

Irene places her hand on the thick glass and watches the magpies wheeling overhead. The weeks, months, years roll out before her like the undulating hills outside the window. She takes a deep breath and holds it as she imagines all those years alone.

Irene slides out of the ute, locks the door and looks towards the hair salon. She sees her hairdresser through the window, moving between her clients. Gorgeous Zola with her deep brown skin, her head piled with dozens of tiny, meticulously-woven plaits. What will she say when she sees the remains of Irene's hair sticking out in awful tufts?

Irene wraps her grey cardigan around herself, pulls its hood over her head, and ventures towards the building. The bell jangles on the door as she opens it and steps inside.

Zola turns and smiles. 'Here you are, my friend.'

Irene lifts the hood of her cardigan and lets it slip to her shoulders.

Zola freezes. Her smile slips. She peers at Irene for a few moments before lifting her chin.

'I can fix that,' she says.

Irene sinks gratefully into the salon chair and waits until Zola is ready for her. The hairdresser wheels a trolley up beside Irene, drapes a cape over her shoulders and says, 'Alright darling, I'm all yours. How shall we proceed, eh?'

Irene glances apologetically at Zola in the mirror. 'Don't you want to know why I did it?'

Zola smiles, showing her perfectly white teeth. 'You're a woman. You do what you need to do. You need to cut your hair, you cut your hair.' She jerks her head to the side and frowns. 'Sometimes it might not be the best idea, but you have Zola to fix your mistakes.'

She stands behind Irene, places both hands on either side of her head and studies her in the mirror. 'May I make a suggestion?'

'Please do.' Irene has trusted Zola with her hair for many years and has no doubt she'll know what to do with this latest dilemma.

Zola nods thoughtfully. 'No more auburn, I think. How about something more sophisticated for the next stage of your wonderful life? Perhaps a silver pixie cut with a little colour at the ends?'

Irene grins. 'Why not?'

Zola cuts, paints, foils and makes coffee. Irene's shoulders relax into the chair as she enjoys the soothing ministrations. When the hairdresser leaves her with a head of foils and a magazine, Irene glances about the salon at the other patrons. There's only one face she recognises—a young woman who works at the bakery here in Durrunby. Such a contrast to Crayfish Cove where Irene lives. There, every face is someone you know with the occasional stranger thrown in.

Irene hasn't been into Durrunby since Bill died. It's a quaint town with a meandering river cutting through its centre, stone bridges, convict-built cottages, picturesque parks and arty shops. Lately attracting more retirees and tree-changers from the city, especially creative types—painters, writers, sculptors, poets. What would it be like to live here in a little cottage nestled amongst the shops? Or tucked away in the trees by the river but close enough to join the bustle when one felt like it? It isn't the first time Irene has had such thoughts.

A laughing couple wander hand-in-hand past the window of the salon and Irene watches their reflection in the mirror. The woman stops to bend over and fix her heel strap. As she stands, her companion wraps his arm around her shoulders and they lean into each other as they go on their way. An ache starts in Irene's chest. Her life is being squeezed into a new shape now, pummelled and scraped into something she isn't sure about. Though it has been three months since Bill's death, still she struggles to emerge from the fog of her grief.

A buzzer sounds and Zola hurries back to Irene's side. 'Ready to see some magic?' she says as she starts to unwrap the foils. After a wash and blow-dry, Irene and Zola admire Irene's reflection together.

'What do you think?' Zola asks. 'Magic, yes?'

Irene can hardly believe it is herself she sees in the mirror. She puts her hand to the side of her head and brushes the tips of her hair with her fingers.

Zola laughs. 'What did I tell you? I knew you were in there somewhere, my lovely.'

Irene smiles at the beautiful woman in the mirror. The one with the silver pixie cut with light pink highlights. A butterfly emerging from a cocoon. She nods.

'*There* I am,' she says.

Irene again contemplates her reflection in the floor-to-ceiling mirror. The homeless person is gone, replaced by a confident-looking woman in denim jeans and a black T-shirt, bare feet, painted toenails. And a stunning new haircut.

The cut is similar to a wig she used to own—a short, red one. Back in the days when the big decision for the day was which wig to wear. *Do I feel like a blonde or a redhead today?*

Irene strokes her silver hair with the pink tips. Like newly sprouted feathers. What a strange metaphor to pop into her head. She thinks of a scarf she sewed years ago from a piece of fabric she'd loved—sky blue with a pattern of butterflies, their wings in flight. That scarf had power, helping her to hold onto her dignity when she lost her hair with the chemo and, later, both breasts. She'd worn the scarf all spring, until it vanished.

Irene clenches her hands by her sides. *Breathe in for four, hold for eight, let it out slowly. Repeat.*

She looks down at the discarded pile of Bill's clothes at her feet—shirts, jackets, overcoat, belts, shoes. A ridiculous number of garments. Bill was never one for throwing things out. Having pulled Bill's clothes off the hangers, she can get a better look at her own and starts taking down some of her clothes and dropping them into another pile—dresses, skirts, blouses, cardigans. If she's going to declutter, she may as well do it properly.

Soon she has another mound of clothes at her feet, a veritable garden of florals in pinks, purples and greens. Many of them Bill had bought for her. She feels a pang of guilt but pushes it down. Some of these clothes she hasn't worn in years. Most of them, if she's honest, she doesn't even like.

Irene regards herself in the mirror again. There is something of her younger self in the reflection. A certain luminance, as if the discarding of unnecessary things—hair, clothes, possessions—has unearthed something long buried.

Reaching her hand down the front of her shirt, she removes her knitted bra-stuffers and drops them onto the pile of discarded clothes. They can go too. Itchy things, she's sick of them. She stands motionless for a moment—steeling herself—before pulling off her T-shirt and bra.

Irene studies her scars in the mirror. It has taken a long time to accept her altered body. To recognise the beauty in it, the strange, unfamiliar lines. To stop seeing them as reminders of trauma and embrace them as evidence of a battle fought and won.

She runs her fingertips across her flattened chest and down the sides of her body. Her torso appears as an unfinished sculpture in pale, mottled clay. As if the artist has paused mid-creation to ponder their next move. To decide where the beauty lay and how to reveal it.

The question of breast reconstruction surgery had come up, but she'd never felt ready. And now the pressure is gone. She pulls her shirt back on, minus the knitted bra-stuffers. She is a new creature. One with wings.

Irene leaves the mounds of clothes on the floor and exits the walk-in-robe. Tomorrow is Saturday and Helen will be over to help her finish the bedroom. The drawers and cupboards are still full of Bill's belongings. How had the man collected so much stuff?

The collecting had started after he'd retired and handed the dairy farm over to Caleb. He developed a sudden fancy for dress shirts, silk ties and leather shoes. Then came the golf clubs, books, small painted landscapes and odd pieces of pottery. Recently, he'd started collecting old coins. Then, in the middle of all this collecting, his new lease on life, he'd died. Keeled over on the grass, in the middle of a cow paddock.

Irene turns to look through the bedroom window. Just out there. She saw him fall like a felled tree through the thick glass.

Irene goes to Bill's side of the bed, sits down and opens the drawer where his pyjamas are kept. She takes out a top and holds it to her face. The flannelette, soft on her cheek, retains a faint smell of him. She closes her eyes and tries to conjure his face, but the memory is clouded.

Irene doesn't cry. She cried at first—one big, short fountain. A sudden flood and an equally sudden drying up. Ever since, she has been stuck in a numb space.

A weariness envelops her as she thinks about tomorrow. Her daughter will be here early, armed with garbage bags and determination. Helen will be thorough.

Irene glances about the room. Yes, she does feel ready to sort everything properly. But there are things Helen needn't know. Not yet. Irene pulls open the bottom drawer of the tallboy and dips her hands under her winter woollens until her fingers find the spiral-bound notebook. She takes it out and goes into the yellow room—named for the cheerful daisy coverlet on the spare bed.

Under the bed is a camphor wood chest. She pulls it out and lifts the lid. Moving a pile of fabric aside, she slips the notebook underneath with the others, covers them back over with the fabric, closes the lid and slides the chest back beneath the bed.

There, now she's ready for Helen.

HELEN 2024

Helen holds her mother's shirt to her face and breathes in her lingering scent. The past roars up like a wave. She wipes her eyes with the soft, cotton fabric and lays it back on the sofa.

She stands, arms by her sides, looking about the living room in her mother's tiny flat. White. Neat. Sparse. The bare bones of a life. Yet, it's a welcoming space despite the lack of clutter. There's a crocheted blanket draped across an armchair, photo albums and board games stacked in the bookcase. One of Sing's ceramic creations stands on a shelf—an odd woman with a bent back. Helen never did understand it.

It won't take long to pack up the rest of her mother's stuff and clean the place. Such a contrast to the farmhouse where Helen and Caleb grew up and the big house their parents had occupied for the final ten years of their life together. Those homes were places where things accumulated. Rooms filled with stuff, with life.

Helen picks up her bucket, takes it to the kitchen sink and fills it with water and detergent. Last weekend, she and Pete cleared out the kitchen and bathroom cupboards and all they need now is a wipe down. She gets to work.

The kitchen and bathroom combined take less than an hour. Tomorrow, Caleb will bring a truck and they'll move the few bits of furniture out.

Now only the bedroom remains. Helen has avoided her mother's bedroom. Such an intimate space. It tends to make her cry when she'd really rather not. Crying takes up too much time and plays havoc with your make-up. Helen prefers to get on with life, one foot in front of the other at a steady trot. Things like this... well.

Helen decides to rest for a few minutes. She unlocks the sliding door to the deck, steps out and sinks into a chair. It's peaceful out here, a different kind of peace to the farm. The deck overlooks a tranquil section of the river overhung with willows. Her mother used to sit here for hours listening to the burbling river and children playing in the park on the other side of the trees.

Helen still didn't understand why her mother moved here. Why she had been so determined to leave the farm and everything behind. She hadn't even finished cleaning out Dad's stuff. But over time, especially on the days the two of them sat out here together, Helen had witnessed her mother unwinding like a spring. She hadn't even realised her mother had been wound up. How she berated herself for that. It was only after Irene's cheeks started turning pink and the angles of her body filled out that Helen recognised a healing taking place. Healing from what? Helen still doesn't know.

Best get on. She stands and goes back into the living room. There's the wooden chest her mother used as a coffee table. She remembers, a long time ago, Irene pulling out folds of fabric from its depths, ready to sew. All those scarves and bags and belts. Helen thinks of that time as her mother's heyday, when her business was booming. She could barely keep up with demand for her upcycled pieces, constantly zipping up and down between home and the city, glowing with energy. Until the cancer happened.

In the new house Helen's parents built, the wooden chest was kept in the yellow room. Helen wonders again why her mother chose to bring it to the flat. The actual coffee table would have suited this space well enough. She kneels on the floor, flicks the catch and opens the lid. Inside she finds some blankets and a few pieces of fabric. Closing the lid, she decides to have a better look when she and Pete take it back to the house. The bedroom can't be put off any longer.

Helen braces herself and opens the door. The bed is draped over with the old sunflower coverlet, an indent in the middle as if her mother has just been sitting there. Helen's breath catches in her chest.

She ventures in, slides the door of the built-in-robe across and scans the space. There's hardly anything in it. Three men's shirts, one black jacket, a pair of brogues.

Oh Mum.

Helen slides the door closed, sits on the edge of her mother's bed and buries her face in her hands.

No sooner does Irene hear Helen's car pull up to the house than seven-year-old Poppy's voice carries through the front door—'Reenie. Where are you, Reenie?' Her little feet clatter up the hallway.

'In here, monkey.' Irene is kneeling on the floor, folding a pile of Bill's shirts into a neat pile.

Poppy bounds through the bedroom door, flops down next to Irene and gazes at her head. 'Reenie, you look beautiful. You've got fairy-godmother hair.'

Helen stops short at the bedroom door and gapes. 'Wow, it suits you. Whose idea was the pink?'

'Zola's. I like it.'

'It looks great.'

'Mummy, I want hair like Reenie's.'

'Darling, you have beautiful hair,' Irene says. She reaches out to stroke her granddaughter's long, straight brown hair from which her ears poke out at right angles. Poppy's ears had prompted Bill to nickname her monkey and the name had stuck.

'I've come to help you sort out Granddaddy's stuff.'

'How are you going with it?' Helen kneels beside Irene and picks up a shirt.

'This is the easy part. The office will be the challenge, all those books.'

'Maybe we should box them up without looking at them, and send them to Bea's.'

'Pah! I'm not taking anything else to those gossips. I'll take them into Hobart next week. I have to go in and sort my bank cards anyway.'

Another job to be done. The thought is like a deadweight pressing on her, as are all the other tasks jostling for space on her to-do list. There are too many. Irene's list is growing quicker than she can mark things off. Every time she has to add something to it, it lands thick in her chest and sucks a bit more energy out of her. Some days it's like pushing through quicksand. This is normal, her doctor assures her. She's still processing her grief and learning to trust her new circumstances. Her energy will return in time.

'Don't forget what I told you,' Helen says as she lifts another shirt from the pile. 'Make your appointments on a Tuesday and I can take you in.'

'I know, thanks.' The truth is, Irene prefers to drive to town alone in the ute with the windows down and her thoughts to herself. But this, she doesn't say.

Helen folds meticulously, lining up the shirt sides and pressing the fabric down with her hands between each fold. The shirts look like they have just been taken new from a package. She places the one she has finished folding on top of Irene's growing pile and pushes herself up from the floor.

'Anything left in here?' she asks as she wanders into the walk-in-robe. 'What's this, are you cleaning out your stuff too?'

'Yes, take what you want.'

'Your green dress? That was Dad's favourite.'

Irene clicks her tongue. 'And the last place I wore it was his funeral.'

'You could make a scarf out of it.'

Irene studies the purple shirt in her hands which would also make a lovely scarf. In fact, there's enough fabric in Bill's shirts and silk ties to make dozens of scarves. She could start up her business again. *Irene Flower: Fashion Accessories from Repurposed Fabric.* Upcycling, they called it nowadays. She'd sold well in some of the city shops and made a name for herself. Perhaps that shop in Durrunby, Artful Earth, would sell her creations on consignment.

But there is no excitement stirring in her chest. No desire to plan and cut and sew. All the running up and down from the city. Irene is too tired for that.

She folds the shirt and places it on the pile. Poppy watches and mimics her, and together they finish the job. Helen has brought the anticipated roll of garbage bags and starts tearing them off and filling them with clothes. Soon there are five filled bags lined up against the wall.

'What's in here?' Helen opens the drawer of a small cupboard.

'That's your father's.'

'What, the whole cupboard?'

Poppy helps her mother lift the drawers out and turn them upside down on the carpet. They do the same with the contents of the plastic tubs from inside the cupboard. Helen tips one tub cautiously on its side to empty a collection of glass jars.

Poppy scoots over on her knees to investigate. She lifts each jar in turn to inspect the contents. 'Marbles. Oh, look at this one. What's in it?'

'Matchbooks,' Irene says. 'Your granddad collected them from hotels and souvenir shops. See, each one has the name of where it came from.'

Helen looks up. 'Gosh, I haven't seen a matchbook in years. Hard to believe nearly everyone smoked once.'

'You mean, like, cigarettes?' Poppy pulls a face.

'Hey, look at this.' Helen holds up a bunch of envelopes, slightly yellowed and tied up with a ribbon. 'Secret love letters?'

'Huh. I thought we'd lost those. We used to write to each other in our courting days.'

'Dad kept them. How romantic.' Helen passes them to Irene, who sets them beside her on the floor.

As they sort through the stuff from the cupboard, they make separate piles—keep, donate, discard. There are books, packs of playing cards, a few loose screws, old neckties, empty cardboard pill packets and toffee wrappers.

Poppy tips a jar of coins out onto the floor and lies on her stomach to inspect them. Helen leaves the room to find some cardboard packing boxes and Irene continues to look through an assortment of eye-glass cases. She had tried to convince Bill to donate the glasses but he could never seem to part with them. She opens the cases one by one and checks each pair of spectacles. They look sound. She's heard the community centre in Durrunby collects them for charity.

As Helen wrestles three packing boxes through the door, Irene spies something glittering amongst the mess on the floor. She reaches over to pick it up. Poppy giggles, says something about a funny picture on a coin, but Irene barely hears. In her hand is a gold ring set with a red garnet. She recognises it instantly and puts it in her pocket.

By late afternoon, they've finished sorting the main bedroom. Bill's clothes have been neatly folded into bags and cardboard boxes, along with some of his collections, and stashed in the shed. Irene will take them into Hobart next week in the ute.

Helen and Poppy climb into their Toyota, Poppy clutching a small box of her grandfather's belongings—a paperweight, a jar of marbles and a collection of foreign coins—and they wave goodbye.

As the car disappears into the main road, Irene takes the garnet ring from her jeans' pocket and holds it up to the light. It had been her grandmother's. Not valuable in a monetary sense, but something she'd treasured.

'You've misplaced it,' she was told. As she'd misplaced many other things.

She takes the ring into the bedroom and puts it in her jewellery box where it will be safe. The ribbon-wrapped letters, she places in one of Bill's empty drawers. To think of all the time she'd spent searching for those. She should have insisted on a big cleanout a long time ago.

The bedroom is very neat. After sorting, Helen had dusted and vac-uumed and straightened the furniture—working methodically, saying little. Sometimes it was best just to let Helen do her thing.

Though most of Bill's belongings are gone, Bill is still here. In an antique clock on top of the dresser and a leadlight lamp on his bedside table. In the absence of curtains and the thick glass windows. Irene wraps her arms about herself and surveys the room.

'Too big.'

She speaks the words aloud and they echo strangely off the walls. A new emptiness. The walls so far apart, yet closing in on her. Outside, the sun is already heading below the treetops and casting imposing shadows across the paddocks. Aloneness creeps over her. She is a small person alone in a large house and she hates it.

There, she has admitted it. She hates it here. She hates this room and the mass of glass with no way out. Damn you, Bill. Why did you have to go and die right outside the bedroom window?

Irene gathers her nightclothes, underwear, tomorrow's clothes and her bedside clock and takes them into the yellow room. She opens a drawer in her sewing cabinet, moves the few things into a space in another drawer, replacing them with her clothes. Next, she sets her clock on top of the bedside table.

That evening, Irene climbs into the bed in the yellow room. She will sleep in here from now on beneath the daisy coverlet. Tomorrow she will wake up as usual with the day opening up before her like a gaping yawn, the hours stretched out. She'd had plenty to fill them once, in the period of life she remembers as a burst of confident colour. Before cancer came calling.

Irene thinks about it as she lies there, eyelids fluttering. If she's honest, something had gone awry long before the cancer. A long and drawn-out slipping away. Was it right to have kept her secrets?

Her eyelids droop and close. She has ideas about how she will fill her days from now on. She is healthy, strong, intelligent, creative. Tomorrow, she'll start planning.

With this thought half-formed, Irene drops into the soundest sleep she's had in a very long time.

HELEN 2024

The flowers on the grave have wilted. Helen tips up the vase to empty it and refills it with water from her drink bottle and a bunch of marigolds she's brought with her. She fusses with their arrangement. Why they remind her of the pretty heads of small children, she couldn't say. Strange thoughts have been sliding into her head since her mother's death.

She'll never get over it, she's convinced of that. Who knew being orphaned at her age would feel like this? That it would rattle her bones and turn her innards to mush. Oh, why couldn't she have broken herself open and said all the things she should have said. The kind words she hadn't thought to utter, now bursting into her consciousness like newly-formed buds. As if they had lain dormant like seeds inside her until brought to life by the very tragedy that rendered their blossom too late. She can never say them now.

Helen refuses to cry in public. She could easily crumple, sprawl her body over her mother's grave and sob fat tears into the earth. But she won't. She's a school teacher in a small community, a model of good manners and respectability.

Tears slip uninvited down her cheeks. She has cried and cried copious tears already, you'd think she'd have emptied herself. But still those blasted things come, sometimes at the most inconvenient times. In the supermarket as she picks up a cheese her mother liked. In the middle of a class so she has to dip her head and pretend to be immersed in marking someone's awful assignment.

Helen stands before the gravestone with her hands clasped. She can't bring herself to speak out loud in the cemetery, but she speaks to her mother silently inside her own head. Tells her everything she wishes she'd said when she was alive. Helen hopes her mother hears her now, wherever she is.

But that's the trouble, Helen doesn't know where she is. Whether she exists only as disintegrating flesh and bone, or has somehow connected with the God she talked about in her later years. Helen shudders at the memory of her mother's body in the funeral parlour—the lifeless shell already beginning to decay, sinking in on itself, closing the space once inhabited by its vital life.

Where has she gone? Helen won't—can't—believe her mother no longer exists at all. Irene could no more cease to exist than Helen could turn herself into a cat. Her spirit was something too precious, too solid, too wild to slip away into nothing.

Oh, why this terrible grief? She hadn't felt like this when her father died. Sad, yes, but not this wretched squeezing as if her own life were ebbing out of her.

Bill's body lies next to Irene in the soil, his bones devoid of the flesh which has long since rotted into the ground. A renewal in a sense. Irene's body will also be renewed in this way and that's something, at least.

A sob escapes Helen's lips. She bites them shut and clenches the feeling in. Her body quivers and she hopes no one has witnessed it. Holding her shoulders rigid, she lifts her head and turns towards the gate.

IRENE 2014

Irene has the distinct impression she's asked a stupid question.

'Uh—' The bank clerk behind the desk tilts her head to the side and scratches her cheek. 'No, that's your everyday account, Irene. It's separate, do you see?'

The clerk points to the computer screen, which is swivelled around so Irene, sitting on the other side of the desk, can see. Across the top of the screen are the words *Good morning Irene,* which is disconcerting in itself. Beneath the greeting are numbers and geometric symbols. Irene puts her hand to her chest where a familiar fluttering begins, and takes a deep breath.

The clerk peers at Irene, her forehead crinkled. 'Would you like me to write this down?'

'Yes please. Just the steps for getting into the accounts.'

'Of course.' The clerk writes on a sheet of paper. 'This is your client number—'

'Where do I put that?'

'On the bank homepage. Remember I showed you?'

Irene leans forward. 'How do I find the bank?'

'Type this into your browser—'

'That's the bit at the top when I'm on the internet, isn't it?'

The clerk looks up and blinks at Irene. 'Um, yes. Irene, do you have someone who can help you with this?'

Irene nods. 'My daughter.'

'Ah, good.' The clerk appears relieved. She finishes writing and hands the piece of paper to Irene. 'Everything's set up. You'll receive your cards in the mail and the letter will explain how to activate them. Any questions?'

Irene is full of questions. But nothing she wants to ask this young woman who oozes competency and looks about a third of Irene's age.

'I'm sure I'll figure it out.' Irene gives the clerk what she hopes is a confident smile.

'Goodbye Irene. And again, I'm sorry for your loss.'

Outside the bank, the city of Hobart is all abustle. Engines roar, cars honk, pedestrians weave their frantic dance along the footpath. Irene stands beneath the eaves of the bank building, gathering herself. Figures dance in her head. Large figures. Irene had no idea of the extent of their savings. She thrusts her hands into the pockets of her coat and decides not to think about that for the time being. At least she won't have to worry about money. That's something.

She's completed most of her errands—delivered the boxes and bags to an op shop, filled her prescriptions at the pharmacy, sorted out her internet banking. With an hour to spare until her next appointment, she goes for a wander down a shopping arcade crammed with fashion stores. You didn't find these kinds of shops in Crayfish Cove. Not even in Durrunby, despite the influx of resident creative types.

Irene inspects the window displays. Frayed denim, faux fur, designer sneakers and mod boots, jumpsuits, crop tops, bomber jackets. She sighs and keeps moving. A boutique specialising in fashionwear for older women showcases skirts and blouses in various shades of fawn and peach. Irene passes these by without a second glance.

A profusion of rich colours catches her eye and she's drawn to a row of shirts hanging outside a store. Vivid blues, greens, purples, white with bold stripes. She looks up at the sign above the door and recognises it as a popular menswear store.

Irene sidles up to the rack and flips through the hangers, admiring the patterns, feeling the fabric between her fingers. She looks into the store and sees more racks of lovely shirts. She edges her way in and up to a rack of floral prints.

What an array of colours and patterns—from tiny periwinkles and baby's breath to bold hibiscus flower prints. Far lovelier than any women's fashion prints Irene has seen lately.

A young salesman with a round face and glasses, wearing a polka-dot shirt approaches her. 'Good morning, madam. Aren't they gorgeous?' His cheeks dimple in a smile. 'I can see you appreciate fine fabric.'

'I do indeed.' Irene's creative spirit is twirling. 'These are wonderful.'

'We have some paisleys over here in the same brand.'

'Ooh.' Irene hurries to the rack and lifts a hanger holding a shirt in forest greens. 'I don't suppose...' Irene licks her lips. How to say this? She hopes she isn't blushing.

'Are you looking for something for yourself?'

'Ah—' Irene is sure she's blushing now.

'I suggest trying on an extra small and yell out if you need me to grab another size.' He smiles broadly.

'So...' Irene clears her throat. 'Women do purchase your clothes, then?'

'Oh, we get all genders in here. If you like, I can help you find pants and jackets, ties, scarves, shoes, anything you like.'

Irene grins. 'Thank you—' she looks at his name tag— 'Sebastian. I'll try this one on first.'

Forty-five minutes later, Irene walks out of the menswear store with a large carry bag and a brand new excitement in her spirit. She is a creature metamorphosing. She hangs onto her butterfly moment as she walks the half block to her appointment with her optometrist.

HELEN 2024

Helen goes to the corner of her living room where she and Pete have placed Irene's wooden chest. It's heavier than she remembers. There's obviously more in there than fabric and blankets. Helen has dealt with everything else. The flat has been cleaned from top to bottom ready for the real estate agent to re-let the space. Besides the filing cabinet, this box is the last of Irene's items to sort.

Helen kneels beside the chest and lifts the lid. On top are a couple of blankets which she lifts out and places on the floor. Next she removes a few folded fabric pieces and a scrap of material that sparks a memory—blue cotton with a pattern of butterflies.

At the bottom of the chest, she finds a pile of notebooks of various shapes and sizes. Taking hold of one, she opens it to a random page, expecting a diary or journal or perhaps poetry. She stares at it for a moment, turns the page, turns another. Memories surface of Irene scribbling in the kitchen, jotting down recipes, phone numbers, to-do lists. Each page contains something different. Aunt Ruth's quick scone recipe... a list of appointments and dates (dentist, car service, parent/teacher meeting)... a page of doodling... some business notes.

Helen runs her finger over a drawing of a tote bag which has been coloured with green and pink stripes. One of Irene's many creative business ideas. Helen smiles to herself. These books could make for some interesting reading. But not yet. Helen doesn't think she can read her mother's words yet. She'll sort them out when she has more time. When she feels stronger.

Out on the kitchen table is another more urgent pile. Twenty-two student assignments to mark. Not for the first time she asks herself, who in their right mind would be a teacher?

IRENE 2014

Irene stands in the middle of the living room and looks around. What did she come in here for? She turns to stare at the book-case—nope, can't remember. She turns again to face the kitchen and, as always, her attention is drawn to the knives. The row of razor sharp blades grip the wall, their lethal points raised as if preparing for action. She tried using them once, years ago, when Bill had first hung the magnetic strip on the wall and attached the new knives. Awful things—the damage they could do. Irene can't leave the living room for the hallway without those knives flashing at her.

It's a family joke, how Irene insists on using her supermarket knives that she keeps in their individual sheaths in a kitchen drawer. How they're always blunt. Irene prefers them blunt. *Blunt knives are more dangerous,* they've all told her. But Irene knows different.

Her gaze travels over the bench tops, cupboards and walls as she tries to remember why she came in here. When nothing jolts her memory, she returns to the yellow room and the drawer she'd been sorting. Maybe she can trick her brain into slipping back to the moment before she'd vacated the room.

She moves a few items around in the drawer, pushes it back into the sewing cabinet and sighs. It's no use. She gives up trying to remember and returns to the kitchen.

Irene's kitchen appears as something from a home magazine. Polished marble bench tops, soft-closing drawers, high-end cooktop and oven, every kitchen appliance a person could wish for. Behind the oak cupboard doors, inside every drawer, are stacks of crockery, utensils, heavy pots and pans, appliances. Most of it, Irene hasn't touched in years.

Royal Doulton resides in the sideboard for special occasions. Crystal glasses, the 'good' cutlery, serving platters, Christmas platters, expensive bowls. Things Bill had presented her with, wrapped in gold paper, at every birthday and Christmas, despite her insistence that she didn't need any more things.

Some of Irene's most treasured memories are of cooking in the kitchen in the old farmhouse. Beating butter with a wooden spoon. Stirring a stew in a huge pot on the original woodstove and dishing it up to the farmhands. All those fruit pies she made from scratch and baked in cast iron pie tins. When they built the new house, Bill insisted she have everything of the finest quality. Everyone who came to the house for the first time remarked on the kitchen. How lucky she was. How they'd kill for a kitchen like Irene's.

Irene opens a bottom drawer and shifts the kitchen paraphernalia to the side to create some space. She reaches up and takes each expensive kitchen knife gingerly by the end of its handle and places it carefully into the drawer. There. All that remains on the wall is a magnetic strip. She won't ever have to look at those knives again.

Irene looks back towards the living room where the bookcase bulges with books and photo albums, and two glass-fronted cabinets proudly display Bill's collections. There's still so much to sort. Irene hasn't ventured into Bill's office yet. The filing cabinet needs going through. And more books. So many books.

Then there's the double garage bursting with stuff. Even the laundry has been used for storage. Why had he built such a large room for a laundry? Shelves of plastic containers jammed with pieces of life. Spare crockery (for what?). Photographs. Wads of fabric from Irene's sewing days.

That was it. The thought pops into Irene's head… Claire.

As Irene had been sorting through her sewing drawer, she found a pin-cushion she'd made a long time ago from a remnant of fabric—a leftover piece from the scarf she'd sewn when she was going through chemo. The pincushion had, near its rim, the orange tip of a butterfly wing which was what had triggered her memory of Claire.

How Irene had loved that scarf. It was the one she'd worn most when her hair started to fall out. Claire figured out how to wrap it stylishly around Irene's head and tie it with a bow above her ear. Irene remembers them looking into the mirror together, Claire kissing her on the cheek and saying, 'How gorgeous you look.'

Irene hasn't seen Claire for a long time. Longer than she has owned a mobile phone which is where she stores her contacts these days. That's what Irene had gone into the living room for—to find her address book and look up Claire's number.

Irene searches the bureau drawer where she's always kept the book, but it isn't there. Nor is it in the cupboard underneath, or in the coffee table drawer. She scrabbles about, pulling out puzzle books, biros and pieces of fluff, tossing everything out onto the floor.

The book has vanished. Like so many things over the years.

Helen has laid out her mother's notebooks on the living room floor and is sorting them according to date. They start from the early 1990s, around the time Irene commenced her business.

Pete pokes his head in from the hallway. 'I'm taking off for a run.'

Helen looks up to see him grabbing the doorframe with one hand and reaching into the room to take his wallet from the sideboard with the other. She chuckles at the sight of him balancing on one skinny leg with the other lifted out behind him so he won't dirty the floor with his sneakers.

'You should buy another tracksuit, my sweet. That one belongs in another century.'

Pete slips the wallet into his pocket and rocks back on his heels, grinning.

'How many are there?' he asks, indicating the books spread out around Helen.

'About twenty.'

'Just a lot of lists and stuff, you said?'

'Hmm, not sure. There's more, but everything's mixed in together. I guess she treated them as day-to-day diaries, recording anything she needed to keep track of, like appointments.'

Helen studies the spiral-bound notebook in her hand. Most of the books have the year written inside the front cover. This one is dated the year before Helen's father died. Irene seems to have abruptly stopped writing in notebooks from that point.

Pete's voice pulls her out of her thoughts. 'Earth calling Helen.'

'Sorry?'

'Want anything at the shops?'

'No, all good.'

Pete blows her a kiss and heads off, and Helen keeps sorting. She arranges the notebooks into what she believes to be the right order, stacks them together and slots them all except one into a space on the bookshelf. She makes a cup of tea, curls up on the sofa and opens to the first page of the oldest book. The year 1990 is written inside the front cover.

It's immediately apparent why her mother started the notebook at this time. On the first page is a list of business names she was considering.

Irene Blackford Creations

Irene's Fashion Accessories

Belts and Bags (scribbled out)

Irene Flower Fashion (Flower being Irene's maiden name)

Irene Flower: Fashion Accessories from Repurposed Fabric (This one was circled and became the name of the business).

Following this was a list of products she was contemplating.

Scarves (which became the best sellers)
BeltsBags—hand, shoulder, purse, strap/handle (both).

Irene had designed a sizeable range of scarf styles. Helen recalls going with her mother to op shops to scout out second-hand fabrics and clothes that could be cut up and sewn together. Her mother had a knack for placing contrasting patterns together and creating cohesive and stunning designs.

Helen flips through the rest of the book, pausing at a recipe here, a to-do list there, design ideas, pages of doodles. She recalls her mother doodling absently while talking on the phone. Who was she talking to as she sat and drew... potential customers, friends?

As Helen reaches the end of the book, she finds a photo tucked inside the back cover of her mother and another woman. She turns the photo over and reads the inscription: *Irene and Claire, Market, Hobart.*

Irene is stunning. She would have been about thirty-five or six, long red-brown hair, wearing a floral dress and wide sunhat. And Claire—blonde, big sunglasses and blue jeans. The women stand behind their market stall, coloured scarves hanging from the awning, stands of costume jewellery adorning the table. Their arms are around each other's shoulders and they grin openly into the camera.

Helen remembers Claire who had been her mother's best friend for years. Irene told her Claire had left to live overseas, but Helen no longer remembers where she went.

The photo sparks Helen's own memories of the markets when she was a young girl—taking off in Claire's Volkswagen and singing to cassettes all the way to Hobart, helping set up the stall, exploring the other stalls with her mother. Helen closes her eyes and recollects the bustle, the exotic wares, the buskers. Her mother's vibrant energy that drew people to their stall.

Helen opens her eyes and gazes again at her mother's image in the photo, at the expression of wild joy on her face.

Until the last few years of her life, Irene's joy had waned considerably. When exactly did her mother change? And why hasn't Helen thought more about it before? Perhaps it began with the cancer.

But the more Helen thinks about the time of the cancer, the more she is convinced the change had already begun.

IRENE 2014

The morning sun glows dully through the curtains, casting a golden hue about the yellow room. It's an altogether different sensation to waking with the whole day crashing in through the vast panes of glass in the main bedroom, bright and urgent.

Irene has been escaping into Durrunby lately in Bill's ute. She stretches and contemplates the idea now. A walk along the river to wake her senses so she can sort through some items on her list—finances, appointments, her car that has been sitting in the garage all this time waiting for a new… what, spark plug? Something. Irene can't remember. They'd booked it in, Bill had died and Irene had forgotten about it. How rude they must think her, to make an appointment and not show up. In the meantime, she's been driving Bill's ute which she doesn't mind, it's easy enough to drive. However, it will be good to have her own car running again.

Irene rugs up and heads off, steering the ute up the gravel drive, over the cattle grid and onto the main road. She gazes out at the new-ly-washed world. The sun has spread its pale light determinedly across the rain-soaked landscape where everything shimmers—rain-slicked leaves on the eucalypts, the damp asphalt, paddocks where puddles lay like scattered oases.

In Durrunby, Irene parks by the bakery, grabs a pastry and coffee and wanders down to the river. She treads cautiously across the wet grass as she leaves the path, the sodden earth yielding sponge-like beneath her feet. At the riverbank she pauses, her gaze drawn to two mallards dabbling in the water beneath the branches of a willow.

She stands motionless, breathing deeply... in, out... using her senses to intentionally hone in on her surroundings: the glittering interplay of water and light on the river, twittering bird-calls overhead, a distant dog's bark, petrichor scent rising from the damp earth, a hint of eucalypt on the breeze blowing across her cheek, coffee cup warm on her palm, and... she takes a sip of her coffee... a taste of heaven. The Durrunby Bakery makes excellent coffee.

There, now she can tell Helen she's practised that mindfulness thing she keeps going on about.

Irene walks back up to the path and finds a bench seat to sit and enjoy her breakfast. This is her favourite time of day, when the world is just waking up. When, for whatever reason, her heart glimmers with optimism. The feeling tends to wane as the day progresses until, by the evening, she finds herself battling a heaviness in her chest no amount of practised mindfulness will budge.

Irene bites into her pastry as a family hurries by. The mother is chasing a recalcitrant toddler while her husband trundles a pram along behind. Irene shouldn't assume he's her husband, of course. These days you weren't supposed to assume anything. He could be a lover, a friend, not necessarily even the child's father.

Were things more straight-forward when her own children were small, or did she just remember it that way? Bill and Irene—married, two children, living together in the same house. Most of her friends had been in the same situation. There were a few divorces, of course, and deaths that left one spouse on their own. Bill said young people these days lacked commitment. Irene isn't sure. Sometimes she wonders whether, rather than possessing less sticking power, they simply have more courage. It takes courage to admit something is wrong.

'Irene?'

A middle-aged woman hurries up to her with her hand to her forehead like a visor. Hair in a bun, smart suit sporting the Hix Real Estate logo, runners on her feet.

'Miranda,' Irene leaps to her feet as she recognises the local real estate agent.

Miranda Hix gives Irene a hug. 'I wasn't sure it was you at first. You look amazing.' She gazes at Irene's hair. 'Zola, right?'

Irene pats her head, still self-conscious but becoming used to the frequent remarks.

'And your clothes—is this a new look? Gosh, I love it. Sorry, I'm gushing. I haven't seen you since Bill's funeral, how are you holding up?'

'Alright. You know...' Irene shifts on her feet.

Miranda nods gravely. 'I'm sorry.'

The women sit together on the bench seat, turned towards each other.

'How's business?' Irene asks.

'Not bad. I'm about to show a home to a young couple. It's getting quite busy round here. People escaping the city rat-race. Not many young families though. There isn't much work about.'

'It might pick up with all the new touristy things happening. I often think I wouldn't mind living here myself.'

Miranda's back straightens. 'Why don't you?'

Irene is caught off-guard. 'Uh—I probably shouldn't have said anything. It's just a thought that keeps popping into my head.'

Miranda crosses one leg and leans towards Irene. Her professional pose, Irene thinks. 'Would you sell your place? I can help you with that.'

'No, I'm leaving my house to Helen. It's on its own title and Caleb has the farm, you see.'

Miranda nods and tilts her head.

'However...' Irene gazes across the river for a few moments before turning back to Miranda. 'What do you have in the way of rentals?'

'Funny you should ask. There's a glut at the moment, if I'm honest. Although, I don't have anything resembling your lovely place. Nothing that big or modern. But I'm guessing you're thinking of downsizing?'

'What I'd really like, Miranda, is something small but comfortable. Close to the main centre but quiet. Near the river if possible. Something so compact it would be impossible to fill it with clutter.'

Miranda chuckles. 'You *have* been thinking about it. Do you know, I may have just the place. Can you call into the office later, around eleven?'

Irene leaves the river for the carpark with a fluttering in her abdomen. What is she doing? Is she really thinking about moving house at her age? Impulsive decisions tend to lead to chaos, don't they? Like the time she and Claire rented an apartment together in Hobart that turned out to be next door to a drug dealer.

'You want to find out what your soul needs?' Claire had asked her once. 'Write down two choices on two pieces of paper, fold them up and pick one out of a hat, bowl, whatever. Tell yourself, the one you draw out is what you're going to do. Now—this is important—as soon as you read what's written on the paper, check the feeling in your body. You'll know by what you feel whether it's the right or wrong choice.'

What does Irene's soul need? She could try the exercise—write the choices down on a paper napkin at the bakery (*stay in her own house / rent an apartment in Durrunby*)—and randomly choose one out of her pocket. Perhaps she'll pull out the Durrunby one and feel immediately worried or sick. But what if it excites her?

She'll go and see Don Batty about her car now, and meet with Miranda later. She may as well take a look at the rental. She might hate it and that will be her answer. After all, she has a perfectly lovely house with an enviable kitchen and beautiful views. A peaceful abode.

So why is it that to feel at peace, she needs to escape that house and drive into Durrunby to walk by the river with the ducks?

Don Batty of Batty & Son Auto leans over the counter, tapping away at a computer keyboard. 'Let's have a looksee. About three months ago, was it?'

'Something like that. It was booked for sometime in late January, but Bill died on the fifteenth and it slipped my mind.' Irene rubs the tops of her arms with her hands. 'I'm really sorry about it.'

'Absolutely no need to apologise. I don't remember a missed appointment but if it happened, it'll be here.'

'I can't remember if Bill said it was a spark plug or maybe something to do with the battery?' Why can't she remember? She should be on top of these things.

'Right, here's your BMW.' He reads out Irene's number plate. 'Last service was November twenty-ninth and everything was in order. Nothing was booked after that.'

'Are you sure?'

'Yep, nothing here.' Don looks up and leans his head to the side. 'You alright, love?'

Irene blinks rapidly. 'Yes, of course. I thought... well, I was sure I made the appointment but it must have slipped my mind.' She attempts a light-hearted laugh.

'Look Irene, I'm booked out this week, but I have to head into the Cove next Tuesday. How about I shoot out to your place and take a look. Then I'll know whether we can drive it in or I need to organise a tow.'

'Thanks so much, Don.'

'Never a problem. You take care, alright?'

Irene goes back out into the daylight with a sinking feeling. The appointment hadn't been made after all.

Irene and Miranda stand before a wide, converted weatherboard home with two distinct entrances.

'I think you'll agree the location is excellent?' Miranda says. She stands straight-postured, holding a clipboard.

Irene turns around and takes in the street. Rows of maples either side are already ablaze with crimson leaves. The homes are neat—clipped lawns, meticulously tended gardens. It's very quiet despite being a short walk away from the main road with its vibrant bustle.

'It's certainly pretty.' She turns back to the house which is tucked comfortably amongst a variety of trees and bushes like a giant bird in its nest.

'As you can see, flat one is the larger dwelling.' Miranda indicates the lefthand side of the building with a sweep of her arm. 'It's been recently tenanted by a young woman and her son. They have the yard and the garage. A carport has been added onto the other side for flat two.'

Irene nods as she takes in the property—fenced yard on the far left next to the entrance to the first flat, a single garage and a low wooden fence separating the dwellings. On the other side of the fence is the entrance to the second flat and a carport attached to the righthand side of the building. The driveways run parallel to each other, either side of the fence.

'Would you like to view the inside?'

Irene follows Miranda as she unlocks the door and steps through into a short passage.

'You'll notice it's accessible, no steps or tripping hazards.'

The passage opens into a small open-plan living area—kitchen at the road end, bench in the middle and a carpeted space with windows and a sliding door out onto the back deck.

'Oh my.' Irene scoots over to the door.

'Thought you'd like that. Your own private view of the river. Here, I'll unlock it so you can see the deck properly.'

The house is built on a downward slope and from the wooden deck, Irene gazes down at a quiet section of the river, overhung with willows.

'Apparently, there's a resident platypus, though I haven't seen him myself.'

'This is gorgeous. I can hear the river from here. Oh, I love it, can I sign today?'

Miranda laughs. 'Irene, you haven't seen the rest yet.'

Irene hardly notices the rest. She tries to take in what Miranda is saying. The adjoining wall has been properly soundproofed—yes that's important. Walk-in shower—wonderful.

When she arrives home later, she has a vague recollection of crisp, clean lines and just enough space. The one bedroom next to the lounge also has large windows facing the river. The bathroom is accessed from the bedroom but she doesn't care about that. It will only be herself living there. She'll buy a sofa bed and Poppy can stay over. The fun they'll have.

Oh dear, what has she done? This impulsive behaviour could be becoming a habit. Cutting off her hair and leasing a flat. What will Helen say?

But Irene can't stop thinking about the wonderful space outside the sliding door. She'll be able to sit there on the deck—she'll buy a nice setting—and listen to the rush and burble of the river.

She doesn't need to do the 'choices on pieces of paper' exercise. She knows what her soul needs. The flat is perfect.

Helen has read the first few of her mother's notebooks. For several years Irene's business flourished and Irene employed two sewists, giving her more time for designing. Then, at the height of the boom, she and Bill took off on an overseas trip.

The book Helen holds in her hands, dated 1996, appears to be dedicated to their holiday. They were away for a few weeks and Helen and Caleb had stayed with relatives.

Helen flicks through the pages, finding herself drawn into her mother's excitement and chuckling at her commentary. Her vivid re-tellings are filled with people, feelings, food, smells. Not so much about the places themselves, but more the impressions they made on her.

Bill insisted on posing in front of the Eiffel Tower... Veronique (a woman they met) *lost her hat to the wind and I joined her in the chase down Rue Saint-Dominique...* The Cinque Terre villages along the coast of the Italian Riviera—*oh, the colours!* Irene had sketched and coloured in the huddle of vibrant buildings hugging the coastline.

She describes Antoni Gaudí's *gorgeously-shaped* buildings in Barcelona (again her words accompanied by sketches) *like something from a fairy-scape. I could have jumped from the bus and taken a bite out of the La Pedrera-Casa Milà...* descriptions of food from everywhere they visited: the *wonderful schnitzel* in Austria, and in Germany, *all those sausages!*

She has written some notes on London and the hotel they stayed in—*windows looking out onto the River Thames, so extravagant. And Buckingham Palace—Bill is taken with the architecture. The gates alone are a work of art he says.*

An obvious highlight of their trip is a tour to Winchester Cathedral. Irene has included the story of the west window, whose stained glass was destroyed by the Roundhead soldiers in 1642 and later pieced back together by the townspeople. Being impossible to recreate the Biblical scenes with all the broken pieces of glass, they gathered it up, added some plain glass pieces, and created an abstract mosaic. *It's breathtaking,* she writes. *Something so completely broken, mended in such a way that it becomes a new work of art, just as beautiful.*

There is sadness in Irene's next words: *We didn't go to the Cotswolds, a place I was desperate to see. I've been dreaming about it for years. But Bill went back to the palace to see the changing of the guard and we missed the coach which threw everything else out. I'm so shattered I could crumple.*

Nearing the end of the trip, Irene writes of a missing ring. *I must have lost it in the hotel somewhere but we've searched and searched.*

After this, her entries dwindle. Had she lost interest in recording their adventures? Or were they having so much fun, she didn't have time to write?

Helen closes the book and clasps it to her chest. There is so much of her mother here. She wants to curl up and read it properly from cover to cover. Bring out the photo albums and look at the pictures at the same time. Live vicariously through the one big trip Irene made in her lifetime. Read her mother's words and soak them into herself.

Oh, how she misses her.

IRENE 2014

The concrete steps of the old farmhouse are worn down in the middle like a dented pillow. Irene's feet feel their familiarity, muscle memory conjuring up the years.

To think of all the feet that have trodden upon them. Four generations of Blackfords—Bill's grandparents, his parents, Bill himself when his father retired and now Caleb and Sing. Their friends, family, employees.

The back door leads straight into the kitchen, a narrow space taken up with a table at the centre. Irene grabs hold of the doorjamb with one hand, feeling the rough, chipped paint brushing her palm as she takes the last step in. The room is warm and rich with spices. Her daughter-in-law swings towards her.

'Oh, thank you! That looks so delicious.' Sing holds out her hands, delight filling her face as though Irene's bowl of potato salad is something exotic. 'Come in Mum, sit down.'

Irene is still getting used to Sing. Her tiny frame. Long, dark hair, brown skin, fine features. Yet such large gestures—her wide smile, the way she laughs at everything, her generosity.

She calls Irene "Mum" and her own mother, "Mama". Sing's mother lives in the city and the two speak daily on the phone. Irene tries to imagine herself and Helen talking on the phone that often. What would they say to each other?

When Irene first met Sing, she couldn't resist asking about her name. 'Mama had wanted me for so long,' Sing replied. 'When I finally arrived, she was so happy she couldn't stop singing.'

Irene slips into a seat at the table and watches Sing bustling about the kitchen.

'Caleb's on his way, he had to fix something at the milking sheds.' She sets a covered plate of home-baked bread in the centre of the table.

'You've been busy.' Irene lifts the tea-towel and steam rises from the bread. 'What's in the oven? It smells wonderful.'

'Just chicken, nothing fancy.' She whips around the table, setting down placemats.

That was Irene once, cooking and baking in this same little kitchen. Many meals have been shared in this room. The hot lunches Irene cooked for Bill's farmhands, everyone squished around the narrow table. These days, Caleb's employees bring lunch boxes and eat in one of the sheds he's set up with a kitchenette. Times change.

There's a rumble of engine, the sound of car doors slamming and Helen arrives with Pete and Poppy. Caleb follows them in, scrubbing his boots on the mat outside the door and bellowing a greeting to everyone. The tiny kitchen fills with voices, the walls swallowed up with bodies, Caleb's wide shoulders taking up half the kitchen.

'I'm sitting next to Reenie,' Poppy announces as she drags a chair closer to Irene's. She flings her arms around her grandmother's neck and kisses her several times on the cheek.

Caleb bends to kiss Irene's other cheek and she slips him an envelope. 'Happy birthday, sweetheart. There's a bit of cash in there so you can buy what you like.'

'Thanks Mum, but you needn't have.'

Irene dismisses his remark with a flick of her hand. 'I can't take it with me.'

Sing places a roasting dish on the table which is filled with chicken pieces glistening under a sticky sauce.

'Doesn't look like "just chicken" to me,' Irene says.

'It's a Filipino family recipe. Mama made it a lot when we were growing up.'

Irene's belly rumbles.

As they tuck into the meal, the room fills with the easy chatter born of familiarity and comfort in each other's presence. Warmth blooms in Irene's chest as she regards her family. The dynamics of their diminished clan—reduced by one—has shifted subtly. Caleb appears larger with his father gone, the two no longer jostling for space. Are they now, as a group, a little looser? As if a screw has wriggled its way out of a hinge and left a door swinging open. What will emerge from behind that door, Irene wonders?

'This is Sing-*sational*,' Poppy says, and everyone laughs.

Opposite Irene, Helen takes small, quick bites of her meal, leaning forward as if braced to spring into action should a disaster arise. Dear Helen, if she could relax a little. Like Pete, who slouches beside her, chatting easily with Caleb. Pete is so thin Irene can imagine him toppling over in a stiff breeze, but rock solid in the ways that matter.

Caleb is thirty-two today. Yesterday, a mewling baby—today towering over Irene. How had it happened? Irene supposes she should feel old but she doesn't. Something has been happening to her lately—new life fizzing up inside her as she emerges from the fog of the past three months.

Caleb catches her eye. 'So...' he begins, and Irene steels herself in the pause. She has been waiting for the barrage of questions. 'What's this about you moving out of the house, Mum?'

Irene can't help but notice Helen squeezing her elbows tighter into her sides.

'I need a change. The house is getting harder for me to manage. It's awfully big for one person.'

'You could take in a boarder,' Helen says.

'I don't want a boarder. No, I'd like to try something different. The flat is in a nice spot.'

Poppy jigs up and down on her chair. 'Reenie said I can have sleepovers. Did you know there's a platypus living in the river?'

Sing clasps her hands to her chest and beams. 'It'll be an adventure.'

'We'll all pitch in and help you move,' Pete says. 'You say the word and Caleb and I will bring in the trucks.'

'Thanks, but I reckon I'll manage with the ute.'

Caleb lays his cutlery on his empty plate and shifts the plate to the side. He leans forward. 'Mum, you won't fit your furniture in the ute.'

'She's getting new furniture,' Helen says drolly.

'How exciting,' Sing says.

Caleb gazes admiringly at Sing, turns back to Irene and says, 'Well, it's your life, Mum. You should live it how you want.'

'Hear, hear.' Sing raises her water glass.

The table erupts with more chatter and Helen mumbles something Irene doesn't hear. Irene leans towards her, about to ask what she'd said. But before she can, Caleb stands and taps his glass with a spoon.

'What's this?' Pete asks. 'Shouldn't someone else be toasting the birthday boy?'

Caleb and Sing lock eyes for a moment, a silent message passing between them, and Caleb turns back to the group. His cheeks turn a little pink.

'My darling wife and I have some news.'

There is a general audible sucking in of breath.

'I knew it,' Helen says. 'How far along?'

'Three months. We wanted to wait until—'

Caleb's words are swallowed by cheers and congratulations, leaving him speechless. Irene springs from her seat and hugs him tightly.

'Oh, that is wonderful news!'

Irene's heart swells with the thought of another grandchild to love. A grandchild Bill will never meet. She swallows the sudden pang and draws away from Caleb, sitting down to wait for Sing who is locked in an embrace with Helen. She studies the face of her son as he scruffs Poppy's hair and shakes Pete's hand. Will he be a good father? Is he kind enough, gentle enough? Irene mustn't worry. This little family will be fine.

As Helen and Sing draw apart, Irene witnesses the fleeting expression of sorrow that crosses her daughter's face. Helen has dearly wanted another child but her dream has not eventuated. Irene aches to talk about that and so many things with Helen, but Helen doesn't talk. Helen holds her grief close, hugged tightly to her own chest. Irene has learned to keep her mouth shut and wait for the rare moments when her daughter chooses to open up.

As Helen sits down, Irene stands and moves towards Sing, holding out her arms to hug her daughter-in-law and the new child growing within her.

IRENE 2014

Irene stands at the corner window watching Sing as she wanders over the hill from the farmhouse. If you had no idea of the distance, you might think it was a leaf blowing up, bright and golden. Now twirling its way across the paddock, shapeshifting as it draws closer and morphing into a yellow dress and a swinging basket.

Irene opens the sliding doors of the living room and steps onto the verandah to greet her as she approaches.

'Goodies for you, Mum,' Sing calls as she takes the steps and meets Irene on the verandah.

'What's this?' Irene takes the basket and sets it on a chair.

Sing pecks her cheek. 'For your move. You don't have to keep the basket, I know you want to go minimal. The rest is to help ease you into your new place.'

Irene fingers the gifts, arranged like a boutique hamper. A loaf of fresh-baked bread, biscuits, a jar of Sing's jam, some apples from their tree. Even a couple of the puzzle books Irene likes.

'You're always so thoughtful, Sing. I—' Irene can't find the words.

'It's alright.' Sing smiles and rubs Irene's arm. 'Anytime.'

They take themselves and the basket of goodies into the kitchen. It's not long before they hear the familiar sounds of a car engine and tyres crunching on the gravel. Helen strides in, hands in her cardigan pockets. She eyes the cardboard boxes lined up against the wall.

'You're packed then?'

Irene gives her a brief hug. 'If you could help me get these into the back of the ute, I can manage the rest.'

'Is that Don Batty I saw revving your car in the garage?'

'Oh good, he's got it going?'

'Sounded pretty healthy.' Helen wanders to the kitchen bench and absently picks at something stuck to its edge. 'We should have helped you with the car. I didn't even think of it, sorry.'

Irene shakes her head. 'It's alright, we were all grieving. I don't mind driving the ute, anyway. It's kind of macho, don't you think?'

Helen snorts and turns around to survey the living area. 'I still don't get why you're leaving all this.'

'It's just for a while.' Irene pats her on the arm. 'Until I figure things out.'

Helen goes over to inspect the bookcase. 'You've left your photos and your albums. Don't you want those?'

'Yes, I will take some now, and come back for anything else I need later.'

Helen picks up a photo album and flicks through the pages. 'Look at this. Your world trip. There's Dad in front of the Eiffel Tower. Such a cliché, that.'

Irene chuckles. 'You wouldn't visit the Eiffel Tower and not take the picture, would you?'

Helen replaces the album and returns to the boxes lined up against the wall. She shifts one an inch along the floor with her foot. 'May as well get on with this then.'

'Can you help me with the chest first?'

'What chest?'

Helen and Sing follow Irene into the yellow room where Irene stoops to pull the camphor wood chest out from under the bed.

'I remember this,' Helen says. 'You used to keep your sewing fabric in there.'

'There's still some in there. Who knows, I might start sewing again.'

Helen smiles and Irene gazes at her daughter's transformed face. Those cupid-bow lips. Irene traced those lips countless times with her finger when Helen was a baby and lay in her arms, surrendered and trusting. Even now, Helen's mouth curves and dips in a full-grown version of the cherubic lips of her babyhood.

Helen raises her eyebrows. 'Why are you looking at me like that?'

'You really are beautiful when you smile.'

Helen lets out a 'Pfft,' and bends to lift the chest.

Irene takes one end and together they wrestle it out to the ute. Though awkward to carry, it doesn't weigh much, as Irene has temporarily emptied it of the notebooks. She'll return those later when she's alone in the flat.

As Helen manoeuvres the box up against the sides of the ute tray, Don Batty comes out of the garage, wiping his hands on a rag.

'Ladies.' He nods to Helen and Sing, and turns to Irene. 'Car's good to go, love. Spark plugs are fine, everything else is in good order. Funny thing though, one of your cables was disconnected from the battery.'

'Oh?'

'Maybe Bill was doing some tinkering and forgot to put it back?'

Irene pauses for a moment and nods. 'You're probably right.'

'Well, I'll head off. Car's safe, you can take her out now.'

As Irene walks Don to his truck, she says, 'I'm sorry to put you to so much trouble.'

'It's no trouble. Call me if you have any concerns.'

'I'll drop in and pay you this afternoon.'

Don waves his hand in the air. 'No need, I was coming out anyway.'

When Don has left, Helen tuts. 'To think, you could have been driving your car around all this time.'

Irene shrugs and walks back towards the house. 'No harm done. Let's grab these boxes.'

Irene and Helen fill the ute tray with boxes while Sing, forbidden to lift anything heavy, retrieves the gift basket from the kitchen and some garbage bags Irene has filled with soft items. When they've finished loading everything, Irene attaches the tray tarp, stands back and slaps her hands together.

'Done. Thanks for your help, ladies. Now, who's coming with me?'

'You two go in the ute,' Sing says. 'I'll grab my car and meet you there.' As she twirls and claps her hands together, Irene can't help picturing her with wings and surrounded by fairy dust.

'I'll drive you down to yours,' Irene says.

But Sing replies, 'No need. I like the walk over the hill.'

Irene and Helen take off in the ute. As they trundle over the cattle grid, Irene glimpses Sing's dark head through the rearview window, bobbing back towards the hill. She thinks of the child growing inside Sing's body. A whole new person in a state of becoming.

Yet weren't they all in a state of becoming? Growing, morphing, edging towards an unknown tomorrow. Irene shivers. Who knew what she was opening herself up to by leaving the property where she'd lived for thirty-four years? Was she being ridiculous? The way Helen looks at her lately suggests she is.

'What are you thinking about?' Helen asks.

Irene catches herself frowning. She turns briefly to smile at Helen. 'I'm wondering what tomorrow will bring. You never know, do you?'

Helen sighs. 'I just hope it's something good.'

Irene leans on the deck rail gazing out over the river. On the other side of the weeping willows lining the bank is Durrunby Park from where Irene hears the distant shouts and laughter of children. Closer, the burble of the river is like a song and she breathes it deeply into herself.

While helping Irene unpack her few boxes and bags, Helen had made pointed digs about the tiny size of the flat. Irene had expected it, of course. She didn't know herself exactly why she'd chosen such a small space, but it had felt like home the moment she'd walked in, something she couldn't explain.

When they'd finished unpacking and Sing offered Helen a lift home in her car, Irene breathed an inward sigh of relief. Now, she's enjoying time alone with the river. There's a lot to think about.

She needs to read through her notebooks. She'd like to be sure of what she remembers. There's still doubt in her mind about certain events and she wonders if she'll ever truly shake it. She has the feeling that putting some distance between herself and her house—and yes, her family too—will enable her to unravel certain tangled threads.

As she goes back inside and secures the sliding door, a jarring bang erupts from the street, sounding like it has come from right outside the building. She hurries to the front door and looks out.

A faded green station wagon has backed into the wooden fence between the two flats. The car lurches forward and straightens with a jerk onto the neighbouring driveway, leaving the waist-high wooden fence sagging towards Irene's side of the building.

The driver, a young woman, cuts the engine and leaps from the car. Rushing around to the fence side, she sees Irene and her hands fly to her cheeks.

'I'm so sorry! I'm trying to get the—thing—ugh.'

Irene goes to the fence and gives it a wiggle. 'No harm done. I reckon we can fix it.' She smiles at the woman. 'I'm Irene. I'm moving into flat two.'

'Zoe. I live there.' She jerks her head to indicate the other flat, glances back at Irene and her shoulders slump. 'I'm a single mum.'

Irene senses an enormous weight in those four words.

The back door of the station wagon opens and a small, pale face with a shock of black hair peeks out. Irene waves and calls out, 'Hello there.'

Zoe heads back to open the car door for the boy. 'Milo, come out and meet the nice lady.'

As she helps him out, Irene notes the woman's short, uneven hair and wonders if she cuts it herself. She's wearing tracksuit bottoms with a misshapen T-shirt and well-worn flip-flops. Irene feels a jolt of surprise when the young boy emerges from the car dressed in smart corduroy trousers, a collared shirt and lace-up shoes. He squeezes his body against his mother's and looks shyly up at Irene.

Zoe puts her arm around his shoulders. 'This is my son, Milo. This is Mrs...?' She peers at Irene.

'Bl—' Irene hesitates before deciding on her maiden name. 'Flower.'

'Flower? Mrs Flower?'

'Yes. But please, call me Irene.'

Milo's face breaks into a grin and he says a quiet, 'Hello.'

Zoe kisses the top of his head and moves towards the garage. As she pulls the door up she says, 'I had this bright idea, to reverse the car into the garage. Save me backing onto the road, see.' She shakes her head. 'I've got crap spatial awareness.'

Irene pushes the fence up into a standing position and slowly moves her hands away. The wooden slats stay for a moment before drooping back down.

'I'll call the real estate agent,' Zoe says.

But Irene shakes her head. 'No need. I'll ask my son to fix it. He runs a dairy farm and fixing things is right up his alley.'

Milo has scuttled up next to Zoe and semi-hides behind her as he peers at Irene.

'Tell you what,' Irene walks around the fence and into Zoe's driveway, 'How about I help you navigate?'

Zoe sends Milo to wait by the door away from the car, and Irene gives directions as Zoe reverses the station wagon into the garage.

'Perfect,' Irene says as Zoe emerges from the car. 'All you need is some practice.'

Zoe pulls a face. 'Thanks. Hey, do you want to come in and have a cuppa?' Her invitation seems sincere so Irene accepts.

Like Irene's, the home appears to have been recently renovated with new carpet and fresh paint but is a more spacious dwelling. The living area is larger and Irene spies a good-sized yard through the sliding glass door where a trampoline and a three-wheeler bike are on the grass. She sits on a fabric sofa that dips in the middle.

'Show Mrs Flower your train, buddy,' Zoe says as she sets about making Irene a cup of tea. 'He got it for his birthday. He's just turned four, haven't you?'

Milo pulls a wooden train engine and several carriages from a toybox and brings them to Irene to inspect. She turns the pieces over in her hands and asks the boy questions, and it's not long before words are tumbling out of him as if he's known Irene forever.

Zoe carries a cup of tea to Irene and sets her own cup and a glass of milk for Milo on the coffee table, before sinking into an armchair. As they chat, Irene learns they recently moved into the flat after a failed attempt at living in a share house with friends.

'It wasn't the best situation for Milo. I can afford this place since I got a job at the local grocer. It's not the most exciting work, but they pay well.'

Milo pushes his train along the carpet, crawling along on his knees and making chuff-chuff noises.

'What lovely pants he's wearing,' Irene says. 'Sorry, I've got an eye for nice fabric, can't help myself.'

Zoe gives a short laugh. 'There's a really good op shop in Durrunby. Someone around here buys expensive kids' clothes and donates them, I guess as soon as their kids grow out of them. I try and get in first when they put the new stock out.'

'That's handy.'

'Sometimes I wonder if they see Milo around town wearing their kids' cast-offs.' She pulls a face. 'I usually have to take the trousers down, though. Milo has long legs.'

Irene looks at Milo's trousers as he shuffles past with the train. An even section at the bottom of each leg is a darker brown than the rest, showing they've been lengthened.

'Did *you* take the hem down?' she asks. 'I can't even see the stitches.'

'You like my invisible hem? That's one thing I remembered from school. What do you think of his shirt?'

On closer inspection, Irene spies certain unique signatures of a handmade item. 'You made it?'

'Uh-huh.' Zoe's chin comes up.

'Do you like sewing?'

'I do, actually. I've got a machine but it badly needs a service. Just another thing...' Her voice trails off.

'It must be difficult,' Irene says. 'I mean—' Irene isn't sure what she meant to say.

Zoe wraps both hands around her teacup and takes a sip. She shrugs her shoulders. 'Being a single mum?'

Again, Irene feels the weight of those words in the way Zoe expresses them.

'I can only imagine what it's like to do it on your own. But from what I see of Milo, you're doing a good job.'

Zoe gazes over at her son. 'I try.'

Irene stands. 'I should go and leave you and Milo to enjoy your afternoon.' She takes her cup to the kitchen sink and heads to the front door where Milo and Zoe wave her off. As she approaches her own side of the building, she turns back to find Zoe staring at the leaning fence with an expression close to despair.

Inside, Irene gazes about the empty space of her flat. Her new furniture will arrive tomorrow. One more night in the big house and she can move into the flat properly. While thinking about her house, she feels the familiar tightening in her chest. She imagines herself going back this afternoon—entering through the front door, checking the keys, moving through the vast rooms. She thinks of the cupboards, shelves, drawers, tubs, and everything contained within them. Things that, by the fact of their existence, she must hold in her head and give space to. She can't hold it all anymore.

Irene realises she hasn't once looked up to check the security keys in the flat. She checks them now and of course, they are where they should be—hanging above the doors and windows.

Irene makes a decision. She goes into the bedroom and sorts through the garbage bags where she's packed her bedding. She shakes out a thick quilt encased in a removable cover. It's soft enough to sleep on, she decides. She lays it out, doubled over, on the floor and places her pillows at one end. Retrieving some blankets and the daisy coverlet from another bag, she puts these over the quilt. There, a makeshift bed. She'll sleep here tonight.

Besides, except for swapping the ute for her own car, there's nothing else she must go back to the house for. In fact, she may not need to return at all for a while.

This is her home now.

HELEN 2024

Helen studies the pages of her mother's notebook, trying to make sense of the drawings. It's her day off and she should be marking assignments and lesson planning. Instead, she's curled up on the couch, wrapped in her dressing gown against the April chill, flicking through Irene's notes.

She's perused the seven years of books dating from her parents' overseas trip in 1996. After they'd returned home, her mother's business had slowed and it took her a while to resuscitate it. But, within a year it was again flourishing. She writes of markets and shops and orders and plans, her creativity at its peak.

The book in Helen's lap is labelled 2004, the year Irene was diagnosed with cancer and had chemotherapy. Helen remembers coming home from university on the weekends to find her mother weak, vomiting, losing her hair, trying to be brave.

Despite her deteriorating physical health, she had tried to keep her business afloat. Helen read determination and courage in the pages of jottings, mind maps and to-do lists. Her mother was still planning and creating—*red & white polka-dot scarf / belt... forest green bags for Monday... buy 2 metres of blue Searle.*

By the end of that year, Helen's father had started building the new house. Helen was twenty at the time. She remembers the planning, the excited discussions, the thrill as the foundation was laid and it started to come together. Irene was to have comfort and the best of everything. 'I've got to look after your mother,' Bill had said. Helen can hear his voice, thick with worry, as plain as if he were still alive. Irene's illness had clearly shaken him.

There's nothing in Irene's notebook about the new build. By that time, she was too sick to write. What puzzles Helen are the small drawings she keeps finding here and there, tucked amongst the writings. She peers at the one she has discovered in the bottom corner of the currently open page—a hand-drawn rectangle divided into sections, each section containing a written list. Helen recognises it as a miniature map of Irene's kitchen drawers, the lists an inventory of their contents—cutlery, utensils, food wraps, knives. The number of drawers correspond to those of the old farmhouse where her parents were living at the time.

Helen recalls how the chemotherapy treatment had affected her mother's short-term memory. She was constantly losing her keys and her phone, and forgetting where things were kept. Was it because of her faulty memory that she'd sketched the drawers, to remind herself of the contents? But why not open up the drawers and look?

The lists are meticulously written in a small, tight hand as if the record holds particular importance. The only explanation is that her mother was testing herself—drawing up the list from memory as a way of checking her recall.

Helen flicks ahead to the other sketches she found this morning. Circles and arrows, dotted throughout the book, which make no sense to her. These aren't the only strange entries she has found within the pages of the notebooks. Scattered amongst Irene's to-do lists and business notes are odd combinations of words, written in tiny letters along the page edges or in corners, or underneath drawings. As if they are semi-hiding—not noticeable at first glance, but easily found once you know they are there. Helen can't make sense of them.

Irene didn't write much during 'the year of the cancer' as Helen thinks of it, and she skims through the rest of the pages. After the chemo treatment, her mother had tried to keep working but when one of her sewists left, business dwindled. The notebook Helen is reading stops abruptly half-way through, leaving the rest of the pages blank.

On the last used page is a drawing, carefully sketched and coloured in with pencils. It's a picture of a scarf, folded lightly across diagonal corners, each end floating. Irene has drawn butterflies on it, and coloured the background blue.

Helen recognises the pattern. She recently found a piece of the blue fabric in the chest where the notebooks were hidden. Her mother used the material to make the scarf that covered her head when she lost her hair. Irene had worn wigs as well, but more often than not, her head was wrapped in the blue scarf.

Helen runs her finger over the drawing as if she can conjure her mother through the touch. As she does so, she notices a string of tiny letters running around one corner of the scarf like a trail of ants. She brings her face close to the page and squints to read her mother's words:

Where did you go?

IRENE 2014

Despite having no mattress beneath her, Irene sleeps well on the first night in her new flat. She wakes to the quacking and splashing of ducks in the river below her bedroom window and bounds out of bed to look. Oh, what beauty is spread out before her! She dons a robe and goes out onto the deck to gaze at the river. Sunlight spills through the branches of the willows and dapples the water's surface with winking flecks of gold. Is it her imagination or have her lungs expanded? She breathes deeply, filling her body with beautiful air.

Her stomach rumbles and she realises she's had nothing to eat since yesterday afternoon, when she ate some bread and jam from Sing's gift basket. She dresses warmly and wanders over to the main road where a handful of people dot the street and businesses are beginning to open. She buys a coffee and pastry and takes them down to her favourite bench by the river, where she breakfasts to the sounds of birds and river-song. Her furniture will arrive this afternoon and she'll be able to sit on her own deck looking out over this same river, listening to the ducks and the wind and the river notes. What had Sing said?—*it'll be an adventure.* That's exactly how Irene feels, as if she is at the very start of an adventure, one toe dipping into it.

An elderly man walks past her with a dachshund on a lead and calls, 'Lovely morning.'

'Indeed it is,' Irene calls back.

Irene has a sudden urge to call out 'Lovely morning!' to everyone. She actually gets up and looks about, searching for someone to greet. But it's early yet and walkers are few.

On the way back to the flat, she stops at the grocery store to pick up some staples. She spies Zoe stacking shelves in one of the aisles and greets her cheerfully.

'And don't you worry about the fence,' she says as she takes a jar of peanut butter from the shelf and adds it to her basket. 'My son's coming to fix it this evening.'

'Oh, thanks.' Zoe's body visibly relaxes and Irene makes a mental note to find ways to encourage the young woman.

Irene's new furniture arrives in the afternoon—a sofa bed and armchair for the living room, lamp table, bookcase, a new bed and bedside table, comfy outdoor setting for the deck. While the delivery people are putting the bed together, she arranges the living room pieces to make the most of the view. The wooden chest containing her notebooks will serve as a coffee table. She sets some family photographs on the bookcase and her lamp on the table.

Irene is so happy she could dance, but resists the urge until the delivery people have left. Once she's on her own, she spins around the living room, nearly upsetting the lamp, and flops down on the sofa. She could do with a couple of cushions, a good excuse to take Poppy out. They can go shopping together and check out the crafty stores in the main street. Poppy will love that.

Irene sighs happily, robustly.

With nothing else to do, she decides to drive into Crayfish Cove to retrieve her car. As she turns the ute through the farm gate, she casts her gaze over the attractive brick bungalow she's lived in for nearly ten years. She has a strange sense of being an intruder. Perhaps *visitor* is a more apt word—as if her heart has already turned itself away from the old, and towards a new life.

After retrieving her car from the garage and replacing it with the ute, she goes up to the front door with her keys. Should she go inside? There's nothing she needs right now and, if she's honest, she doesn't want to go in. She'll have to at some point. There's a lot to sort and rooms to clean.

She decides instead to walk down the side of the building and look across the paddocks to the milking sheds in the distance. She watches the men for a few minutes as they round a herd of Holsteins, and makes out Caleb's Akubra hat amongst them, bobbing into a shed. Sing's car comes into view, travelling up the gravel road from the farm house, and Irene remembers Sing has her ceramics class today.

Irene returns to her car and leaves, driving over the cattle grid, through the gate and onto the main road. The street winds away from Crayfish Cove, snaking through farmland and orchards and rolling hills, turning into the quaint tree-lined streets of Durrunby.

There is adventure here. Irene feels it in her bones. Already she senses her creative spirit pulling together threads of ideas—gossamer-fine and fragmented as yet, but readying themselves for the clinging and weaving together.

She thinks of Zoe next door with her gift for sewing. Zoe's young son, Milo, painstakingly loved and cared for. On the main street is a community house, an op shop, any number of small businesses. And Irene has spied at least one vacant building peering out from an exciting vantage point.

She just needs to learn about her community, make friends, get involved, ascertain the needs, the pulse points, the heart of the place. This is the stuff she's good at.

Irene pulls into her carport and fancies she can already hear the river singing. Inside the walls of this building is a haven where she feels comfortable and safe. A place she can be herself, and from where she can venture out to live and grow and be useful.

Here, she can be Irene.

IRENE 2014

There is frost on the deck this morning. It sticks to the wooden floor, the table and chairs. Irene touches the deck rail and pulls her hand back, her fingers leaving their mark as an imprint in the ice. She stands in her bathrobe, her cheeks chilled, gazing at the river.

What a transformation. A mist rolls across the surface of the water like a great fantastical creature with swirling arms. Irene's breath billows out in a cloud as if she is also part of the magic. She hurries inside and grabs her phone to take photos. How exciting to think of the many moods of the river she'll be able to capture in pictures from her own deck.

Later in the morning, when the mist dissipates and the sun beams down gloriously from a clear sky, Irene goes exploring. It turns out Durrunby has more than craft shops and cafés to offer. It has grown considerably over the last few years and she finds a cake shop, a florist, two street libraries and a pet shop she didn't know were there. Also, tucked between the cake shop and a jewellery store, a shop called Riddles that sells puzzles and games. She purchases some wooden puzzle toys in anticipation of her new grandchild and some games Poppy and Milo might like.

She continues her ramble down to the bottom of Main Street where the road curves and turns into a stone bridge. Irene stands on the bridge and looks into the grounds of the old church building on the corner. She has heard it holds services on Sundays. She remembers, a very long time ago, holding her mother's hand and walking through that very door. Perhaps after she's settled into her flat, she'll pop in for a visit.

On her way back, she stops at the grocery store and finds Zoe serving at the counter. While she's between customers, she asks if Zoe and Milo would like to come to hers for dinner.

'It'll be takeaway,' Irene warns, 'but healthy.'

Zoe laughs. 'I don't care what it is, if I don't have to cook it.'

'I heard The River Café is good?'

Zoe briefly closes her eyes and sighs. 'Joss is an amazing cook. You have to try their wagyu beef ball risotto.'

'Right. Wagyu beef balls it is.'

Irene finds a whole afternoon stretched out before her. She eats bread and jam for lunch. Unpacks and studies one of the games she bought for the children. Sits on the deck listening to the ducks and the voices of families carrying up from the park on the far side of the river.

She imagines her body as a sponge soaking up the peace. The peace expanding her lungs. This quiet life is simply an interim. She plans to rest for a while. Get to know her community. Make some friends. After that... Well. Irene has plans.

Before the café closes, she picks up the meals she has ordered, takes them home and keeps them warm in the oven. Zoe and Milo arrive soon after and they eat on their laps in the living room. Zoe fusses when Milo drops a meatball but Irene waves her hand and says, 'Don't worry. I'm not worried.'

After the meal, they play one of the games Irene bought—a memory game consisting of pictures of doors with knobs or handles, where the players must remember in sequence how to turn the handles to open each door—clockwise, anti-clockwise, up or down.

Milo becomes highly animated and keeps playing the game by himself after Irene and Zoe's interest wanes. They sit back with hot chocolates while Milo, on his knees on the floor, jiggles up and down, flipping cards. 'Up, up, up... down ... left... no, right.'

Zoe shakes her head and sighs. 'He's exhausting.'

'He's a clever lad,' Irene says. 'My granddaughter sleeps over on Friday nights. If you ever want a break, he could come over and I'll play some games with them. She's seven, but she's good with younger children.'

'How about that, Milo? You can come and play at Mrs Flower's sometimes.'

'Reenie,' Irene says.

'Pardon?'

'Poppy calls me Reenie. Milo can too, if that's alright.'

Milo squeals, 'Right... down... no, up... left...'

Zoe rolls her eyes and takes a sip of her hot chocolate.

'Is that another of your shirts?' Irene asks.

Zoe calls to Milo. 'Come and show Reenie your shirt, buddy. It's actually a second-hand one I did up. Added pockets and a matching collar.'

Irene lifts Milo's collar for a better look. 'Gosh, it makes all the difference. I wouldn't have thought of that.' Irene winks at Milo and says, 'You can go back to your game.'

To Zoe, she says, 'Have you ever thought of sewing as a business?'

Zoe's face lights up. 'Have I ever. But where to start?'

'I had a business for a few years.' Irene tells Zoe about *Irene Flower*. How she worked from home and sold at markets and fashion stores in the city. 'There was a lot of travelling to and from Hobart.'

'Are you thinking of starting up again?'

'Not exactly. I have other ideas. Nothing solid yet.'

Zoe grins. 'Whatever it is, let me know if you can fit me in.'

Irene nods. 'Leave it with me and I'll let you know.'

'Right... Yes, right...' Milo raises his arms in a victory pose. 'I did it!'

When they leave, Irene watches them from the doorway as Milo skips through Irene's gate and his own, waving enthusiastically all the way to their door.

Irene closes her own door and stands for a moment, feeling the silence of the space. A silence still imbued with the echo of a small boy's excitement.

HELEN 2024

Helen stands before the shelf in her living room where she has set some of the items from her mother's flat.

A framed photo of Pete and Poppy dressed in pirate gear is her favourite. She decides to keep this on display and sets it next to a photo of Bill and Irene on their wedding day.

A stack of Irene's photo albums can go in a cupboard. There are so many of them. Helen looks through them every now and then. Seeing pictures of her mother stirs up a raw-edged feeling, but she keeps looking at them, purposefully conjuring up the love and the pain that exists all muddled up together.

Then there's the ceramic lady Sing gave Irene as a gift. Of all Sing's ladies, this one has to be the weirdest. Helen can't think why she gave her this one when Sing is usually so thoughtful. Irene said she liked it but Helen suspects she was just being polite. What should she do with it—give it back to Sing? Helen certainly doesn't want it.

Helen has dealt with everything else from the flat. She kept her mother's blankets for the spare room which they still call the yellow room, though until recently it hadn't had anything yellow in it for years. Helen goes in there now and looks at the old daisy coverlet she has returned to the bed. It stirs up so much emotion, she thinks she should change the cover to something else.

There's Irene's filing cabinet to go through which Helen will have to find a whole afternoon to tackle. It took them ages to find the keys which were stuck between two drawers of Bill's desk. They must have fallen through a crack where the sides of the top drawer were coming apart. Helen has no excuse now. She really should start sorting it out.

Helen goes back to the shelf in the living room and studies the ceramic lady again. She takes hold of it and shifts it around, viewing it from different angles. No, there's no saving it.

She picks up the ornament and sets it on a table by the back door, ready to take down to Sing and Caleb's.

'Sorry,' she says to the bent woman, who appears to be trying to stand. 'I just can't figure you out.'

IRENE 2014

Irene opens the door to her flat one Friday afternoon to find Helen on the doorstep, waving a bottle of wine in the air.

'School's out, the weekend's here. I've come to sit on your deck.'

As she steps inside, Pete and Poppy come up behind her. They're dressed as pirates in stripy tops, cardboard hats and eye patches. Poppy carries a silver cardboard sword and Pete has a toy parrot attached to his shoulder.

'Ahoy there,' they both say at once.

'What's this?' Irene says.

'Aarrr. It's talk like a pirate day, Reenie. Dad and me's going to the pirate picnic.'

'At the community centre,' Pete adds.

Helen calls out from inside the flat, 'See you two pirates later.'

'Fair winds, Lubber,' Pete calls. To Irene, he says, 'We'll be back in an hour to pick Helen up and I'll leave Pirate Poppy with you.'

'Wait. Can I take a photo?' Irene grabs her phone and comes back to take a snap of them by the door before waving them off.

Poppy skips down to the gate, jabbing her sword at the air.

'You didn't want to go to the pirate thing?' Irene says as she goes back to her living room.

'I'm too tired,' Helen says. 'Pete offered to take her and he'll enjoy it.'

'I'll get some glasses, then.'

Helen stands in the middle of the room with the bottle of wine in her hand, turning around in a circle and shaking her head. 'I'm still getting used to it, this tiny space of yours.'

Irene takes two glasses from an overhead cupboard in the kitchen. She likes her new place. It might be minimalistic, but she has her own personal belongings around. Her books and photo albums, the ceramic woman Sing made and gave her as a gift.

Helen studies the ornament with her head tilted. 'Why did Sing give you that particular lady, I wonder? She's a strange one.'

'A bit like me, then.' Irene heads for the deck with the wine glasses. 'Grab some cushions on your way out.'

Helen pours the drinks. Irene plumps her cushion and leans back with her glass, looking over the water. The low acrylic-glass sides of the deck give an expansive view of the river with the rows of willow trees either side whose leaves have turned a buttery yellow. In the distance, the purple hills and stone bridge give the scene a fairytale air. It would make a wonderful painting, Irene thinks, but photographs will have to do.

Helen says, 'It is gorgeous out here, I'll give you that. However, the view from your house is spectacular too.'

'I know, but I needed a change. I've lived on that property for thirty-four years.'

'You don't need to explain. It's your life.' She sighs. 'I am going to miss the big family get-togethers at yours, though. The big space and all the food.' She looks behind her at the sliding door. 'You can't very well do that here.'

'I have been thinking. Why don't you and Pete move into the house?'

Helen frowns and shakes her head.

'It'll be yours when I'm gone, anyway. You could move into it now.'

'No.'

'Why not? *You* could have the family get-togethers. I'd help with the cooking.'

'You might change your mind about this place. You might want to go back.'

'That won't happen.' Irene takes a long, slow sip of her wine.

'You think so now. But what if your landlord sells the flat, or wants it for themselves or something?'

'Your father left me very well off. If that happened, I'd be in a position to buy something else.'

'Goodness, the farm must have done alright.' Helen pours more wine into her glass and holds the bottle out to Irene.

'Thanks. He had investments too. He was very good at making money. As it turns out.'

Helen looks sharply at her. 'Didn't you know?'

'I didn't know everything, put it that way.'

After a pause, Helen says, 'He would have wanted to make sure you were looked after, should something happen to him.'

Irene smiles. 'Of course he would.'

Helen curls her feet underneath herself and leans back into a cushion. 'If you can afford to buy something else, why don't you? Instead of paying rent.'

'I rather like knowing I can live here and someone else is responsible for repairs and that sort of thing. It's—' Irene searches for the right word. '—freeing.'

'Fair enough. All the same, we won't be moving into your house. I'm happier knowing you have it to return to, if you need. Pete and I are okay, we can manage our mortgage easily enough.'

'Well, the offer's there,' Irene says.

They both stare out at the river for a few moments, and movement catches Irene's eye. She grabs Helen's hand beside her and whispers, 'Shh, don't move.'

She slowly raises her hand and points. 'Over there, beside the big rock jutting off the bank. Can you see it?'

Helen sucks in a breath as a slick, brown creature darts across the rock. It slips over the grassy bank and stops for a moment to scratch itself with a webbed foot, before diving into the water bill-first. They watch its tail vanish beneath the branches of a willow.

'Oh, that was adorable. Poppy will be envious,' Helen says. 'How many sleepovers has she had with you? And no sign of the platypus.'

'Maybe she'll see it tonight. If she can keep quiet long enough.'

'I did tell her she has to be quiet.'

'She tries,' Irene says, and they laugh.

'Oh, look.' Helen points.

There it is again, climbing back up onto the rock. Its dark fur glistens, almost camouflaged against the descending shadows, and it sits poised as if it knows its strange beauty is being admired. As it slips back into the river—soundlessly, elegantly—Irene thinks she has never before felt such peace.

IRENE 2014

It's a risk, of course it is. But oh!—what if she can make it work?

Irene sits at a table outside The River Café, drinking coffee and gazing across the street at the vacant building on the other side. It's perfect—glass storefront, accessible, located on the main road amid the bustle. The visions in Irene's head have been keeping her awake at night. The more she thinks about the possibilities, the more animated she becomes. She's at the point where she either does something with her ideas or they'll wear her brain out with their relentless frenzy.

She finishes her drink and makes a decision. Waving her thanks to Joss through the café window, she hurries down the street and into the real estate office. Miranda Hix welcomes her heartily and ushers her into a cubicle.

'Have a seat. It's great to see you,' she says. 'How're you finding the flat?'

Irene tells her she loves the flat and they make small talk for a while, before Irene says, 'I have another request.'

Miranda leans forward, nodding.

'I'm looking for a commercial property to rent. I want to open a retail business, a kind of gift shop. I was wondering about the building opposite The River Café. It's for lease, I noticed.'

'Ah.' Miranda's expression dulls. 'The owner is asking a lot for that one. Because of its prime position.'

When Miranda tells Irene the amount being asked for the rent, Irene almost gasps.

Miranda nods. 'I can tell by your face what you're thinking.'

'That's way too much.' Irene shakes her head. 'What a pity.'

'The only other one I have on Main Street is number two. It's up at the hill end near the cat rescue. Not really a good location for a gift shop.'

Irene shakes her head. 'No, that wouldn't work. Never mind.'

'Do you have your heart set on the main road? I have another idea.'

'I'm open to hearing it.'

'Right.' Miranda jumps to her feet and grabs her handbag. 'Come with me.'

Miranda takes keys from a cupboard and leaves a message at the front desk, before opening the door for Irene.

Outside, the street is bustling. No matter the weather, Durrunby stays busy with not only local shoppers, but tourists, holidayers and weekend escapees from the city. A recent surge in overseas tourists has added a new vibrancy to the town. Now would be a good time to open a retail outlet.

Miranda leads Irene across the street and heads along the footpath in the direction of the river. They walk through the busiest part of the street and into a quieter section. As they pass the op shop, Miranda says, 'I've thought about this place quite a lot.'

Irene looks about. 'What place?'

'Bear with me.'

The op shop is attached to the community centre, which sits on the corner of a tiny intersection. Miranda turns into the narrow one-way lane joining the main road—Maple Lane. The main entrance to the community centre is located here and next to the centre, as Irene now discovers, is another vacant building with a glass shopfront.

'Ta-da.' Miranda waves her arm towards the building.

Irene stops and looks it over. At first glance, it appears old and neglected. The paint on the window frames is peeling, the grass overgrown. But its bones look solid and as she takes it in, the shabby exterior transforms into something else in her mind's eye. She sees possibilities.

Miranda, astute businesswoman, waits silently until Irene turns to her.

They lock eyes and Miranda grins. 'You see what I see.'

Irene nods. 'Nothing a bit of TLC won't fix.'

'And the location?'

'Not in the hub as most would consider to be the hub...'

'But...'

'But next door to another hub—the community centre and op shop. A possible partnering with those places, chances to be involved with the community, mutual benefits...'

'I knew you'd see it,' Miranda says. She turns back to the building and sighs happily. 'There is potential here, and not everyone would see that. Let's look inside.'

The inside needs work, but the rent is a fraction of the other building. It'll take some elbow grease, minor repairs and a fresh coat of paint to make it shine, but shine it will.

'It's roomier than it looks from the outside,' Irene says. She pictures shelves on the walls, a counter, a sewing table and racks for children's clothes. There's an adjoining room for more stock or storage, and a functional kitchen and bathroom at the back.

She turns to Miranda and nods. 'I'd best make a visit to the council.'

'You won't have any issues with them,' Miranda says. 'Anyway, I know people.' She taps her nose with her finger. 'How about we go back to the office for a chat.'

Irene does one more turnabout, taking in the whole space. She can see it, as if she has vision into the future. It's there as solid as anything she's ever believed in. The business she has wanted for a very long time is going to happen.

The four women stand inside the building, looking around the main room— Sing wide-eyed, Irene's neighbour Zoe thoughtful, Helen with arms folded. As Irene observes them, a sudden wind gust rattles the window making them all jump.

'It's risky,' Helen says.

'Life is risky,' Irene replies.

'You should be cautious.' Helen squints at the ceiling as if searching for cracks.

Irene tries to keep the irritation from her voice. 'I'm sixty years old, Helen. I'm tired of being cautious. The reason we're here is not about *whether* to start a business, but about *who* may like to be in it with me.'

Sing turns to the largest wall and opens her arms wide. 'This. I see shelves, a display of handicrafts, lots of colour.'

'Exactly what I thought,' Irene says. 'I can see your ceramics up there, Sing. Your pots and your lovely ladies. We can sell local hand-made items on consignment. We'll buy some racks for Zoe's creations which we can arrange anywhere in the room.'

'Where would I set up?' Zoe asks.

'You decide,' Irene says. 'Walk around and get a sense of where you'd feel the most comfortable and inspired. You'll be our main attraction. Customers can come in and watch our resident sewist at work.'

Zoe grins, her cheeks pinking. She wanders around the perimeter of the room, touches the walls, looks at the window. 'The light's good here. Maybe a long table against this wall so I'll have the light from the window. And I could use the wall as an ideas board.'

'Perfect,' Irene says. 'I have multiple tubs of fabric stored at the house, I'll bring those in for you. And my sewing machine and over-locker are in pretty good nick. You can start with those and make a list of other items you need as we go.'

Helen clicks her tongue. 'It's rather spur-of-the-moment, isn't it?'

'Actually, it's been in my head for more years than I can count.'

Sing swings around to face Irene. 'Really?'

'Why didn't you do it before, then?' Helen asks, as she pokes her head into the adjoining room and pulls a face.

'Oh, many reasons,' Irene says.

Zoe wanders about some more, does a final inspection of the back room, and returns. She appears to be trying to keep the grin from her face when she says, 'Count me in.'

Sing claps her hands and says, 'Me too. I'd better get creating, I only have a couple of months before this one comes.' She pats her stomach affectionately.

'Well, congratulations everyone,' Helen says. 'You're all mad but I kind of envy you.'

Sing says, 'Do you think you'd like to—'

But Helen interrupts, shaking her head. 'I'm a teacher. It's what I love, as much as I complain.'

Irene takes the key to the building from her pocket and moves towards the door. 'Well, that's it. There's a lot to organise before we can even think of opening. Cleaning up this place, planning, legal paperwork. We'll take it step-by-step.'

They leave the building and Irene locks the door. Sing points across the road and says, 'We're not the only ones tucked away here, anyway.'

It's true. The pharmacy sits on the opposite corner, its main entrance on Main Street. Next to the pharmacy, in Maple Lane itself, are two businesses—one selling antiques and the other wood crafted items. From there, the lane contains only residential buildings.

'At least we're close to the main drag,' Zoe says.

Sing twirls and says, 'I have a good feeling about this.'

As they walk back towards the main road, the wind picks up, sending a flurry of blossoms spiralling down the lane. They flutter past the women like a cloud of white wings. A good omen, Irene thinks.

HELEN 2024

Helen has navigated death and grief. Her mother's death. Her father's. The miscarriages she never told her mother about. Each time, the slow and painful crawl from the Slough of Despond, back to life, duty, responsibility.

Today she buries Banjo, the budgerigar. A tiny life, an insignificant death. But somehow it crashes into those other past griefs and tangles itself up in them, dragging them back to the surface. Oh, how it hurts. In the garden, she shovels earth over the little box. The tiny body once filled with life—a flurry of feathers and chatter and frequent bad temper—is silent and still. The stone in Helen's gut that has been there for so long re-emerges, pushes itself upward. She sits flat on her bottom in the dirt and howls.

By the time Pete is due home from his Saturday shift at the hospital, she has pulled herself together and baked biscuits. These emotional roller-coaster moments have been happening more frequently since her mother died. She'll be cruising along, happy as you please, and bam! down she goes. Up again within a few hours or a day, but already anticipating the next crash. Who'd be a woman? If she'd been given the choice, she might have chosen to be a man. She thinks for a moment, chuckles at the irreverent pictures darting into her imagination and shakes her head. Being a man was probably no easier.

She makes herself a coffee, sits on the sofa and picks up a photo album. She's been looking through her mother's albums lately. Funny how she calls them her mother's, as if they belonged more to Irene than to Helen's father. Her mother was the meticulous record keeper in the family. Her latest were photobooks she'd created online from digital images, but she'd still referred to them as her albums.

The one Helen looks through now begins with the lease of the building in Maple Lane. There they are, cleaning, sanding, painting walls. It was intense work. Helen was sore for ages afterwards.

The next page showcases the building after its repairs and facelift. There is one taken after the shop name, *Maple Lane Gifts,* was painted onto the window. They're standing outside with their arms up, pointing to the sign with big smiles. The following few photos show the space decked out with the first lot of merchandise, and the rest of the book is filled with pictures of them doing various tasks around the shop.

Irene was a remarkable business woman. The way she connected with the community, marketed the business, managed the finances and partnered with the community centre. All those free sewing courses she ran at the centre that attracted business back to the gift shop. She was truly amazing.

It's a puzzle why she hadn't done something like it sooner. What was it she'd said on the day they first saw the building—that she'd wanted to run a business like that for a long time? So, why hadn't she?

There's a noise at the front door and Pete calls out, 'Hi honey, I'm home,' in a sing-song voice.

'In here,' Helen calls back.

Pete comes into the living room in his socks and bends to sit next to her. When almost seated, he glances out the window and straightens up again, staring out.

'Oh,' he says.

'Yes,' says Helen.

'When?'

'This morning. I found him just after you left.'

Pete lowers himself onto the sofa and wraps his arm around Helen's shoulders. They both look out the window at the empty cage on the table where Poppy's budgie used to live. The door is open as if Banjo has simply hopped out and flown away.

Helen can't help herself. 'Oh Pete,' she says, and bursts into tears again.

IRENE 2016

It takes two years for Irene to convince Helen she won't be moving back into the house. 'It's yours,' Irene kept saying. 'I *want* you to have it. Move in, sell your place, save yourselves some money.'

Finally, Helen and Pete agreed to move into Irene's house. However, they've rented out their own in case Irene decides she's made a mistake about the flat, even though she's been living in it for two years. She won't convince them otherwise.

Irene stands at the window of what is now Helen and Pete's home, gazing out at the lush, green paddocks of the farm. In the distance, between two outcrops of eucalypts, the scrap of sea glistens. Slick and calm today, like a tiny paradise. She moves to the corner window and looks out at the milking sheds, the roof of the old farmhouse, a herd of Holsteins grazing in a paddock. Caleb will be out there somewhere, working hard. Irene feels a swell of pride in her chest as she thinks of her son.

'Here's your tea, Mum.'

As Helen sets a cup and plate of biscuits on the coffee table, Irene folds herself into an armchair.

The house looks different with Helen and Pete's belongings in it. Helen teases Irene about the sparseness of her flat, but Helen is quite the minimalist herself. No clutter in this room. A smart leather lounge suite, chrome coffee table, a couple of modern shelves and a

TV mounted flat to the wall. Irene likes it. Since Bill's and her own belongings have been moved out, Irene finds she can breathe easier in this house. She relaxes in Helen's armchair, enjoying the view from the windows.

Helen has gone back to the kitchen bench and Irene hears the clink of a spoon as she stirs her tea. Helen calls out, 'We've put your filing cabinet in the shed. Let us know when you want to go through it.'

'Oh that. I suppose I should.' Irene can't think of anything she wants to do less. All those papers, she can't be bothered.

'There's a box of loose photos in the spare room too. I'll keep holding onto them until you want them, shall I?'

'Thanks.' Irene thinks about the photos she couldn't fit into her albums. It would be fun to go through them with Helen sometime.

She can't help feeling guilty about leaving her family to clear out the stuff from the house, but in the end, she couldn't face it. Helen was good about it, of course, but she must have been annoyed. Irene would have paid for a professional service to sort everything but Helen insisted they could pitch in and do it themselves. At least they all scored a share in the high-end kitchen appliances, not to mention the Royal Doulton.

Helen flops onto the sofa with her drink. She lies back against the headrest and sighs. 'This is nice.'

Irene watches her daughter's slow smile and the way her shoulders sink back into the sofa. 'You needed this holiday,' she says.

Helen nods. 'No Kayden Skinner for two whole weeks.'

Irene guffaws. 'That bad?'

'Oh yes. You wouldn't believe.'

'In my day, that kind of behaviour got you the cane. That's showing my age, isn't it?'

'I can't condone physical punishment, but I do fantasise about giving some of them a good dressing down.'

'Well, take it easy for the next couple of weeks. Buy yourself some pre-made meals from The River Café like I do. They let you use your own containers.'

'Don't you get sick of bought food?'

'Why would I? No effort, no mess, minimal washing up. And Joss is an excellent cook. If I do feel like something different, I can buy a burger or a souvlaki or anything I like, all a short walk away. Did you know there's a vegetarian café opening soon?'

Helen shakes her head. 'You used to love cooking.'

Irene shrugs one shoulder. 'It's different when you're on your own.'

They're both quiet for a moment. Perhaps Helen is thinking of her father and how she misses him. Or maybe she's feeling sorry for Irene. She needn't. Irene hasn't felt this invigorated since her market days back in the nineties. A bit slower of course, she is sixty-two after all.

'Actually,' Helen says, 'I was thinking of coming to help you in the shop.'

'That wouldn't be much of a holiday for you.'

'You know what they say about a change.'

'I won't say we wouldn't appreciate your help. But do make sure you have a rest.'

'I will.'

As Helen sets her cup down, she bumps it on the edge of the coffee table and tea splashes onto the table. She wipes it with her fingers, flicks her hand so the droplets spatter over the carpet, and leans back into the sofa.

Irene wonders whether she's done this because she feels relaxed. Or if she's just too tired to care.

IRENE 2016

'Morning, Brenda.' Irene waves to a stout woman arranging a bucket of cut flowers outside the florist shop on the other side of the road. Brenda waves back.

Next, she blows a kiss to Zola at the hairdresser's window. Zola keeps Irene looking smart. These days, Irene prefers her short cut as an overall silver-grey without the pink highlights. However, one day she might try a red. Why not? You only live once.

Irene calls 'good morning' to several other people as she hurries along the street, heading for her own shop in Maple Lane. As she enters the building, Sing pokes her head out from the side room and greets her.

Zoe is sitting at her sewing table, her machine humming. She looks up and says, 'Before you ask—busy, busy, busy.'

'Well, that's good, good, good.' Irene does a silly dance. 'I'm happy, happy, happy.'

Zoe swings her swivel chair around. 'You're in a good mood.'

'Why wouldn't I be?' She takes a hanger from a row of children's clothes and holds up the tiny pair of hand-sewn denim pants with embroidered pockets. 'Look at these. You're amazing, Zoe. You have more talent in your little finger—'

'—than you've got in your whole body. So you keep saying.' Zoe rolls her eyes. She turns back to her sewing bench, but Irene catches her grinning.

Sing emerges from the back storeroom, carrying a stack of fabric shopping bags, followed by a toddler hugging an armload of the bags to his chest. She turns to smile at the child. 'Come on, my sweet boy. You can do it.'

Irene can't resist scooping him up in her arms. 'How's our chief shopkeeper today?'

'Ree,' Tobias says, giving her a sloppy kiss on the cheek. 'Down.' He wriggles until she places him back on the floor where he waddles wide-legged after his mother.

Irene watches Zoe as she stitches the tiny pieces of a shirt together, her lips pressed together in concentration. Irene will never forget the moment she suggested the idea for the gift shop to Zoe—the sudden blaze of Zoe's cheeks and shower of tears. It turns out Zoe's love of sewing was an actual starving passion. And here she is making a name for herself all over Durrunby and Crayfish Cove.

Sing, of course, was a natural addition with the online handicraft store she had already established. And Irene has really taken to internet banking. Who knew it could be so easy? In fact, Irene has never had so much fun in her life.

She gazes about the shop at the racks of handstitched and upcycled children's clothes, shelves of handknits, candles, ceramics and jewellery. Sing creates the soap and the ceramic tableware, but her best talent lays in her quirky ornaments—women in various kinds of dress carrying baskets, flowers, babies, placards and boxes. They are hugely popular.

Rather than playing music, they fill their space with their own sounds—sporadic chatter, the tinkle of the bell on the door, the hum of Zoe's sewing machine. No need to add anything to what is already a joyful space.

Could Irene have done this earlier in her life? Perhaps Zoe and Sing were the elements she needed, the three of them merging their talents to pull the dream together. She wouldn't have done it if Bill was alive and this knowledge exists as a dissonant jarring, evidence of a complicated grief.

The bell on the door sounds and two women enter. Sing greets them and in her non-intrusive way, introduces them to Zoe and invites them to watch 'our sewist' at work. The customers are, of course, delighted and one of them buys a shirt with printed Tasmanian devils. By the time they're leaving the shop, they've purchased several other items and their carry bag is bulging.

'We're going on a cruise,' one of them says on their way to the door.

'A *cruise?*' Irene says.

'To New Zealand,' the other one says. 'We have family there, that's who the gifts are for.'

'Actually, the soap's for me,' the first one laughs.

They're obviously excited and Irene feels a fluttering in her own abdomen.

'Well, have a lovely trip,' she says as she waves them off at the door.

When they've left, Irene says, 'I've always wanted to go on a cruise.'

Zoe swivels her chair about to face her. She lifts one knee onto her seat and laces her fingers around it. 'Where to?' she asks.

Irene shrugs her shoulders. 'I don't really care, to be honest. It's the cruising itself I'd like to experience—sitting around doing nothing but eating, reading and watching the ocean.'

'Did you ever suggest it to Bill?' Sing asks as she re-folds a knitted blanket.

'It wasn't Bill's thing. He called cruise ships "germ incubators". I guess there's nothing stopping me now.'

'You should do it,' Sing says.

Irene nods. 'Maybe I should.'

Sing bends to pick Tobias up and swings him onto her hip. 'Well, I'd best be off. Ladies to make.' She glances at the diminishing row of ceramic women on the shelf behind her.

As she's heading out the door, Helen arrives with a box of donuts from the bakery. Sing takes two and within seconds, Tobias has stuck a chocolate covered donut to his face. Sing scurries off, licking her fingers.

Irene and Zoe drop what they're doing and zone in on the donuts.

Helen sets them on the counter. 'There, don't say I don't look after you. So what's new?'

Zoe mumbles through her mouthful, 'Your mum's going on a cruise.'

'What? Clues...?'

'Cruise.'

'A cruise. Really, when?'

'Maybe later in the year,' Irene says.

Helen's face lights up. 'There's one from Sydney to Cairns during the next school holidays—a round trip. One of the teachers is going. That'd be perfect for us. Pete wants to take a week off and take Poppy camping, so you and I can go.'

Helen grabs a donut with pink icing and takes a huge bite. She's so animated and brimming with cheerfulness that Irene hasn't the heart to say what she should say right now before this idea goes any further.

Irene can imagine Helen on a cruise—organising, directing, creating itineraries. She'd have them signed up for all the dinners and shows. And look out, cabin staff, if anything isn't exactly as it looks on the website photographs.

'You look tired, Mum,' Helen says, and Irene almost laughs.

Yes, it would be a very tiring cruise with Helen. Irene would much rather go alone.

HELEN 2024

Helen blinks at the eleven-year-old with the clenched teeth standing before her.

'What? Sorry, can you repeat that, Briony?'

'Ugh, what is *wrong* with you?' The child rolls her eyes.

'I beg your pardon?' Never, in Helen's many years of teaching, has she had a student talk back to her like this girl.

'I said that Mum said to tell you I *did* do the assignment. It got accidentally deleted and it's *not* my fault.'

Helen purses her lips as her mind is accosted by an image of this child's mother. Is another encounter with the woman worth the hassle of holding Briony to account for her actions (or in-actions)? Whatever happened to teaching children responsibility for their behaviour? She really shouldn't let Briony get away with this again.

Helen sighs inwardly and turns away to her desk. 'Bring it to me as soon as you can,' she says wearily.

As she glances back, she catches a smirk on Briony's face as she heads out the door.

Teaching feels too hard today. The truth is, Helen can't get her mother's notebook out of her mind—the one she was reading this morning before she left for work. She's been wrestling with it all day. She even sent a text message to Pete to make sure he's home when she gets there so she can talk to him about it. She feigns a migraine so she doesn't have to attend the after-school staff meeting, and heads home.

'Hey, babe.' Pete wraps his arms around her as she walks in the front door and almost attempts to lift her into the air.

'Don't even try,' she grumbles, batting him away. 'I've put on two kilos in the last month.'

'And you are as beautiful as ever, my bonny sweet Helen, light of my life.'

Helen fails to stifle a giggle. Pete is the most ridiculous man she's ever met, precisely the reason she fell for him. And married him. And if she's honest, she's still pinching herself that he fell for her as well.

'What's this discussion we need to have?' he asks.

She jerks her head towards the living room. 'Come on.'

When they're seated together on the sofa, Helen takes a spiral-bound notebook from the coffee table and opens it. She points to the page and holds it out to Pete.

'Read that.'

Pete takes the book and reads. *Lost things: Scarf, Garnet ring, Letters, Keys, Amethyst earrings.* 'What's troubling you about this?'

'Do you remember how Mum was always losing and misplacing things?'

'When she was having chemo, yes. We know the chemo affected her short-term memory. I assume by keys she's referring to the security keys?'

'That's my guess. She had an obsession with them ever since she locked herself in the house that time. Do you remember?'

Pete frowns. 'Yeah, it was a bit weird.'

'A bit weird is an understatement. When she rang me from her mobile she was so distressed I couldn't get any sense out of her. I got there just before Dad came up from the sheds and used my key to get in. Mum was literally shaking, saying she couldn't get out of the house.'

'The keys were missing, right?'

'No, that was the thing. Don't you remember me telling you? When Dad came in, he looked above the door and the key was hanging there. Or maybe it was caught up where she couldn't see it. I don't know, it doesn't matter. The point is, the keys were there all along.'

'All of them?'

'I believe so.'

'So how did she manage to deadlock herself in?'

'No idea. She was always losing stuff, forgetting where things were kept. Dad was so worried. She'd go into a room and forget why she was there.'

'Everyone does that. I do it, don't you?'

'I suppose.'

Pete leans back, puts his arm across the sofa behind Helen and strokes her hair. 'I agree she was unwell, especially during the chemo. But she got better and had a good life. I don't know that we need to worry about it now.'

Helen takes the notebook from his hand and flicks back to the first page. 'Look at the date,' she says.

Pete frowns. 'Two-thousand-thirteen.'

'That's at least eight years after the chemo. Probably closer to nine.' Helen pauses, watching Pete's face as the information sinks in. 'Why has she written a list of lost items in twenty-thirteen? You're the nurse, could her brain still have been affected?'

Pete puts on his thinking face. 'It's possible. Some cancer patients report permanently impaired cognitive function.'

'From chemotherapy?'

'Not necessarily. It can be caused by the cancer itself.' Pete places his hand on Helen's knee. 'But honey, a list of lost things doesn't constitute cognitive dysfunction.'

'Alright, how about this?' Helen picks up another notebook from the table. 'Here's one of her earliest books. This one was written years before the cancer. I found weird stuff in there. And not just in that one, but in many of her notebooks, spanning years and years.'

'What do you mean by weird stuff?'

'Mostly strange drawings and lists. I've figured out that some refer to contents of cupboards or drawers. Others I can't make head nor tail of. But they're kind of hidden amongst her business notes as if she didn't want anyone else to read them.'

'Show me.'

Helen flicks through the early notebook, points to a picture looking vaguely like a ladder containing words relating to linen—*sheets, cotton blankets, wool blankets, pillow cases, table cloths.*

'Looks like a list of cupboard contents to me,' Pete says.

Helen clicks her tongue. 'Yes, but why is it here? And look at this.' She takes the book from him, flicks to another page and hands it back.

Pete frowns over a string of letters that make no obvious sense.

Helen shows him several other cryptic entries and says, 'What if her impaired cognitive function wasn't caused by the cancer?'

'I don't know. She seemed fine in her later years.'

'What—suddenly moving out of her house and squeezing herself into that awful flat? That wasn't fine. And what about how she didn't cook anymore when she'd always loved cooking? I tell you, she wasn't herself.'

'The flat wasn't awful.' Pete closes the notebook and runs his hands over the cover.

Helen's stomach clenches. 'And something else. What if she was still unwell when she moved? It might mean she wasn't thinking right when she went on that cruise.'

She watches Pete's expression alter as realisation dawns. 'You don't think—?'

Helen nods. 'The cruise, and what happened to Poppy.'

IRENE 2016

As it happens, as the school term draws to a close, Helen catches a bad case of flu and can't go on the cruise with Irene. Half of Crayfish Cove and Durrunby have come down with it. Pete is asked to do extra shifts at the hospital so Pete and Poppy's camping trip is also postponed.

Irene makes the most logical decision and offers to take Poppy on the cruise. Helen is grateful and Irene feels energised. Why hadn't she thought of it before? Poppy and Reenie sailing the ocean together.

Sing and Zoe have the shop under control. After two years of their hard work, the business almost runs itself. And Irene must admit, she's due for some time off.

On the day they depart, Poppy is wild with excitement. She sleeps over at Irene's the night before and Caleb picks them up early in the morning to drop them at the airport. Poppy chatters incessantly all the way to Sydney on the plane and bombards Irene with questions.

'How fast is the plane going, is it faster than a racing car?... Are they actual *clouds*? How come they're under the plane and there aren't any on top?... Who's that, is that the pilot? Which one's the pilot?... What are you doing?' (Irene was winding her watch.) 'Why hasn't your watch got a battery?' She admires one of the flight attendants— 'She's so pretty. Doesn't she look like a movie star?' —and decides to be a flight attendant when she grows up.

'Here, have some barley sugar,' Irene says, and enjoys some peace and quiet as the plane descends.

Poppy conks out on the bus from the airport to the cruise terminal and Irene strokes the sleeping head in her lap. She hopes she'll actually be able to rest on the cruise. She feels like she could sleep for a week.

They line up at the terminal shed with a crowd carrying backpacks and trundling carry-on cases. Poppy holds onto Irene's hand and seems to have finally run out of chatter. Nearby, a group of young women travelling together have pulled out their phones and are ignoring each other. Next to them, an elderly group laugh uproariously at something a woman in a red sunhat has said. No guesses as to which group are going to have the most fun.

Ahead of Irene is a young man with a shaved head and an elaborate tattoo snaking up his neck and over his scalp. Is it safe to tattoo your head, she wonders? He's travelling with an older gentleman with silver hair. Irene notes similarities in their facial features—high cheekbones, a certain slant to the jawline—and wonders if they're father and son. The older man, Irene can't help noticing, is very handsome. She almost giggles at herself. He turns his head and Irene darts her eyes away just in time.

Finally, they reach the check-in desk, receive their pass card and are ushered through a final roped-off area before boarding the ship. Poppy clings to Irene, leaning into her with evident exhaustion. Irene navigates her way up an escalator, down a corridor or two, and eventually finds their cabin.

'Choose your bed,' Irene says.

A new burst of energy bubbles up in Poppy. 'This one. I love it. What's that, is that a TV? Oh wow, we've got a balcony.'

Irene lies down on her own bed.

'Are you tired, Reenie?'

'I am a bit.'

Poppy skips off to investigate the bathroom, comes back and says, 'I'm hungry.'

Irene sits up. 'Before we do anything, we have to go to the muster station for a safety drill. Then we'll go exploring and have something to eat. How does that sound?'

'Can I look at the balcony first?'

On the balcony, Poppy stands and gapes. 'Wow, I can't believe it.'

How glad Irene is that she brought Poppy. To think, her original idea was to go on a cruise alone. What a stupid idea, adventures like this were meant to be shared.

She puts her arm around Poppy's shoulders and kisses the top of her head. 'Monkey, you and I are going to have the time of our lives.'

Irene wakes late the next morning and Poppy is still fast asleep. She looks at her watch. Plenty of time before the kids' club starts. Poppy has been eagerly anticipating spending time with the other children onboard and Irene secretly relishes the prospect of a few quiet hours to herself.

By the time Irene has showered and dressed, Poppy is stirring. She blinks, looks about, sees Irene and sits up. 'We're on a cruise,' she says. 'And I'm hungry.'

Poppy asks if they can have breakfast at the bistro where they'd eaten the evening before. There are mountains of food. Irene hasn't seen anything like it. Poppy piles croissants and jam sachets onto a plate. Irene, overwhelmed by choice, chooses muesli. She can always try something more adventurous later.

They find a table. From Irene's seat, she has a clear view of the doors and sees the handsome man with the silver hair and his companion enter the bistro and head towards the breakfast buffet. Irene mentally kicks herself for the fact that she notices him. He's only a man. Handsome, yes, but so are lots of men. There isn't anything particularly special looking about him. Even so, she enjoys surreptitiously observing the easy way he walks—leaning slightly forward, relaxed, his neck craned as if listening intently to what the younger man is saying. There's a kindness about him. Silly, Irene is sure, to be thinking in this way. After all, how can you really tell whether a stranger is kind, just by looking at them?

Irene thinks of Bea from the op shop in Crayfish Cove—her pinched features and the gossipy way of her. Some faces do tell a story—creases and lines in telling places. Of course, there are also faces that lie.

Irene keeps her eyes on her muesli, deliberately averting her gaze from the buffet. Nevertheless, her peripheral vision—seemingly on high alert—catches movement at the table nearest hers and Poppy's. She turns casually to glance over just as Handsome Man sets his breakfast tray on the table and looks her way. He catches her eye, smiles and nods his head in greeting. Irene automatically nods her own head and quickly looks away.

Poppy is struggling with a jam sachet and Irene peels the foil lid away for her. Poppy digs the tip of her knife into the tiny container, attempting to scrape the jam onto her croissant. She gives up and uses her finger, spooning out the blobs onto her breakfast and sucking the jam from her finger. She takes a large bite of the croissant, widens her eyes at Irene and makes a 'mmm' sound while nodding her head.

'Good?' Irene says.

Poppy's eyes crinkle in a smile, then shoot sideways. Her eyebrows go up and Irene turns to find Handsome Man standing beside them.

'Excuse me,' he says. 'May I bother you for some sugar? We don't appear to have any on our table.'

'Of course. Help yourself.' Irene hands the container of sugar packs to him.

'Just a couple will do, thanks very much.'

He takes them to his table and sets them down. Irene keeps watching as he takes hold of his trousers at the knees and hitches them upwards before he sits down. Irene almost giggles. The last person she remembers doing that was her grandfather.

The man turns to her again and says, 'I'm Max,' at the moment Irene fills her mouth with muesli. She nods and puts her hand up to shield her mouth as she chews.

'And this is my son, Gregory. Pleased to meet you.'

Irene gulps, coughs and gestures with her hand.

'Oh, I'm sorry—'

Irene shakes her head and clears her throat. 'Quite alright. I'm Irene and this is my granddaughter.' She's not about to go divulging her granddaughter's name to strangers, so she smiles politely and turns back to Poppy.

Poppy, with her mouth full, bursts into a giggle and pieces of flaky pastry spray across the table. She slaps one hand across her mouth and points to Max's table with the other.

Max has jumped up and is wiping vigorously at his shirtfront with a serviette while his son laughs.

'Can't take you anywhere, can we, Dad?'

Max glances at Irene and grimaces. 'Coffee.'

'Oh dear.' Irene stares at the splotch of brown dribbling down the front of Max's white shirt. Max sits down and drops the soggy napkin on the table.

'Are you alright?' Irene asks. 'You haven't burnt yourself?'

'No, no. Thank you, I'm fine. I'm a bit grubby though, I'll have to change.'

Gregory shakes his head. 'I swear, Dad, you've got the same stain on every shirt. You should patent it.'

Irene can't help chuckling. 'I've got just the thing for that.'

'Oh, really?' Max's eyebrows shoot up.

'My daughter-in-law's handmade soap. Gentle on skin, tough on stains. I'll grab it for you as soon as we've finished our breakfast.'

Max thanks her profusely and they return to their own breakfasts. When Irene and Poppy have finished and stand up to leave, Max jumps to his feet, gesturing towards the exit. 'Do you want me to—er—'

'No, no. I'll bring it to you. Won't be long.'

When they're out of the dining room, Irene allows herself a backward glance. Max has re-seated himself. His son leans back in his chair, grinning and running one hand over his bald head. Irene calculates that Max must have had Gregory later in life. Unless Max is younger than he looks. Not that she cares, of course.

In the cabin, Irene grabs her bar of Sing's soap.

'Are you going to give that man your soap? What will you use?'

'I have an idea.' Irene hurries Poppy back out the door.

On the way into the bistro area, Irene stops to collect a small plate and knife and returns to Max's table. Max jumps up from his seat again and Irene gestures for him to sit. She sets the plate on the table with the soap on top and slices a piece off one end with the knife. The rest, she puts into her bag.

'There you are,' she says, pushing the plate towards Max. 'Wet the shirt, rub in the soap, leave for a few minutes and rinse. The stain should come out easily.'

'Thank you very much, that's awfully kind of you.'

'You're welcome. You can keep that piece for future mishaps.'

Gregory laughs loudly.

As Irene turns to leave, she says, 'I'd get onto it as soon as possible.'

'Oh. Yes, of course.' Max continues to thank her as she puts her arm around Poppy and steers her away.

At the kids' club rooms, Poppy is greeted by a club host named Taylah, and introduced to a group of children. She skitters away happily with only a cursory glance back at Irene. However, after a moment, she removes herself from the group and hurries back to smack her lips against Irene's cheek before taking off again.

Irene stands at the door for a few minutes watching the children mill around a table where the hosts start explaining a planned science experiment.

Well. Irene has a few hours to herself. What first? It's a glorious day so she travels up the escalators and heads for the pool deck. On the way, she passes food stations, bars, shops and sitting areas with ocean views. When she sees a gelato station she wishes she wasn't still full from breakfast.

She finds a sun-lounger on an upper deck above the main pool with a generous view of the sea and settles in for a lazy morning. Book, sunscreen, towel folded into a pillow for her head. Even this far above the sea line, the air is salt-edged and ripe with holiday vibe. She breathes it in deeply, holds it within herself and lets it out on a slow breath.

Irene opens her book and begins to read. A few pages in, she finds herself re-reading the same sentence, her vision swimming. The warmth of the sun is full and wraps around her, melting into her skin until her body pulsates with its heat. She drops her book and pulls off her top, rubs in more sunscreen and lies back in her shorts and bathers. Shards of light slip between her fluttering eyelids, glinting through her lashes. Bringing visions of buttercups (why buttercups?) and a small puppy, its tongue lolling.

Irene wakes with a jolt and glances about. Only a few people are dotted here and there on the sun-loungers and no one seems to have noticed Irene's sudden awakening. She thinks she may have been dreaming about her childhood dog. She shakes the sleep from herself and checks the time. Not even close to lunch time; she has a couple of hours before she needs to pick Poppy up.

The sun has mounted further into the dome of the sky and Irene's body glows with it. She swings her legs to the side of the sun-lounger, her thigh indented with a criss-cross pattern from the weave of the chair. She picks up her bag and towel. Time to move into the shade. Even better, go for a swim. She pulls off her shorts and her watch, and wraps her towel around herself, before going down the steps to the main pool area. There's more bustling down here—movement and chatter, the plashing of pool water, ice clinking in glasses.

Irene finds a seat near the pool where she can keep an eye on her bag. Within moments she has slipped into the water and immersed her whole body. The coolness is a pleasant slap that turns her skin to pimply gooseflesh. She swims lazily along the length of the pool and back, treads water for a few moments, before lying on her back and floating. Her head fills with the muffled outer sounds and the splotch and fizz of the water around her. When the acrid smell of chlorine fills her nostrils to the point of annoying, she side-strokes her way to the steps and exits the pool.

Irene dries off, wraps her towel around her middle and finds a seat away from the main throng. She flops down in a patch of full sun and soaks it up. She could become very used to this kind of life. She vaguely wonders how much it would cost to live on a cruise ship full-time.

Why she looks up at that particular moment, who can say, but it gives her time to hastily arrange her towel to cover as much of herself as possible before Max comes close enough to see her. Pretending she hasn't noticed him, she scrabbles in her bag for her shirt and pulls it on, for the first time in two years regretting the discarding of her knitted bra-stuffers.

Irene is doing up her buttons when she hears him speak.

'Hello there, Irene. I thought you should know, your soap worked a treat.'

She looks up and smiles. 'Morning, Max. I'm glad about that.'

'No sign of the coffee. I might try it on some of my other shirts. I'm afraid I've rather messed some of them up.'

'I use it all the time.'

'Ah.' Max stands with his hands in his pockets, looking around and nodding absently as if trying to think of something else to say. 'It's a lovely sunny spot you've found there.'

'Are you by yourself?' Irene asks. Did that sound like an invitation for him to join her? She hopes she isn't blushing.

'Greg's in the fitness centre. Working out and that kind of thing, you know.'

'Ah, yes I see.'

'Not for me, I'm afraid. I'm more a lazing about kind of guy. I probably shouldn't admit that.' His expression is so endearingly helpless, it makes Irene chuckle.

'Would you mind if I sit for a few moments?' he asks.

Irene gestures with her hand and he pulls a sun-lounger closer. 'Ah, that's better. Getting a bit stiff in the joints.'

'Have you been on your feet this morning?'

He nods. 'Thought I'd take a look around the ship while Greg's doing his thing. Did you know there's a running track, on a cruise ship of all things?'

The sun, now higher in the sky, blinds Irene with its glare. She places her hand against her forehead like a visor. 'Have you been on a cruise before?'

'No, never. You?'

Irene shakes her head. 'First time.' She takes her sunhat out of her bag and puts it on. 'It's nice spending some time with my granddaughter. I'm guessing that's why you brought Gregory, for some father-son bonding?'

Max's face softens into a warm smile. 'That's right. Although, Greg's technically my nephew, not my son. My wife and I brought him up after my sister died. He doesn't know who his biological father is so...' Max shrugs. 'He was young and it was a no-brainer, of course. We have a daughter as well but she wasn't able to join us. We're thinking of doing another cruise when she's free—the three of us.'

'Not your wife?'

'Ah, she's my ex-wife now. Unfortunately.' There's a sadness in his eyes and he looks away.

'What happened to your sister?'

'She had cancer.'

'Oh.' Irene feels her face flush.

'It's a terrible illness.'

'It is.'

Max meets her eye. Perhaps he sees the tell-tale flush on her face. 'I'm sorry,' he says. 'Did I—do you know someone—?'

'I'm a cancer survivor myself,' Irene says matter-of-factly. 'Had everything—chemo, radiotherapy, double-mastectomy.' (There, that's out in the open.)

'I'm sorry—'

'I've been cancer free for...' Irene counts in her head. 'Nine years now. It's alright, I don't mind talking about it.'

Max's body seems to meld into the sun-lounger. He pulls one knee up and leans back. Irene suspects she's in for a longer conversation than originally anticipated.

'It snuck up on Karen. By the time she knew she had it, it was too late.'

Irene nods. 'That happens. I'm sorry.'

'She had first rate care though. And a terrific cancer support group. They became like a second family for her in such a short time. They all came to Kaz's funeral. One of them sang.'

Max absently picks pieces of lint from his trousers and rolls them around in his fingers. There's a patch of bristles on the side of his jaw he's missed with the razor, giving him a vulnerable air. Suddenly, he sits upright and swings around to place both feet on the ground. 'What a fool I am. I shouldn't be talking about that. I do apologise. I should go and—well—' He shakes his head and stands.

'It's quite alright.' Irene blinks slowly at him, feeling her own body relax trustfully into the moment. 'You must miss Karen very much.'

Max nods, his lips pressed into a thin line.

'I don't mind listening.' Irene lifts her bag from the floor and takes out her shorts. 'Excuse me while I slip these on. Perhaps we could go in search of some food. I'm actually getting peckish.'

Max's face opens into a lovely smile. 'Oh, I would love to.'

'Come on, then.'

And Irene and Max weave their way around the sun-loungers, into the corridors and bright, welcoming spaces of the ship, in search of food.

IRENE 2016

'Tell me what you did today.'

Poppy waves goodbye to her new friends and skips down the corridor beside Irene. 'Science experiments. You know Taylah? She showed us how to make volcanos and they *spewed*.'

'Don't tell me. Baking soda and vinegar.'

'How did you know?'

'I reckon I've learnt a thing or two in my sixty-two years.'

'Sixty-two?'

'I know, it's a huge number isn't it?'

Poppy grins. 'Well, you act young.'

Irene bursts out laughing. 'Thank you. So do you.'

Reaching the promenade deck, they find a crowd gathered around a mini acrobatic show. Poppy gapes as a man in a brightly coloured costume tosses a woman into the air and holds her up by her hands so she's upside down with her feet in the air.

'How do they do that?' she asks as the woman flips about and lands on her feet on the man's shoulders. They watch the rest of the short show, which includes a juggling act and a trick with hoops. When Poppy yawns and visibly wilts, they go back to their cabin for a rest.

In the evening, they eat in the bistro, piling their plates with meats, pasta, salad and creamy pastries. They even manage a piece of chocolate torte each and Irene wonders if she'll be able to stand and waddle away.

There's no sign of Max and Greg, and Irene imagines them tête-à-tête in a restaurant somewhere. She wonders if she'll see Max tomorrow.

After their meal, Irene and Poppy watch a family movie on the pool deck, wrapped in blankets on two lounges set together. By the time the film has finished, Poppy's head is nodding. They retire to their cabin and Poppy falls asleep on her bed almost instantly. Irene covers her and kisses her gently, before opening the sliding door and stepping out onto the deck.

The air is crisp and its sharp fingers cut through her tiredness. She sits on a deck chair, enveloped by the night. Above her, the sky is a dome of velvet darkness punctuated with a million stars. Her chest expands with the beauty of it.

She closes her eyes and concentrates on the sounds around her—the deep, steady thrum of the ship's engine, the whoosh of the sea as the hull sluices through it. A sprinkle of laughter drifts up from a hidden balcony. She breathes in the scent of the ocean, opens her mouth to welcome the salt tang on her tongue.

Here she is, perched on the side of a huge ship like a barnacle clinging to a rock. What if the ship were to list and fall, crashing into the deep? Would her death be quick? Would she feel pain or would it be over in an instant? On her first cruise, she can't help thinking of the Titanic. She wonders if other people do too.

Why is she thinking of death all of a sudden? Perhaps the conversation with Max has shifted something inside her and set it off kilter. Death. There it is, an incontrovertible event on the calendar, date unknown but unerasable.

She thinks of Max's face when he spoke of his sister. The crumpling of his cheeks. 'We got to say goodbye. But it isn't enough, is it?' he'd said, before scrubbing his face with both hands. 'There were too many things I *didn't* get to say. Regret. It's the hardest thing.'

Irene hadn't known how to reply. There's no hope in regret. No way to change what has already passed. Death is the end, isn't it? The place where hope ends. How cruel when it catches people off-guard. It caught Max's sister off-guard, leaving her with no choice but to entrust her young son to the care of others. Barely time to register what was happening, let alone put her affairs in order, say goodbye, do everything she wanted to do in her lifetime.

How precious each moment of life is when you don't know how many moments you have left. What else would Irene like to do before her end? This cruise was a desire but not an important one. She wouldn't have minded if she hadn't had the opportunity. The shop she opened with Sing and Zoe was the stronger dream, one she'd only found the confidence to try once she was widowed.

Her mind tilts, unsettles. Like something sliding from an upturned table, caught the moment before it falls. She opens her eyes as a pale spectre flits by in the dark, illuminated momentarily by the moonlight or light from the ship. Surely not a bird way out here in the night? Perhaps something escaping from a balcony into the wind. She hopes it isn't a plastic bag or some other human rubbish spiralling its way down into the ocean.

Irene stands and holds onto the railing, looking out into the night. And wonders about life—its beginning, its end, and all the spaces in between.

Irene isn't surprised when Max seeks her out the next morning. She almost expects it as she sits on the pool deck in the sun, thinking about him. Poppy is happily immersed in whatever the kids' club is doing this morning and Irene will pick her up after lunch.

Max wanders over in shorts, a loose-fitting shirt and wide-brimmed fedora. He takes off his hat as he approaches her. 'Good morning. It's a beautiful day,' he says.

'It is. Greg working out again?'

Max nods. 'His morning routine. He does his thing and we meet for lunch.'

'Same with me and Poppy. Only she stays to eat with the kids' club. Apparently their lunches are more exciting than ours.'

Max chortles. 'Mind if I sit down?'

He settles himself on the seat next to Irene, leans back and looks out over the pool area. Irene spies the elderly travelling group from the check-in terminal on the first day. They're sitting together in a bunch and appear to be drinking cocktails already. There's a sudden explosion of laughter that turns heads their way.

'They're having a hoot,' she says.

'How old do you think they are?'

'Seventy plus, I'd say. I wonder how they know each other.'

'Nursing home?' Max replies, and they both laugh. 'It would be a lot of fun I imagine, travelling with a group.'

Irene opens a tube of sunscreen and slaps some more on her arms. 'How are you finding the cruise?'

'Relaxing. It's nice to be away from the grind for a while.'

'What do you do?'

'I teach woodwork in a high school just outside of Sydney.'

'Do you like it?'

'I do, very much. I enjoy teaching young people.'

Max asks about Irene's life and she tells him about the gift shop, about pooling her talents with Sing and Zoe. She becomes quite animated as she describes fixing up the building ready for business. 'We're online too. Sing manages our online shop.'

'I'll have to check you out,' Max says. 'Do you sell your soap on there?'

'We certainly do.'

'Well, I might need a store of it.' Max gives his eyebrows a playful wiggle and they both erupt in laughter.

Irene is surprised at how relaxed she is in Max's presence. Their conversation flows as if they are old friends catching up. Even the lines and contours of his face have taken on a pleasant familiarity.

Max clears his throat. 'Have you seen much of the ship yet?'

'No. There's a lot of it, isn't there?'

'I was wondering if you feel like exploring?'

Irene waits for the anxiety to bubble up, but it doesn't. Instead, a wave of excitement. It feels like the most natural thing in the world to go exploring with this man.

'I'd love to.' She gathers her few items into her bag and stands. 'Where to first?'

'Perhaps we could wander and see what we find? And have some morning tea when we're hungry?'

Irene smiles warmly at Max and together they amble across the pool area, send a greeting to the elderly group who lift their glasses in response, and make their way into the vast corridors and spaces of the ship.

At one point, she even takes his arm.

By the time Irene goes to collect Poppy, she feels like she has walked a few miles. Perhaps she has. She and Max have explored a lot of the ship and eaten a substantial morning tea comprising mostly of carbohydrates. Irene could do with a nap, but exercise is probably the better option.

Irene takes Poppy around the parts of the ship she and Max explored earlier—the art gallery, the shops, the library and the glass walkway jutting out from the side of the ship with transparent panels on its floor. Poppy stares down through the windows at her feet, turns back to Irene and says, 'Aren't you coming?'

'I'll wait here. Go to the end and come back.' She'd had to grip Max's arm and do her deep breathing to cross it earlier. All that sea below her feet. It almost sent her into a dizzy spell. Heights were not her thing.

Poppy hops along, looking at the water below as she goes, and skips back. 'It's not scary,' she says.

'No, of course it's not. Reenie's just tired.'

As they're heading back to the bistro, they stop at a demonstration outside an ice creamery which results in them filling their tummies once more. There's no way either of them will fit another meal in for a long time, so they go back to their cabin for a rest and order room service later in the evening.

'I'm having so much fun, Reenie.' Poppy yawns and snuggles down in her bed.

'Me too, monkey. I'm glad I brought you along.'

'I'm glad you brought me along too.'

'What big adventure should we go on after this?'

'Hmm. Maybe explore the Antarctic?'

'There's a thought. What do you think we'd find there?'

'Penguins and icebergs and whales and stuff.'

'You know a bit about it already, then?'

'Mum showed me on the internet. It's not like the real thing though, is it?'

'It certainly isn't.'

Poppy sighs. 'I *really* want to see all the icebergs.'

Poppy closes her eyes and appears to be drifting off to sleep. Irene prays she will dream of icebergs and a penguin or two.

IRENE 2016

The kids' club members are gathered at the waterslide. Irene watches them from her deck chair as the hosts run through a kid-friendly safety drill. Poppy keeps turning to wave to Irene and Irene waves back.

Funny how Irene imagined this cruise as a chance to laze about by herself and yet, here she is having enormous fun hanging out with Poppy. Gadding about the ship, swimming, eating, taking in the family shows, watching movies in their cabin at night or star-gazing on the balcony.

Then there's Max, and whatever it is they're doing together. What is she doing with Max? A lot of eating and talking. Every morning, while Poppy hangs out with the kids' club and Gregory does his workout, Irene and Max meet in the bistro or a café to sample the cuisine and talk. Irene is surprised how much she talks. How cracking open the layers of herself has been strangely effortless with Max. Oh, the secrets that have tumbled out of her.

Perhaps it's the fact of him being a stranger, someone she'll never see again. There's a certain safety in that knowledge. Now, this stranger knows intimate details about her—the building of her life on the farm with Bill, the peace she loved there, her hopes for her own business and how it was ripped away, her struggle back to health after the cancer. And Bill's death. She hasn't told Max everything about the day he died—how she watched him through the window, and the questions the police asked her afterwards.

In return, Max has poured out his own story to Irene—his history, his griefs, his longings. And it is like the passing of two tender souls between each other, hearts quivering in cupped hands. More intimacy than Irene has experienced in a long time.

The children are taking turns down the water slide now, squealing in the spray, crashing into the pool where adults in fluorescent lifesaver vests stand guard. Irene opens her book and alternates between watching Poppy and trying to read. In the end, she sets the book aside and simply enjoys watching her granddaughter.

The pool activities draw to a close and the hosts assemble the children. Poppy skips over to Irene, holding a towel around her middle. Her hair sticks in strands around her ears, dripping water onto her shoulders.

'They're having games after lunch. Can I stay?' She glances back at a huddle of girls wrapped in beach towels and back to Irene. 'Can I, please?'

'Alright. Do you want me to come and get you?'

'Abeba's room is near ours. I'll come back with her afterwards.'

'Which one's Abeba?'

'That one, there.' Poppy points, hopping from foot to foot, in a hurry to leave.

'Which one? They're all bunched up together.'

'The one—the one with the—um—'

The girls look over to Poppy and start moving as a group away from the pool. From the mostly fair-skinned children, a girl with deep brown skin and a red towel gestures to Poppy.

'The girl with the red towel.'

Irene squeezes Poppy's hand. Perhaps the world is improving after all, piece by small piece.

'Can I go?'

'Yes, you can go.'

Poppy scurries off to join her friends.

'Oh, and have a fun lunch,' Irene calls, but Poppy is already skipping away.

It's Treasure-Hunt-Lunch at kids' club today. Yesterday, the themed meal was Build-Your-Own-Edible-Creature. Irene almost envies Poppy the lunches, except that she looks forward to seeing Max.

She glances at her watch. It's nearly time to meet him for their morning tea or early lunch, or whatever it is. She places her book and sunscreen into her bag and goes back to the cabin. Changes her shirt, swaps her shorts for linen pants, brushes her hair. Tries to convince herself she's not going to any extra effort.

On the way to the restaurant, she passes a glass-fronted shop, one of its windows displaying an array of perfume bottles. A sophisticated scent wafts by her nose as she walks past and she doubles back and heads inside. She's enticed by a row of tester bottles. After smelling each one, she gives herself a spritz of a delicate floral and exits the shop.

The restaurant is all plush seats, wood and copper tones. As Irene enters, Max rises from a booth and waves her over.

'You look lovely,' he says.

She thanks him and slips into the seat opposite. She's wearing her favourite blue paisley shirt and hopes he doesn't think she's trying to impress him. As she gets a waft of her perfume, she feels heat rising up her neck.

'So,' she says, 'this is where they make the best pizza you've ever tasted?'

Max hands her a menu with a flourish of his hand. 'Indeed, madam. Made to order any time of the day. You can have pizza for breakfast if you so desire.'

'I must bring Poppy here one morning, then.'

Max lifts his menu and stares at it with exaggerated concentration. 'I was wondering if we should have a bottle of wine with our meal?'

Irene glances at her watch. 'Quarter-past-eleven. Close enough to afternoon, I should think.'

Max chuckles. 'I was hoping you'd say that.'

They order pizzas and a bottle of wine from the waiter. The pizza is indeed delicious—the crust fresh and soft, the toppings flavoursome. Irene hasn't had wine for a long time and the first few sips go to her head. Perhaps Max hasn't either as they fall unusually quickly into easy conversation.

Irene tells him more about her shop, her flat and the river she loves, the weekly sewing classes she runs at the community centre. They swap stories about their children, their own parents and the places where they were raised. Max opens up about losing his wife to another man. They order more pizza, more wine and the conversation moves onto music, politics and the state of the world.

When those topics dry up, Irene asks Max about his sister's support group.

'There was nothing similar for cancer patients in my town,' she says. 'I suppose I could have found one in the city, but it's a long drive from Crayfish Cove.'

Max holds his wine glass to the light and gazes at it before taking a sip. 'You know, I think they saved her. From despair, I mean. They made the end easier for her. Hopeful even, as strange as that sounds.' Max shakes his head and smiles. 'They really were something.'

'Hope?' Irene sighs. 'I can't imagine finding hope at the end of my life. It's a bit late then, isn't it?'

'It depends what you're hoping for. Kaz didn't believe death was the end.'

Irene rolls this thought around in her mind, like food on her tongue, tasting it for flavour. There's a lull in the conversation and Irene looks at her watch. 'Aren't you meant to be meeting Gregory?'

Max grins. 'I told him I was taking you out and not to wait for me. Anyway, I haven't had dessert yet. How about you?'

Irene laughs. 'Why not.'

They complete their meal with Affogato and Irene thinks she's never tasted anything so perfect. 'I can hardly believe this is real,' she murmurs through the melting ice cream in her mouth.

Max is grinning one moment, then his gaze drops from Irene's face and his eyes widen in horror.

'What?' Irene looks down at her shirt and discovers a splodge of icecream and coffee dripping down its front.

'Oh,' she says.

'I've got just the thing for that,' Max says, and Irene bursts out laughing.

'As it happens, so do I.' Irene quickly finishes her dessert, picks up her bag and sets it on her lap. 'I really should fix this, it's my favourite shirt.'

Max sets his spoon down. 'Of course. Thanks for joining me, Irene. I've had a lovely time.' He props his cheek on his fist and gazes at her with a loose smile. Irene wonders if he's a little drunk.

'Me too, Max. I'll go and deal with this Affogato disaster...' Irene is finding articulation difficult and slows her speech down to compensate. '...before it stains good and proper.'

Max stands. 'How about I walk you down?'

'It's alright, I'll see you later. If not later, tomorrow.' She whips one finger in the air as if to make a point.

Max holds Irene's bag as she struggles out of the booth, and hands it to her. She smiles and walks slowly and deliberately towards the door, wondering if he's watching her.

Outside the restaurant, the bright lights daze her. She blinks and glances at her watch. Half-past-twelve, earlier than she thought it was. Poppy will be having lunch, after which she'll be staying for games. Irene has time for a rest, maybe even a nap. The thought of curling up in her bed spurs her on, though her legs feel like lead weights.

Past the shops, down the escalators, into a hallway. She peers at the cabin numbers on the doors, finally finds her own and leans against it while rummaging in her bag for her pass card. She can't find it in the bag so she pokes around in her pockets, but it isn't there either. Weary with wine and too much food, she slumps against the door and closes her eyes. She'll have to go back to the restaurant, though the thought of the long walk exhausts her.

'Irene!'

Irene opens her eyes and sees Max hurrying down the corridor.

'There you are. You dropped your pass card in the restaurant.'

Irene straightens up, takes the card from his hand and sighs happily. 'Thank goodness. I did not want to go all the way back there.'

Max grins cheerfully. 'Good thing I saw it. I remembered you said you were on this level. I wasn't sure I'd find you but...here we are.'

'Here we are. Come in.' Irene swipes the card and opens her door. 'You can rest your legs for a bit.'

Once inside, Irene grabs a clean shirt from the closet and says, 'I won't be a moment.' She goes into the bathroom, swaps shirts and wets the dirty one before rubbing soap into the stain. She leaves it in the sink and returns to the main space.

Max is looking about the room with his hands in his pockets. 'I love what you've done with the place.'

Irene laughs. Max laughs. There is an ease between them, a comfortable familiarity. Irene doesn't move away when Max leans down to kiss her. They hold onto each other and Irene lays her face on Max's chest. He is warm and smells like coffee and the cruise ship complimentary body wash. For a few moments, it feels nice.

But underneath is an unfamiliar scent. And Max's arms against her back are a shape she hasn't felt before. His chest, the round of his stomach, his skin on her cheek—all unfamiliar. He is not Bill. It's a disconcerting sensation, how Irene's body knows the shape of Bill and expects it. This man feels like a stranger.

She puts her palms against his chest and pushes him gently away. 'Sorry, I—' She can't find the right words to say.

He reaches out and touches her cheek. 'Irene, I've enjoyed the last few days very much.'

'Me too, Max, but—'

'I don't mind about the surgery, you know. That kind of thing, it doesn't bother me.'

'What?' Irene stares at him.

Max's face contorts. He steps backwards. 'Oh gosh—I've said the wrong thing, haven't I?'

Irene shakes her head. 'I think—it seems we're not on the same page, Max.' She hears a cold edge in her own voice. 'Perhaps you'd better leave.'

'Irene, I didn't mean—I would never presume— Dash it. I'm such an idiot. Forgive me.' He throws his hands in the air and backs towards the door. As he reaches for the handle, he nods slowly in her direction and says, 'You've read me wrong. I do hope to see you again.'

Irene stands motionless, staring at the closed door as the low thrum of the engine pulsates up from the ship's belly. The way Max nodded to her as he left—it was like a scene from a regency drama, a lord bowing his head to a lady. A giggle escapes Irene's lips. Poor Max. She expects she did misread him. She should seek him out tomorrow and apologise, blame the wine.

Irene returns to the bathroom to rinse her shirt and hang it up. After which, she crawls into bed, wraps the blankets around herself and closes her eyes. As the turmoil in her head recedes and her eyes start to droop, she squints at her watch. Twelve-thirty. Is that right? Must be. There's still time. She closes her eyes and succumbs to the weight of sleep.

Irene wakes to a sharp pounding in her head and a mouth like gravel. As she forces herself upright the pounding increases as if there are explosions going off in her brain. She squeezes her eyes shut and grabs her head in both hands, waiting for the barrage to subside. It serves her right. Drinking a whole bottle of wine when she rarely touches alcohol.

She looks at her watch. It says half-past-twelve. She peers closely at it, tapping the watch-face with her fingernail. Her stomach lurches. She has let it run down and it has stopped. She finds her handbag and pulls out her mobile phone to check the time. It's close to three o'clock. Poppy will be wondering where she is. No, Poppy was going to come to the cabin after the games so she must still be at the club.

Irene quickly washes her face, brushes her hair and checks herself in the mirror. She looks awful but it can't be helped. She hurries along the corridors, up escalators, pushing past people as she goes, and finally shoves through the door of the kids' club room. There are still some children there, playing a game of air hockey. Taylah comes towards her and Irene asks where Poppy is. The woman's smile drops slightly. 'She and Abeba left ages ago.'

'What time was ages ago?' Irene tries to keep her tone polite.

'I'll check.' Taylah goes to a desk, picks up a computer tablet and runs her finger across it. 'They signed themselves out a few minutes after two.'

'Poppy hasn't come back to our cabin.'

A flicker of concern crosses Taylah's face but she swiftly schools her expression into a professional composure. 'One moment, I'll check for you.'

She slips into a glassed office area. Irene watches as she picks up what looks like a phone and speaks for some moments. When she comes back, her expression has not changed. But her words cause a cold knot to tighten in Irene's gut.

'Management have been paging you. Have you been in your cabin? Someone tried to find you.'

Irene grips a piece of furniture and leans heavily upon it. 'I was asleep.'

Taylah's expression softens. 'They'd like you to go to the medical facility on deck one.'

'What—' Her breath quickens. 'What's happened, is Poppy alright?'

'Here, this is a map. It's easy to find.'

Irene takes the sheet of paper from Taylah's hand and opens her mouth to repeat her question. But Taylah is already turning away.

Whatever has happened, the woman either doesn't know or isn't going to tell her.

Irene spins about and pushes through the door, a coil of regret rising from her belly and driving her onward.

Irene bursts through the doors into the white, clinical space of the medical centre. A young man in a blue uniform pokes his head around a partition and says, 'Irene Blackford?' The nurse ushers Irene into a cubicle where Poppy sits on the side of a hospital bed, her arm in a sling. 'Here she is,' he says. 'I'll get the doctor.'

Poppy looks up and grins. 'Reenie, I broke my clarricle.'

'Monkey, thank goodness you're alright.' Irene's knees tremble violently and she has to grip the end of the bed to steady herself. 'What happened?'

'I fell off Abeba's bunk bed.'

'What were you doing in Abeba's cabin?'

'Sorry.' Poppy hangs her head, looking up at Irene through her hair.

'Oh, darling. Don't be sorry. I'm just relieved you're alright.'

'I was coming back, but Abeba's mum asked if I wanted to see their cabin. Then Abeba wanted to show me her bunk bed so we climbed up and I fell off. Abeba's mum brought me here.'

Irene sits next to Poppy on the bed. 'How does it feel?'

'It hurt at first but it doesn't any more. Where were you, Reenie?'

'I fell asleep.'

Poppy bursts out laughing, winces and gingerly touches her upper arm with her free hand.

'Mrs Blackford?' A woman in a white uniform appears with the nurse behind her. 'I'm Doctor Nera Gupta. Poppy's fine, she's fractured her clavicle. I've explained to Poppy how if you're going to break a bone at her age, the best one to break is the clavicle.' She winks at Poppy.

'It fixes itself, did you know?' Poppy says.

'Our amazing bodies.' Irene smiles at Poppy and turns back to the doctor. 'What happens now?'

'We've taken x-rays. The fracture isn't serious. It will heal by itself as long as Poppy keeps it in a sling. Braden will show you how to look after it, Poppy.' She indicates the nurse leaning casually against a wall.

'How about another ice-pack?' Braden asks.

Poppy's smile has faltered, a shadow of pain clouding her usually bright eyes, and Irene is grateful to the nurse who notices. While Braden helps Poppy, the doctor shows Irene the x-ray and explains the injury. They finally leave the centre with the appropriate post-cruise referrals and clear instructions around caring for the injury for the remainder of the cruise.

Once back in their cabin, Irene settles Poppy on her bed, propped up with extra pillows supplied by the ship staff.

'Try and have a rest, monkey. Braden will be back soon with another ice-pack.'

'I'm sleepy.'

Irene sits on the edge of Poppy's bed. 'That's the medication they gave you. You might need to keep taking it for a couple of days.'

Poppy nods and her head sinks into the pillow. 'Are we going out tomorrow?'

They'd planned a tour when the ship docked at Airlie Beach in the morning. But Irene notes the strain around Poppy's eyes, a sign she's in pain and trying to be brave.

'How do you feel about us staying on-board? It might be nice with less people about. We can find a hot-tub to ourselves and dangle our feet in it.'

'And eat ice creams?'

'Absolutely.'

Poppy smiles a slow smile and her eyes droop, the painkillers sending her to sleep.

Irene takes her phone and sends Helen an email via the cruise internet app. She keeps the message up-beat: *not serious... doctor's encouraging us to remain onboard and enjoy the rest of the cruise... Poppy's happy and keen to stay...*

Irene watches her granddaughter sleeping, taking in the vulnerable fine bones of her limbs, wisps of hair stuck to her forehead, dark lashes brushing her cheeks.

How stupid Irene has been. She thinks of Max and grits her teeth. He might be a sweet man but he was a stranger. What had possessed her to attach herself to him? Loneliness? It does claw at her sometimes, if she's honest. Married for thirty-four years and alone for two. She's still getting used to it.

She opens the balcony door and steps out into the salt and wind. She grips the railing and looks out. Even if she hadn't met Max, if she hadn't had lunch with him today, Poppy would have gone off with Abeba. She would have visited their cabin, climbed onto Abeba's bunk bed and fallen off. She would still have a fractured clavicle. Nothing Irene did contributed to the injury. So why this terrible feeling of guilt?

Because it could have been so much worse. And if the worst had happened, Irene would always carry the burden of knowing that her attention had been on Max and not on Poppy.

For the next few days of the cruise, Poppy takes it easy. She has round-the-clock care with nurses bringing her ice-packs and checking her vitals. Irene can't fault the medical care and makes a mental note to write a glowing review. It seems all the staff know Poppy. She's greeted by name everywhere they go and offered extra perks and small gifts.

When Poppy goes back to attending the kids' club with her arm in a sling, it's with a certain air of importance. Irene watches as the children mill around her, pressing her for details. To Poppy's credit, she sticks closely to Abeba, the two having formed a firm friendship.

Abeba's mother has approached Irene on several occasions, always wringing her hands and apologising profusely. It doesn't matter how much Irene smiles and tries to reassure her, the woman won't be reassured. Irene has taken to avoiding her.

Max, on the other hand, can't be found, and Irene supposes he is staying out of her way. In the end, she goes up to the fitness centre the day before disembarkation and waits for Max's nephew to emerge. She pretends to be walking past, turns, catches his eye and says, 'Oh hello, Gregory.'

He greets her warmly. A good sign.

'Would you mind letting your father know I've been looking for him? I'd appreciate it.'

'Sure.' Gregory smiles. He goes to walk away but turns back and says, 'Dad's a decent bloke, by the way. I thought you should know.'

'Yes, I know. Thank you.'

Gregory nods and walks away and Irene feels a deep blush warming her face.

Later that morning, Max approaches Irene at an upper pool deck and Irene's body buzzes with anticipation. He greets her and seats himself gingerly on the edge of a seat.

'Max—'

'Irene, I must apologise for the other afternoon.'

'It's quite alright. I—'

'You must think me awful.'

'No, I don't.'

'Really?' Max runs his fingers through his hair. 'Thank goodness for that.'

'Max, listen. I'm guessing you don't know about Poppy?'

'What—has something happened to her?'

'She broke her clavicle. She's in a sling.'

Max's face contorts in horror.

'She's alright, don't worry.' Irene tells him everything that happened that afternoon. 'It wasn't anyone's fault. It would have happened whether you and I were out together or not. I can't help feeling guilty though.'

'I can understand that. To make matters worse, I avoided you. I'm sorry, but I was embarrassed.'

Irene laughs. 'I know. You didn't need to be. You're quite the gentleman.'

Max sighs. 'I can't believe the cruise is nearly over.'

Irene nods. 'One more night.'

'The thing is—' Max clears his throat. 'Do you think you might like to keep in touch afterwards?' He glances up at her almost shyly.

Irene smiles. 'Yes, I would.'

'Ah, I'm glad.' He leans back in his seat and starts tapping the arm rests with his hands. 'In fact, I was wondering if you and Poppy would join Greg and me for dinner tonight?'

Irene accepts. 'Poppy will be pleased to have someone else to share her broken clavicle story with.'

Max chuckles. 'We'll be all ears.'

Irene leans towards him. 'What are you doing now?'

'The usual. Waiting for Greg.'

She stands and picks up her bag. 'Do you feel like some morning tea?'

Max's face breaks into a grin. 'I certainly do.'

Max stands, Irene takes his arm and they wander off together. Past the teenagers on their pool chairs scrolling on their phones. Past the elderly group with their cocktails and sunhats. Past couples, sunbathers and singles with books.

In search of food and a quiet place for intimate conversation.

HELEN 2024

Twenty-six women have died this year in Australia at the hands of a male perpetrator. And it's only April. Helen can't believe it. '…twenty-six women so far…' one news article announced. So far? How many more will there be?

She tugs her jumper over her hips and winds a scarf around her neck. Into a small backpack she adds a beanie, a bottle of water, a muesli bar and an apple. She must attend this End Violence Against Women rally, for her own family and all the women everywhere who deserve to feel safe. To *be* safe.

Helen's stomach knots as she thinks of Poppy boarding in Hobart—what, a hundred kilometres away… more? Does she remember never to walk alone at night? Does she plan ahead, have a friend with her, take taxis? Helen has told her over and over, "If you need a taxi and you don't have money, phone home and we'll organise it. Don't take risks."

Helen swings the backpack onto her shoulder a bit too fiercely and the thump makes her wince. Why are we even having this conversation? What's gone wrong with the world? Maybe the human race is devolving and turning back into animals. Were we once animals? Helen's mother didn't think so. Helen wishes now that she'd talked more to her mother about her beliefs.

Helen's breath catches in her throat as she thinks of the rally and what it means. That her precious daughter isn't safe. Her niece isn't safe. That she, Helen, isn't safe.

Pete comes into the kitchen. 'It's a shame I have to work today.' He puts his hands either side of Helen's cheeks, bends and kisses her. 'You've got this.' Helen wraps her arms around his waist and squeezes.

Helen drives to Hobart and parks near Parliament House. She rewinds her scarf around her neck, having pulled it off on the way as the car warmed up with the heat of her own anxiety. As she gets out, she can smell her deodorant.

She's grateful to find a lot of men standing on the lawns of Parliament House. Men standing up for women. She smiles wryly and nods to a man holding a placard with the words, *Call Out Your Mates.* He nods back.

Not for the first time, Helen feels enormously grateful for Pete. For a man who would move heaven and earth for the safety of his wife and daughter. She doesn't take her good fortune lightly. She knows what other women have suffered from the terrible articles in the news lately. Beautiful women—mothers, wives, sisters, daughters—raped, murdered, knifed, shot, strangled, bodies discarded and left for others to discover.

This rally is a desperate call for the government to step up. To take the epidemic seriously. To support tired women as they try to tame this beast once and for all. How many people are here? A few hundred maybe.

She joins her voice to the others as they chant in unison, '...*five, six, seven, eight, no more violence, no more hate,*' and finds tears slipping down her cheeks.

There's an energy here, pulsating, surging, quickening her own pulse. It throbs in the determined faces around her—the man holding tightly to the hand of a teenage girl, young women with arms around each other's shoulders. Chanting. Rocking. She finds her muscles tensing, an ache in her throat. Near her, a woman lets out a roar—an animal sound, filled with rage. Helen sees both brokenness and determination in the woman's face. What has happened in this woman's life to elicit such a sound?

Later, as the rally draws to a close, the crowd disperses and Helen makes her way across the lawn to her car. She glances at a woman a few paces ahead of her with long, grey-blonde hair and a brown scarf around her neck. She seems familiar.

Perhaps Helen would have looked away and forgotten about the woman, if she hadn't been reading her mother's notebooks lately and seen the photograph of Irene and her friend at the market.

The woman turns to look about and Helen sees her face clearly. Is it Claire, her mother's friend who went to live overseas? She has the same aquiline nose and pointed chin. A certain lilt in her step, triggering a memory. Helen hurries after her.

The crowd is bustling along, heading towards cars and buses. Helen loses sight of the woman as bodies surge forward. She weaves her way through them, searching, and spies a brown scarf ahead. She picks up her pace.

'Excuse me,' she says, as she reaches out to tap the person on the shoulder. Too late, she realises their hair is a lighter shade of grey and shorter. The woman turns and smiles. She's obviously younger than Claire would be—somewhere in her fifties, Helen guesses.

'Yes?' she says, as she stops and regards Helen.

'I'm sorry,' Helen says. 'I thought you were someone else.'

'It's quite alright.' The woman reaches out and touches Helen lightly on the top of her arm. A familiar gesture, born from the past hour of mutual purpose, and the adrenaline still coursing through their veins.

Helen continues to her car. On the way home she thinks of Claire. She has tried to find her on social media, searched her mother's books for an address or phone number or some hint as to where she might be. But no luck. When she gets home she'll continue the search for her mother's phone. There must be someone who will know how to find Claire. Helen is sure the woman she saw in the crowd, but lost, was Claire. If so, she's back in Tasmania. And she would surely want to know about the death of her old friend.

IRENE 2016

I rene is tidying a shelf when Poppy bounds into the shop and gives her a one-armed hug, holding her slinged arm protectively away from her body. She announces she has a new budgie called Banjo 'and a cage and a swing and everything.'

A little voice calls out, 'Pop' from a blanket in the corner, where Sing has placed Tobias with his toys. Poppy drops to her knees and scoots over to her cousin.

As Helen comes in, Irene asks her about Poppy's appointment with the specialist.

'She'll be in the sling for a couple more weeks,' Helen says, 'but it's healing nicely.'

'That's good news.'

Helen flashes a grin at Irene and does an unexpected sashay over to a stool at the counter. 'Sooo...' she says, tilting her head.

Irene sets the blanket she has finished folding on the shelf and asks, 'Something on your mind?'

'Who's Max?'

Zoe and Sing stop what they're doing and all eyes turn to Irene.

'A friend I met on the cruise.' Irene bends down for another blanket to re-fold.

'I know that much.' Helen leans her elbow on the counter.

Poppy calls out from the corner. 'Max is really cool.'

'Cool,' Tobias echoes.

Sing pulls a chair up next to Helen, and Zoe rolls her swivel-chair along the floor with her feet until they're surrounding Irene, who ducks behind the counter and eyes them warily.

'What? He's a friend.'

'A friend you had morning tea with every day,' Helen says.

Poppy reappears and says, 'We had dinner with Max and Gregory on the last night, didn't we Reenie?'

'Who's Gregory?' Zoe asks.

'Max's son,' Irene says.

'He's a grown-up,' Poppy says. 'He's got a tattoo of a dragon on his head.'

'Awesome,' Zoe says.

'And he got me a triple-decker ice cream sundae. It was the biggest dessert you ever saw. Can I get a drink?'

As Poppy disappears into the kitchen, Helen says, 'What's Max's story? Is he widowed too?'

'Divorced.'

'What's he like?' Sing asks.

'He's lovely, but—' and she emphasises the next words— 'he's just a friend.'

Helen shakes her head. 'Come on, we need more information. What did you two find to talk about during all those morning teas?'

Irene sighs and leans on the counter, her cheek in her hand. They weren't going to let her off. 'Max's sister had cancer. I can't even remember how we started talking about cancer, but once we started, we couldn't seem to stop.'

The faces before her are no longer grinning mischievously.

'What happened to his sister?'

'She died.'

Now their expressions are sombre.

Irene says, 'She was Gregory's mother—'

'Wait—what?' Helen's face contorts in horror. 'Max had a son with his sister?'

Irene can't help laughing. 'When Max's sister died, he and his wife took Gregory in. Technically he's Max's nephew, but Gregory calls him Dad.'

'Whew. Had me worried,' Helen says.

Next, they start firing questions at her.

Helen: 'Where does he live?'

'Sydney.'

Zoe: 'What does he do?'

'Teaches woodwork at a high school.'

Sing: 'Do you stay in touch?'

'We email.'

Zoe: 'How often?'

'Once a week or so.'

Helen: 'That often. Sounds like more than just friendship.'

'No, actually it isn't.'

Zoe: 'How old is he?'

'Sixty-four.'

Sing: 'Is he coming to visit you?'

'I don't know.'

Helen: 'I want to meet him so I can give him the once-over.'

'He's just a—'

Helen: 'Friend, I know.'

Irene clicks her tongue. 'Well, he is.'

A customer enters the shop and Irene is saved from further interrogation. As Zoe greets the shopper, Sing stands and leans in to Irene's ear. 'He sounds like a lovely friend.'

'He is.'

And Irene thinks to herself how nice it would be if Max did come to visit her.

IRENE 2016

I rene stands on the bottom step of a community centre building in the city, looking up at the double doors. The edges of the concrete steps are encrusted with frost and the metal stair rail is like ice on her palm. She pulls her hand away and shoves it back into her coat pocket. Typical Tasmanian weather—a frost in spring.

Irene has thought of Max often over the past few weeks. Memories of their conversations have played on repeat in her mind, particularly (lately) the one about his sister's cancer support group. *They saved her from despair and gave her hope,* is what he'd said. Or something like that. Which is why she's here.

She peers back up at the double doors. Her online research has unearthed this possibility—a group in the city where she can meet other people with similar experiences to her own. She's unlikely to bump into anyone she knows this far from Durrunby and Crayfish Cove, but if she does, she can always leave. Yet, she falters on the step, unsure whether to proceed.

A rich, warm voice says, 'Going in?'

A middle-aged woman with round, pink cheeks steps up beside her. She's wrapped in a large faux fur coat and woolly scarf.

'Thinking about it,' Irene says.

The woman smiles and Irene is drawn to her friendly eyes. 'I'm Maggie. Stick with me and we'll do this together.'

Irene introduces herself and walks up the steps with the nice woman beside her. Maggie opens the door for Irene and they pass into a wood-panelled foyer. The building smells of polish and must, with a faint hint of coffee. Maggie indicates a book on a side table. 'We sign in here. It's for safety reasons, no need to add any personal information.'

Irene adds her name to the list. As she places the pen down, an angular woman with a nest of frizzy red hair bursts in from another room and beams at Irene.

'A new member, hello. My name's Ginny and I'm a survivor. And you are?'

Irene backs away and puts her hands in her pockets. 'Irene.'

'Good to meet you, Irene. Come in and join us when you're ready.'

The woman scoots back into the other room and Maggie laughs quietly. 'Don't worry about Ginny. She's harmless.'

'She's very, er, upbeat,' Irene says.

'She always introduces herself like that. But I can assure you, not everyone here identifies as a survivor. We're all at different stages of our very different journeys.'

Irene nods. 'Good to know. Well, I guess it's time to be brave.'

They enter the adjoining room together—a large space, reminiscent of an old-fashioned classroom with high windows and blinds, over-head heaters emanating a dusty smell, a whiteboard shoved up against a wall. At one end of the room, plastic chairs and trestle tables are stacked against the walls. At the opposite end is a roughly circular configuration of armchairs and sofas. Some people are already sitting there with drinks.

Irene and Maggie head to a table laid out with cups, tea and coffee and a bubbling urn. As Irene makes herself a tea, she peers over at the few people seated on the sofas.

Maggie leans in close to Irene and speaks softly. 'See the woman talking to Ginny?'

Irene sees a petite, middle-aged woman in a fluffy cardigan.

'That's Laurel, the facilitator. She keeps everyone in order, including Ginny. Oh, and see this chap coming in?

Irene turns as a large, well-muscled man in overalls and a T-shirt ambles in. He nods at Maggie and heads for the sofas.

'Looks strong and fit, doesn't he?' She shakes her head. 'Bob's story would break your heart.'

As more people trickle through the doors and head towards the drinks table, Maggie picks up her coffee and suggests they find a seat. On their way to the lounge area, Laurel approaches them and introduces herself to Irene. She exudes a warmth and gentleness that Irene is drawn to. As Irene and Maggie sit down together on a sofa, Laurel welcomes another new member, a woman with a scarf around her head and pencilled-in eyebrows. Irene is put in mind of her chemotherapy days when she lost her hair, and wonders if this woman is going through a similar experience.

Laurel pulls up a vinyl-covered chrome chair which hisses as she sits down. She welcomes the group in a quiet but authoritative voice and the room hushes. Each person lowers their cup, or leans forward, or tilts their head in concentration as Laurel holds the room and, in her quiet way, demands attention.

She has them introduce themselves, one by one, before explaining the rules of the group. 'Some members have chosen to share phone numbers for use in the event of an emergency or a situation requiring extra support.' She says this for the benefit of Irene and the other new member, and suggests they may like to get to know the group better before they decide whether to share their contact details.

The topic being discussed is building and maintaining self-esteem and self-compassion. Irene listens as some of the members share their struggles. She notes the established ease amongst them, their mutual trust, the way they hold space for each other and show respect for each other's perspectives. Laurel expertly guides the discussion, pulls in the reigns where needed and ensures each person has equal opportunity to share.

Irene quietly listens. There will come a time when she feels comfortable to share, but not yet. She is drawn to these people with their vastly different backgrounds and personalities, yet similar experiences of loss, fear, grief. As she listens, her own past wounds begin to wriggle, painfully, up to the surface. Her heart feels torn again like almost-healed stitches ripping open. But instead of it being unbearably painful, it is a cathartic experience. As if her soul has exposed its damaged self to the world and received validation and the hope of healing.

She looks around at the bruised faces, the raw souls held out in trust to each other. She has found the place she needs to be. By the end of the session, Irene knows these are her people.

HELEN 2024

How remiss Helen has been. She and Caleb invited everyone they could think of to their mother's funeral, but it seems Irene had friends Helen didn't know about. All those trips Irene made to town, apparently to shop and run errands. Turns out she was meeting people. At least, that's what it looks like.

Helen sits at the dining table, scrolling through her mother's phone. The one she lost, which has recently turned up again in a box of photographs.

There's a Ginny, a Laurel, a Maggie. Helen hasn't heard of any of these people. They all have addresses in the city. As she scrolls through the contact list, Pete enters the room in his nursing scrubs. 'I'd better skedaddle,' he says, coming up to give her a kiss on the cheek. Helen barely notices. She stops scrolling and frowns at the phone screen.

'Huh. You'll never guess,' she says.

'What have you found now?'

'Mum was going to a cancer support group in town.'

'Are you sure?'

'Look.' She holds out the phone and points to the contact she has discovered.

Pete leans in and squints at the phone. 'Well, I guess she had her reasons for keeping it to herself.'

Helen huffs. 'Seems to me she had more secrets than was normal.'

Pete kisses her again and she hugs him goodbye. When he leaves, she finds her laptop and takes it to the table, punching in her password with more force than necessary. A cancer support group—why hadn't she told Helen about it? All these things Helen was only now finding out about her mother. Sometimes she could scream.

At least she has an idea about finding her mother's friend, Claire. Helen has remembered Claire's surname, although it took a couple of days of going through the alphabet in her head and thinking very hard. Eventually, her subconscious dug out the answer and it popped into her mind as she was vacuuming. Claire may have changed her surname since the nineties, of course, but it's a start.

Helen does an internet search for Claire Parry, another search on her social media, combines it with words relating to everything she can remember about Claire. She even does a search of her name paired with 'green Volkswagen.' Or was it blue? Nothing comes up, anyway.

She's about to snap her laptop shut when she remembers something else. She had a sister. Gina... Jillian... Germaine? She's sure the woman's name was Germaine, a bit younger than Claire. The memory of the woman who was Germaine is fine like a gossamer wisp, but real. Long brown hair, freckles? Helen types Germaine Parry into the search engine and clicks on 'images.' Scrolling through, she finds a face that looks like an older version of the person Helen remembers.

She goes onto her social media and types Germaine's name, finds the same picture and clicks on the profile. She lives in Tasmania, that's something. Well, here goes. Helen sends her a message explaining who she is and saying she would like to contact Claire with information about Irene Blackford. Now, all there is to do is wait.

She closes her laptop and scrolls back through her mother's contacts. Should she call these people and let them know of her mother's death—Ginny, Laurel and Maggie? What if her mother didn't want them to know? After all, since re-charging Irene's phone, none of these people have called or left messages. In fact—Helen looks at each one to be sure—the only number showing any recent traffic is the one belonging to Maggie.

Helen switches off the phone and sets it aside. She needs to dress and go to work. Perhaps she'll visit Caleb on the weekend and ask his opinion.

It is an awful thought, and she can't shake it. To think that Helen has neglected to inform these people that their friend has died.

IRENE 2016

Helen has downloaded an app for Irene's phone so she can talk to Max and see him at the same time. What an invention. She has a stand too, so she can set up her phone on the table and talk hands-free. She sits on her deck now, curled up in a chair. Max is leaning back on a sofa grinning.

'How about this, then?' Irene says. 'I suppose it's been around forever and I hadn't noticed.'

'You're never too old to learn, Irene.'

Irene chuckles. 'You look well, Max.'

'So do you. What's new?'

Irene tells him about the support group she has joined. 'I know it's a bit late after the fact. Better late than never though.'

'Terrific. Well done, you.'

'Thanks. I kept thinking about your sister and her group, how it helped her. I never did talk to anyone when I probably should have. When you're in the thick of things, it can be difficult to reach out.'

'Kaz said something similar. When she did find her mob, she said it made all the difference. Sharing with people who were in a similar boat, so to speak.'

'What about you, anything new?'

Max tells her about his work, what's going on in his children's lives and how he's looking forward to a break over summer. 'I might get down your way in January. If it's alright with you, of course. I'd like to visit.'

'It'd be lovely to see you,' Irene says, and means it.

'Any plans for the weekend?'

'As a matter of fact, I'm going to try a local church service.'

Max leans forward, obviously unaware that he's giving Irene a clear view up his nose. 'Really?' he says.

'It's another way of connecting with my community. Good for business, you might say.'

Max grins and shakes his head. 'You can't fool me, Irene. You're not about befriending people for the sake of business.'

'Alright then, I'm curious.'

'What about?'

'Oh, you know. Life, death, eternity... That sort of thing.'

'Ha. Good luck.'

'Do you believe in God, Max?'

Max lifts his shoulders and blows a raspberry sound from his lips. 'I don't believe in *nothing*, put it that way.'

'I'll let you know what I find out.'

'Didn't you say you went to some religious thing a while back?'

'Oh yes, that small group I found in Rosemere, about half an hour from here. I went there thinking to make some friends. Made the mistake of saying something about not wanting reconstruction surgery and one of the women asked what my husband thought about it. That was it for me.'

Max starts to laugh, stops himself and pulls a face.

'You can laugh, it's funny.'

'It is funny. My parents were Catholic,' Max says.

'Oh, I didn't know that.'

'No, it didn't rub off on me at all.'

'Hmm, I think everything rubs off on us in some way. We probably have every experience etched into us somewhere, wreaking untold havoc.'

'You're rather philosophical today, Irene.'

'I like to think about things. It must be taking me somewhere. Maybe it's making me wise?'

'One can hope. There has to be some compensation for all the elderly aches and pains.'

Irene nods. 'Imagine arriving at old age with declining health and no wisdom. Now that would be a tragedy of a life.'

They engage in some silly banter and chat away as amiably as they always do. Just friends, no more. Irene is certain of that.

On Friday, Poppy's sleepover night, Irene and Poppy sit on the deck eating takeaway noodles and drinking bubble tea. Irene swallows a mouthful of her drink, coughs and peers into the cup.

'I'm not sure about this tea, Poppy.'

'Don't you think it's delicious?'

'There are tapioca pearls in it. And I'm not sure it's even tea.'

'It's good to try new things, Reenie.'

'Ha, right you are.'

Poppy stands and plonks her empty cup on the table. She goes to the edge of the deck, sticks her head over the rail and sighs dramatically. 'I don't think the platypus likes me.'

'Platypuses are shy. It might come out if we're quiet.'

Irene joins her at the rail. The willows have flowered and turned a bright golden hue. Irene is about to turn back to find her phone and take a photo of them when a movement on the riverbank catches her eye.

'What's that?' she says, pointing.

Poppy peers downward. 'A plastic bag.'

Irene squints. 'Can you really tell what it is from here?'

'Can't you?'

'Not properly.' She makes a mental note to see her optometrist. 'We'd better go down there in the morning and take it away. We want to keep the riverbank safe for the platypus.'

There's a chill in the air so they go inside where the sofa bed is already set up for Poppy. She clambers onto it and takes one of Irene's photo albums from the coffee table.

'Where was I up to?' she says, flicking through the pages.

Irene pours her bubble tea down the sink and joins her. They snuggle up together on the bed with the album between them.

'Is that really Granddaddy with the queen?' Poppy says as she turns the page.

'The queen? Ah, that's at Madame Tussauds—'

'Oh, that's right, the wax people. They look real.'

'Show me?' Irene lifts the album closer and looks at the picture. Bill looks quite at home amongst the wax figures of the royals. He's making a show of lifting his chin and squaring his shoulders to give himself an important air.

'What's so funny?' Poppy says.

'I was thinking how Granddaddy looks like he wishes he was one of them.'

'A wax person?'

'A member of the royal family.' Irene hands the album back to Poppy and goes to find her laptop. 'How about you have your shower and I'll set up the movie.'

Later, when Poppy has fallen asleep near the end of the film, Irene takes the photo album to her bedroom and flicks through it. They both took photos throughout their European trip. Irene took many of Bill in various places, whereas Bill's photos are of buildings and architecture, so Irene doesn't feature much in the albums.

She finds a favourite one of them sitting at a table in a pub in Scotland. She'd had a waiter take it, and it's one of the few pictures of the two of them together. They sit opposite each other, turned towards the camera. They look tired but happy. Bill has his hands clasped on the tabletop and Irene has her right hand around her glass. A red glint from her ring finger shows she was wearing her grandmother's garnet ring that night.

Irene wears the ring on her left hand now. It's a particularly comfortable one. She hardly knows it's there which is why she never takes it off. And why she's sure she didn't take it off in Scotland either. And yet, it vanished, turning up years later in the oddest of places.

Zoe and Milo join Irene and Poppy for breakfast at The River Café the following morning, as they do most Saturdays. They walk from the flats together, six-year-old Milo hurrying along beside Poppy, his black head nearly level with her brown one already.

'He's going to be a tall one,' Irene says.

'Doesn't take after me, then,' Zoe says wryly.

Milo chatters to Poppy, gazing continually up at her, except when he must check where his feet are. 'What're you having for breakfast, Poppy? I'm gonna have pancakes.'

'French toast,' Poppy says, stopping to look at a frog ornament outside a shop.

Milo stops beside her. 'Me too. I'm having French toast too.'

'With maple syrup,' Poppy adds as she turns and skips along the footpath.

'Me too, I love maple syrup.' Milo trots along beside her until they reach the café, and they enter together.

Joss makes the usual fuss of the children, bringing out their orders with a flourish, a 'sir' and 'miss' and chocolate chips on the side— 'because every meal is improved by chocolate.'

As Zoe and Irene talk about the business and their plans for the following week, Irene hears Poppy telling Milo about the platypus and the plastic bag caught on the rocks. 'It might kill him. We have to go and get it.'

'Mum!' Milo's face is scorched with worry. 'We have to save the platypus.'

Hence, another routine is added to Irene's life—Saturday mornings on the riverbank with Zoe, Poppy and Milo. Donning gloves and picking up discarded fast food wrappers, cigarette butts, bottles and cans and other human refuse. Making sure the platypus's home is kept pristine and safe.

Irene marvels at the natural care and empathy of children and wonders why they have to grow up at all.

That evening, when she's alone, Irene opens her wooden chest for the first time in two years. With the weather warming up, it will be a good place to store the extra blankets she's accumulated.

Looking into the box, she finds some fabric she'd forgotten about. Some of it might be useful for the shop. As she lifts out the pieces to inspect them, she finds a small remnant of her favourite butterfly fabric amongst the pile. What memories it conjures up. She decides to keep it. A couple of the other pieces tug in a similar way at her heart as she remembers sewing clothes for Caleb and Helen when they were little. She decides to keep those also. The other pieces of material, she places in a stack to take to the shop.

Underneath these, of course, are her notebooks. The question is, what to do with them? She had planned to go through them one more time before discarding them. There are entries in there she's yet unsure about, but trying to figure them out might be more hurtful than helpful.

Irene takes one of the books and flicks through it. She knows where the tiny notes are hidden. It's unlikely anyone would be able to decipher her cryptic diagrams and coded words. She imagines telling Caleb and Helen the truth about what was really going on, but she's not sure they would believe her.

Irene replaces the book with the others and piles the fabric on top. They can stay there for now. She folds her extra blankets and puts these in the chest also, before closing the lid.

Time to head for bed. She wants to be fresh for tomorrow when she'll be attending a church service for the first time in many years. Why she suddenly wants to do it now, who knows? Something to do with the questions rattling around in her brain lately. Or because she can't help looking at that lovely old building every time she walks past and remembering a certain feeling—solidness, safety?—she had as a child when she walked in holding onto her mother's hand.

IRENE 2016

The old stone building stands on the corner of Main Street and Pyre Lane, surrounded by clipped hedges and a flat lawn. Behind it, a well-tended graveyard backs almost onto the river. The plaque on the front gate says the building has been here since the 1820s. Probably built by convicts then, Irene thinks.

She waits by the gate until the last minute, when the service is about to start, and slips in behind the last stragglers—a couple leaning on walking sticks. She ducks into a wooden pew near the back wall. It has a cushion attached but it's had so many backsides on it over the years, there's no softness left and the hard seat pushes against her bones. The place looks clean though, polished even. Irene fancies she can smell the polish, laid like a cloth over an underlying mustiness.

A woman across the aisle from Irene smiles and waves at her. Irene recognises Jean, a regular at the community centre, and waves back.

The minister, standing at the front on a semi-raised platform, is also a familiar face. He often pops into the community centre when Irene is there with her sewing students. Andrew—she can't remember if he's a priest or a rector or something else and wishes she'd looked it up on the internet before coming. He's wearing a regular suit with one of those white collars. He's about Irene's age, perhaps a bit older. A slight man with greying hair and a jovial face that looks like it's used to smiling.

He must have already greeted the congregation, as someone is playing an organ and the people are getting to their feet. Irene stands too. She's surprised to see a screen on the wall with the words of the song on it. She'd expected to be flipping through a hymn book.

As she mimes the words of a hymn she doesn't recognise, she looks about the room. Almost every head is grey or white. Not that Irene can talk, with her own silver hair. There are two to four heads to a pew and not all the pews are filled.

The pointed arch windows along the side walls are lovely. Two of them have actual stained glass in them, though Irene can't see them properly from where she stands. She remembers the other windows had stained glass once, but have now been replaced with plain. A pity. Someone would have put a lot of effort into creating those.

Another song starts up and the tune has a vague familiarity. Irene finds she can predict some of the notes of the melody. It's quite nice, but a bit slow. Irene would prefer something with some oomph.

The music stops and Irene sits down before she realises everyone else is still standing. She bobs back up. The minister says something and everyone speaks in unison. She looks to the screen on the wall, but the words aren't there and she doesn't know what she should be saying. The people sit down and Irene follows suit, making a mental note to watch the room carefully so she doesn't mess up again. During the shuffle, as everyone makes themselves comfortable, the minister says something that sets the room laughing, but it must be an in-joke because Irene doesn't get the punchline.

She listens intently during the Bible reading and the prayers. Even the sermon holds her interest for a while, the message being about the inevitability of hardship and trials no matter how good a person is. Well, that's nothing Irene doesn't know already. What did she do to deserve cancer and everything it entailed? When she looks back on her illness, it's as if a significant chunk of her life has been chomped into, leaving ratty pieces she's been trying to pick up and stick back together ever since. What was the point of it, she wonders? Is this great jarring of life really about producing perseverance and character? Irene is sure she could have produced those very traits without the sickness. What with everything else going on.

A ripple of laughter yanks Irene back from her daydream. The minister says something about a talking donkey and Irene assumes he's told another joke. She should be listening, not dredging up memories. Cancer. It's over, she beat it. She has a happy and fulfilling life. The business is flourishing, her home is peaceful, she loves the river.

Irene discovers if she holds her head just right, she can see a section of the river through one of the plain glass windows. Two ducks are swimming there and as Irene watches, one of them stands upright in the water, beating its wings and skimming along the surface. Of course, Irene can't hear it from where she sits, but she imagines it squawking as it goes. When she realises she is listing sideways in her seat with a grin on her face, she straightens up, loses the grin and pastes on what she hopes is an interested expression.

The service finishes with another hymn, a prayer and an invitation to stay for morning tea. Irene grabs her bag and squeezes out of the pew, clamping her eyes on the double doors and escape. But Jean from the community centre jumps from the opposite pew to intercept her.

'Morning Irene. Fancy meeting you here.'

'Hi Jean.' Irene flashes a smile, keeping her body turned towards the door.

'You're going the wrong way, tea and coffee's over there.'

'Actually, I need to get going.'

'Can't you stay for a cuppa?'

Irene and Jean both back into their respective pews to allow an elderly man with a walker to trundle past. Jean shoots out again before Irene can escape and takes her by the arm. 'This way, come on.'

Their progress up the aisle is a slow shuffle, thwarted by people stopping to offer greetings and help each other out of their seats. Jean leads Irene to a doorway through which Irene can see drinks laid out. Right next to it is a side exit which has been opened to the outdoors, and Irene gazes longingly at it. She is about to make an excuse to take this second door, when Jean says, 'Here he is.' She waves at someone over Irene's shoulder. 'Andrew, Irene's here.'

Irene turns to find the minister behind them, smiling warmly and holding out his hand to shake Irene's.

'Good morning, Irene. Lovely to see you.'

'Hello, Andrew. Oh, what should I call you in this setting?' She wishes she'd done that internet search.

'Just Andrew. We don't stand on ceremony here.'

Jean says she'll grab Irene a cuppa and takes off before Irene can repeat her wish to leave.

'I hope you enjoyed the service,' Andrew says.

Irene nods her head but when she opens her mouth, all that comes out is, 'Well.'

The minister's rejoinder is instant. 'Well-executed sermon? I do try, I assure you.' His eyes are actually twinkling and Irene feels her mouth twitch up in a smile.

She glances again at the door to the side lawn and Andrew's eyes follow her gaze. 'How about a tour of the building?' He gestures to the door and they walk outside together.

'Gets a bit stuffy in there,' he says. 'I open the doors at the close of the service so people can escape and enjoy some fresh air with their morning tea.'

As he says this, some of the congregants straggle out with cups in their hands and a couple of gentlemen deep in conversation hoist themselves onto the stone wall that surrounds the rear end of the property.

'It's nice out here.' Irene admires the old-fashioned garden beds bursting with purple hydrangeas, delphiniums and dahlias of various colours.

'Jean does a lot of the gardening. She has quite the green thumb.'

'I didn't realise that. It's a beautiful building. What happened to the windows without the stained glass?'

'That was before my time. Boys throwing rocks, by all accounts. It was too expensive to replace them. Most unfortunate.'

'What a shame.' Irene thinks of the beautiful reconstruction of the stained glass in Winchester Cathedral.

'If you don't mind my asking,' Andrew says, 'what was your reason for attending this morning? I only enquire in case there's some way I can be of service.'

'Oh, a bit of soul searching, I suppose you could say.' Irene meets Andrew's eyes. 'I used to come here a long time ago with my mother. It was a more traditional service back then. Mum loved the bells and whistles.'

Andrew chuckles. 'You didn't, I assume?'

'I arrived at an age, about fourteen I think, when I dug in my heels and refused to go.'

'Has something from that time drawn you back?'

'I think so. Though I'm not sure what. To be honest, I find it all a bit, uh, ritualistic.'

'I couldn't agree more.'

'Really?'

'Oh yes. It's stand up, sit down, prayer, holy communion, the well-executed sermon of course. And I will admit, some of the hymns are getting a bit long in the tooth.'

'So why don't you change it? Spice the service up a bit?'

'I might be run out of town.' His face crinkles up in mirth. 'To be fair, these dear folk come here every Sunday because they connect with the rituals and the familiarity. Their friends are here, they know what to expect, they even sit in the same seats week after week. If this is their way of connecting with God, who am I to change it up?'

Irene watches as one of the men sets out chairs on the lawn for the ladies. How they all appear to be engaged in a well-practised dance, each one moving perfectly in step as they follow the familiar cues.

'I see what you mean,' she says.

'Your own soul searching may take you elsewhere. There's a thriving fellowship in Crayfish Cove. Also a group here in Durrunby who meet in each other's homes. Ask Jean, she can give you their information. Then again, there was a fellow I knew in Crayfish Cove who wouldn't set foot in a church building. He said he could only hear God when he was out in his garden.'

'I do love the river,' Irene says. 'It moves me like nothing else.'

'There's a good view of the river from the graveyard. Let me show you.' Andrew gestures for her to follow him and they go through an open gate into the cemetery. As they pick their way through the neat, well-tended plots, the minister points out the oldest graves and those belonging to people whose descendants still lived in and around Durrunby.

At the far end, the stone wall separates the cemetery from the verge by the banks of the river. On the other side of the river is a flat, grassed area. Andrew waves to a group of picknickers who wave back.

'The cemetery used to go on a bit further, but there was a flood in 1871 that washed away the end of it. A few graves disappeared too, hence the wall. Though, I'm not sure how well it would hold the river back if a similar flood happened today.'

'The cemetery must have been awfully close to the river.'

'Indeed. Legend has it, a young widow was washed away in that very flood while clinging to her husband's tombstone. They all vanished—widow, tombstone, the whole grave and contents therein.'

'Goodness.'

'It could just be a story, of course. I've been able to authenticate the flood and the lives lost. There is a young widow listed, wife of a stonemason. But whether she died clinging to her husband's tombstone or not, I couldn't say.'

Irene and Andrew turn at the sound of Jean's voice. 'There you are. I've made you a cup of tea, Irene. A drop of milk and no sugar, isn't it?'

Irene thanks her and takes the cup.

'Have you been telling Irene about the drowned widow? I think someone made it up to scare the kiddies and stop them playing in the cemetery.'

'Or perhaps a minister invented the story to teach his congregation,' Andrew adds. 'The moral could be, in this life be careful what you cling to.'

'Why do I get the feeling you've used the story yourself?' Irene asks.

'I may have mentioned it.' Andrew chuckles.

They make their way back to the building and Irene finishes her tea on the lawn with Jean. Andrew is literally pulled away by his elbow as someone asks him about a church matter. Irene finds herself surrounded by folk, some of whom she recognises from around Durrunby, others she hasn't met before. They are friendly and welcoming and Irene loses her urge to leave.

Finally, she says she really must be off and Jean takes her cup. As she walks towards the front gate, Andrew hurries up to her.

'I saw you surrounded. I hope it wasn't too unpleasant.'

Irene says, 'They're lovely people.'

'I'm very fond of them. They're the folk the good Lord has entrusted into my care, and I just do my best to pastor them.'

Irene nods. 'Without expecting them to change.'

'Precisely.'

'Well, you're certainly a surprise.'

'Glad to hear it. Well, cheerio.'

As Irene continues through the gate, Andrew calls out, 'By the way, the fourth pew from the back on the right-hand-side has the best view of the river.'

She turns and catches him grinning. Well, really. It seems Irene's lapse in concentration during the sermon didn't go unnoticed after all.

HELEN 2024

When classes finish at three o'clock, Helen finds a missed call and a text message from an unknown number on her mobile phone.

Hello Helen. This is Claire Parry. Germaine said you wanted to contact me about your mother. Not sure where you live but was wondering if you're able to meet up in Hobart? It would be lovely to see you.

Helen wonders if Claire has guessed about her mother's death. She'd probably find the funeral details if she did an internet search. It would be nice to see her again, to reminisce about the market days.

Helen returns a message asking if she is free on Tuesday, Helen's day off. Claire replies in the affirmative with a suggested time and place, and Helen returns an acceptance. There. One job done. It will be a relief to pass on the news that should have been relayed months ago.

She still needs to contact the other numbers in her mother's phone, but doesn't think she can face it yet. One thing at a time. Dealing with anything to do with her mother's death is like lifting an impossibly heavy weight.

Helen immediately recognises the woman standing by the fountain. Long, faded blonde hair with streaks of silver, pointed chin, probably late sixties. She wears linen pants and a long, embroidered jacket.

'Claire?'

The woman turns and smiles as Helen approaches her. 'Helen. You haven't changed.'

'Really?'

'A wee bit older, that's all.'

They briefly hug and Claire kisses Helen on the cheek.

'I detect an accent?' Helen says.

'I've been living in Canada for the past eighteen years. My partner and I moved back in November.' She inclines her head towards a cluster of businesses. 'There's a café over there. How about we have some lunch and talk properly.'

The café is deliciously warm after the chilly outdoors. They choose a booth in a corner with padded seats and peruse the menu.

'I might go with this vegetarian pie,' Claire says.

After a waiter takes their orders, Claire pours a glass of water and says, 'I found the funeral announcement online.'

'I thought you might. I wanted to tell you in person anyway.'

'I do appreciate it. Water?'

'Thank you.'

'I was very sad when I read it. Got the tears over with then.'

'I'm sorry you had to find out like that.' Helen fills Claire in briefly on the circumstances around her mother's death. 'We were overwhelmed when it happened, and I didn't have contact details for all of Mum's friends.'

Claire shrugs. 'We'd been out of touch for a long time. The last time I saw your mum was 2005 when they moved into their new house.

They invited me and Robin to a dinner party to celebrate, along with another couple. Were they still living there?'

'They lived there until Dad died in 2014.'

'Oh, I'm sorry.'

'Mum moved into a smaller place after his death. Pete and I live in the house now.'

'It has gorgeous views, as I recall.' Claire wriggles out of her jacket and lays it on the seat beside her.

'I've been going through some notebooks Mum left,' Helen says. 'They're mostly notes about her business. It's quite fun, actually, reading about her ideas for fabrics and designs.'

'Ha, I remember her books. To think, she kept them.'

'That's one reason I thought of you recently. She mentions you a few times. But there's something else. I thought I saw you at the End Violence Against Women rally last month.'

Claire's face lights up. 'I was there. Why didn't you say hello?'

'I tried but I lost you in the crowd.'

'It was a good turnout, wasn't it? It's a passion of mine. In fact, a lot of my work has been around helping victims of violence.'

They talk about their respective work until their lunches arrive. As they eat, the conversation moves on to stories of their families, before circling back to the market days.

'I remember them well,' Helen says.

'Weren't they fun? Your mum had a way with people, such a vivacious personality. She was the one who drew people to our stall, they couldn't resist her.'

'Mum didn't say why you lost touch. Did you never catch up when you came back to Australia for visits?'

Claire shakes her head sadly. 'To be honest, we had a falling out. It was a personal matter and not something I can discuss.'

'That's alright.'

'But I want you to know, Helen, I've always had a high regard for your mum. She was a person of principle. Our falling out was not her fault. It was just something we couldn't resolve.' Claire fiddles with the edge of her napkin. 'I could have contacted her later, but I didn't. I chose to be offended and it was the wrong choice. I deeply regret that now.'

'If it helps, she talked about you from time to time, and it was always with fondness.'

Claire lifts her eyes and smiles. 'Thank you for telling me. It means a lot.'

They reminisce some more and Helen fills Claire in on the years afterwards. Irene's recovery from cancer, Bill's death and Irene's final ten years in Durrunby.

'A gift shop. That sounds like your mum.'

'She went in with Caleb's wife and Zoe, a young woman who lived next door to her. Zoe and Sing are still running it.'

'How did it fare during Covid?'

'Really well, actually. Their online sales went through the roof. They were a bit worried for a while when the landlord wanted to sell the building. But Zoe managed to buy it which solved the problem.'

'Ha. Smart cookie.'

'Mum helped her. They're currently renovating the back of it, adding some rooms on so Zoe and her son can live there. Mum was thrilled about the whole project. She was nearly seventy and out there every day, getting in the way of the builders. Then suddenly—' Helen shakes her head. 'It happened so quick. Sanding window frames one day, in bed with a drip the next. Then... we lost her.'

Claire pulls a tissue from her bag and dabs her eyes. 'I said I'd done my crying and here I am doing it again.'

Helen averts her eyes and scrapes the last of her pasta from the bowl.

When Claire has recovered herself, she asks, 'What was it like for her at the end?'

'Hopeful.'

'What do you mean?'

'She told us she'd see us again. This wasn't the end, she said.'

Claire nods. 'She always was a spiritual person.'

They settle on coffee instead of dessert, though Helen could easily have eaten a slice of chocolate fudge cake.

'Can I ask you a question?' Helen fiddles with the handle of her cup as she tries to find the right words. 'Do you ever remember Mum having issues with her cognition? Like memory problems or anything like that?'

Claire's expression is thoughtful. 'Hmm, not that I can think of. Why do you ask?'

'There are some odd entries in her notebooks we thought might indicate she had memory issues. Losing things, being forgetful.'

'The cancer?'

'Outside of those times, actually. It could be nothing.'

'I would have thought the opposite, actually. Your mum was very switched on. Intelligent, sharp, witty. I don't remember anything like you're describing.'

Helen shrugs one shoulder. 'That's good then. It was probably part of her to-do lists and plans for her business.'

They finish their meal and rise to leave. As Helen pulls her purse from her handbag, Claire waves her hand in the air. 'My shout. I appreciate you driving all the way up.'

As they leave the café, about to go in different directions, Claire gives Helen a tight hug. 'Goodbye, Helen.'

Helen says, 'We should keep in touch.' But even as she says it, she knows they won't.

Claire goes to walk away, but swings back and says, 'Kind.'

'Pardon?'

'That's what your mother was. She had a kind spirit and people were drawn to it.'

Helen nods. Claire smiles. And they go their separate ways.

The topic today is 'Boundaries in Relationships.' Ginny, her frizzy orange hair clumped into a sort-of bun, has enthusiastically shared her boundary-setting techniques with the group. Irene wonders if Ginny copes as well as she makes out. There's a desperate air about her.

Irene looks for the woman with the scarf and pencilled in eyebrows, but she hasn't attended since her first session. Irene knows not to ask. Laurel is strict about confidentiality and won't disclose anything about group members. Irene was hoping to try and form a friendship with the woman but, as it turns out, she finds herself drawn to Maggie.

The moment Irene opens her mouth today, she dumps. Dumping is okay. So far Irene has seen everyone do it at least once. But Irene has been careful about how much she shares, so is surprised at herself when she can't stop her mouth running on.

'Before I'd even recovered from surgery, Bill started up about breast reconstruction. I didn't know if I even wanted it, but he made it clear what his expectations were. I felt... unloved. I was trying to come to terms with the changes to my own body and needed time to accept them. And he was already making it clear he wouldn't accept me as I was.'

Irene finds herself shaking slightly and Maggie, sitting beside her, rubs her arm.

'What would you say to your husband now, if you could?' Laurel asks.

Irene clenches her fists. 'I'd tell him to go and—'

Irene presses her lips together and feels her cheeks blazing. She can't believe the words that burst into her head and almost jump from her mouth. She has never said words like those. Not in her life, not to anyone.

Bob bellows, 'Go on, you can say it.'

Ginny says, 'Tell him what for, Irene.'

But Laurel, who somehow sees into Irene, speaks. The room hushes. 'What would you really like to say to Bill, Irene?'

Irene takes a deep breath. 'I'd like to say, "Bill, please listen to me and respect my needs. I need you to accept me as I am, whatever decisions I make about my own body. I need—"'

The last words come out in a sob. 'I need you to love me.'

As Maggie rubs her back, Irene weeps. All of her grief pours out of her—for past losses, deep disappointments, all the things she has no words for.

Irene and Maggie go out for coffee later. It's becoming a routine with them. Today they're trying a café on the wharf where the salty air brings back memories of Irene's cruise. Maggie wears her faux fur coat despite the warm weather.

As they sit down at a table outside with their drinks, a young boy throws a handful of chips in the air and a cloud of seagulls swoop down and clack at each other. Maggie laughs and waves at the boy and Irene feels her affinity with this woman deepen.

'Maybe I shared too much today,' Irene says as she stirs her coffee.

'You don't share nearly enough, my friend. It was a welcome change from hearing Ginny go on.'

'Do you think she's as together as she makes out?'

Maggie shakes her head. 'I shouldn't make fun of her. I doubt we know the half of it with Ginny, despite how much she talks.'

'Maybe it's a good thing she managed to get herself onto everyone's emergency contact list, then. It might be herself she's actually worried about.' Irene thinks of the way Ginny sits in her seat, holding her abdomen and struggling to sit still, as if a small animal is crashing about inside her.

'It was brave of you to share about your husband,' Maggie says, pulling Irene back to the present.

'I feel like I've been disloyal.'

'That's because you're such a nice person. The man clearly didn't appreciate what he had.'

Without warning, Maggie takes off her coat, rolls up a sleeve and holds out her arm to Irene. Irene is horrified at Maggie's scars but tries not to show it.

'There are more of the same on other parts of my body. Did you know transgender people are four times more likely to be victims of violence?'

'Oh, Maggie.' Irene's body is all goosebumps.

'In the end, I had to change my name and move states to get away from him.' She pulls her sleeve down.

'I'm so sorry. What I shared is nothing to—' Irene shakes her head.

'There are many different kinds of wounds. You've been hurt deeply, that's obvious.'

'I did love him.'

'I can tell that, too.'

'He took me on a holiday to Europe.'

'Did you want to go?'

Irene looks up sharply. 'What makes you ask?'

Maggie shrugs. 'The way you said it.'

'It wasn't the best timing. My business was booming and I was right into it. Bill got a bee in his bonnet about going at that moment—flights were a good price or something—so off we went.'

'What was the highlight for you?'

'Strangely, the Winchester Cathedral in England. Have you heard of the west window?'

'The one that was destroyed and pieced back together?'

Irene nods. 'Oh, I did love it, Maggie. I thought that window was the most beautiful of the lot. Maybe because of knowing its history. Just because something's broken beyond the ability to be what it was, it doesn't mean it can't be made whole again—just as something different. And beautiful.'

'A bit like us, eh?'

Simultaneously, the women reach out and hold each other's hands on the table top.

Irene nods. 'A lot like us, I think.'

IRENE 2016

The summer holiday season comes around. The business is thriving, both the physical store and online. Irene finds herself stretched in many directions. She's been baking for the community centre and filling hampers for families in need. Helping Zoe with the sewing and Sing with the online orders, as well as working in the shop. By mid-December, Sing has run out of ladies and Zoe's creations are flying out the door almost faster than they can keep up.

All this activity floods Irene with energy—her bones are fairly zinging. What joy it is to be busy and productive and useful. She thinks she could carry on like this forever.

On Christmas morning, Irene attends the special church service. When she enters the building, she doesn't sit in the fourth row from the back with the best view of the river. She can see the river anytime. Instead, she chooses a seat closer to the front where she can hang on the words of the minister.

Andrew is in fine form, preaching the story of the baby born to save humankind. A story so wild, yet so simple, Irene is inclined to believe it. The world is filled with miracles, after all. She only has to look around herself—at the river, the farm, this congregation, her own family—to see the miracle of life. To think, the atoms and molecules that make up her own body began somewhere an unfathomable distance away and burst across space, disconnected yet set on a specific course. And here she is. A body made of actual star dust.

'There are more things in heaven and earth...' Andrew is quoting Shakespeare now. Hamlet, if Irene remembers correctly. He has an interesting style of preaching. Not so much instructing as asking questions, encouraging people to think. He doesn't profess to know the answers and Irene likes that. In fact, she thinks she might come back. Not for the dirge-like hymns but to hear Andrew speak and ply him with questions afterwards.

Irene slips away straight after the service, returning to Helen's as Sing, Caleb and Tobias arrive. Soon after, Zoe and Milo—who have become very much part of the family—arrive with a plate of ginger-bread men proudly carried in by Milo. The gathering is merry, the food bountiful.

Irene gazes at each miracle, breathes them in, her people who are connected by all kinds of threads, familial and otherwise. They all belong. They are all hers.

What absolute joy they bring her.

One warm Friday evening, Irene devises a plan. She sets Milo and Poppy up on the deck with her laptop and an earphone each, and starts a movie. While they're engrossed in the film, Irene watches the riverbank.

With the children quiet, the sounds of the river rise up and Irene leans into the soft trickle and sigh as it plays over the rocks. In the distance, a faint quacking, voices, the tick and rustle of the willow branches as a breeze whips between them.

When the movement on the rocks happens—as she knew it would—she leans over to click off the computer and places her finger over her lips for the children to be quiet.

She smiles and points. They quietly slip off the seat and crawl across the deck, slowly stand and look over the railing.

Beneath them, the platypus paddles through a pool of water by the edge of the river that is surrounded by rocks. As they watch, it flips over onto its back and wriggles, scratching its underbelly with one claw. Over it rolls onto its front, splashing around before flipping onto its back again.

'What's it doing?' Milo whispers.

'Maybe cleaning itself,' Irene says. 'Or just having fun.'

'It's so cute,' Poppy sighs.

The children watch, mesmerised, as the platypus shows off its quirky beauty, doing its magic. How do you explain such a creature? All you can do is accept it is what it's meant to be.

You are perfect, platypus. You are perfect, tree. You are on your predestined course, river. You were created to be filled with wonder, Poppy and Milo.

Later, after Milo goes home and Poppy falls asleep, Irene strips off her clothes and looks into her full-length mirror. She no longer sees an unfinished sculpture. She sees wholeness.

You are meant to be this woman, Irene.

IRENE 2017

Max arrives in January for Irene's birthday. He's staying at a chalet by the beach in Crayfish Cove. Irene is outside checking the mailbox when he pulls up on the road outside her flat in a cheap rental car. As he emerges, Irene shakes her head. 'We're not going out in that,' she says, and backs out the BMW.

'You look fantastic,' Max says.

Irene rolls her eyes. 'Sure. Anyway, you look pretty good yourself. Ready to take off? I'll show you my place later.'

'So where are we going?'

'I booked us into that restaurant in Rosemere I told you about.'

'Oh good, I'm starving.'

Irene drives. Max keeps looking at her and grinning. Irene is surprised she doesn't feel nervous. In fact, Max's presence feels natural as if it hasn't been four months since she's seen him. He chats easily. Tells her Gregory's getting married, and asks if she'll be his plus-one at the wedding. She says she'll consider it.

Twenty minutes later, they turn off the main road into a narrow one that winds its way through seemingly endless hills.

'It's a bit off the beaten track,' Max says.

'It might be a culture shock.' Irene winds the window down halfway. 'Smell that.'

'Eucalyptus. It's very strong here.'

'I love it.'

'This is where you found that religious group, isn't it?'

'I only went a couple of times. They were a bit strange, if I'm honest.'

'I hope the restaurant isn't strange. We do want to get out of here alive.'

'It's agrarian. They plan their menu around what they're growing in their garden, and whatever's available locally. I've been a few times.'

'So you know the owners then?'

'Yep.'

'You know everyone, don't you?'

'Pretty much.'

Max laughs. Suddenly, he swings his head around to peer back behind them. 'What was that?'

'What?'

'A wild bloke, big beard, wearing a—a—not sure what it was.'

'There's a commune up there. A group of folk living off the land. They raise pigs, I heard.'

'I see what you mean by culture shock.'

They pull into the restaurant which looks deceptively like a barn from the outside. The interior is rustic but beautifully renovated—exposed beams, polished concrete floor, shelves lined with rows of bottled fruit.

Irene waves to the chef through the kitchen hatch—Dev from Durrunby—and a waiter shows them to a table by a window. There's a view out to the extensive garden where a woman is picking tomatoes.

Max scans his menu. 'Wood-smoked pork belly. You don't suppose they do business with the commune up the road?'

Irene laughs. 'No idea.'

'Well, I might give the pork a miss. Maybe the barramundi. Should we order vegetables to share?'

'You should try the pinkeye potatoes while you're in Tassie.'

'Oh yes, I wouldn't miss those.'

They chat amiably as they wait for their meal. Max tells her he's planning a renovation on his house. 'The bathroom needs an upgrade. If you saw it, you might run a mile.'

Irene wonders why he imagines her seeing his bathroom.

'The kitchen too. It's pretty outdated.'

'You don't cook much though, do you?'

Max looks a bit sheepish. 'A functional kitchen would be good, though. You know, for when I do want to cook.'

'Planning on cooking for someone?'

'Well, you never know.'

The meals, when they arrive, are impressive. Irene's steak comes out on a sizzling plate and she's suddenly ravenous.

'You're right, these potatoes are good,' Max says.

As they tuck into their lunch, Irene glances towards the door. 'Uh-oh. Don't look now.' She turns to the window in a show of studying the garden.

Max leans towards her and says in a low voice, 'Who is it?'

'Bea from the Crayfish Cove op shop.'

Irene can't stare out the window forever. As she turns back to her meal, a voice calls out, 'Irene. Fancy,' and Bea clops over on her high heels, followed by her husband.

'Bea, Owen. How are you both? This is my friend, Max, holidaying from Sydney.'

Bea gushes her hellos and her husband shakes Max's hand. The exchange is over within a few seconds and they head to their own table.

'They seem nice enough,' Max says.

'By tonight the whole of Crayfish Cove and Durrunby—and for all I know, Rosemere as well—will have heard about you, Max. And believe me, the story will have been richly embellished Bea-style.'

Max chuckles. 'You're not worried about it, are you?'

'Not at all. It might add to my intriguing air of mystery. Good for business.'

After their main meal, Dev the chef brings a flaming plate to their table.

'What's this? Did we order it?' Irene asks.

'Heard it was a special day,' Dev says. 'Happy birthday, Irene.'

'You really do know everyone, don't you?' Max says, when the chef has left.

Though Irene's stomach feels fit to burst, she manages to squeeze in a piece of the Blueberry Tarte Flambé. Neither of them can manage coffee.

They sit for a while until their bellies feel more comfortable, before waddling out to the car and driving back to Durrunby.

As Irene pulls into the carport of her flat, she says fondly, 'My little oasis.'

Once inside, Max goes to the centre of the living room and turns in a circle. 'Not much to it, is there?'

'Suits me perfectly,' Irene says as she fills two glasses with chilled water.

'Yes, I can see that. It looks comfy.'

'Check this out.' Irene takes him out to the deck, bringing the glasses with her.

'Ah, now this is something.' Max goes to the deck railing and looks out over the river. 'Wonderful. I can see why you spend so much time out here.'

'It's home to me, this river. I can't explain why.'

Max nods and sighs. 'Is there any point me asking you to move to Sydney?'

Irene has sat down on a deck chair. Max remains standing and she watches his back. When he finally turns around, his cheeks have turned a light shade of pink.

'Come and sit down, Max.'

Max sits on a chair next to Irene and takes the glass she offers him. He crosses his legs, wriggles his foot and says, 'Of course, I wouldn't be averse to moving to Tasmania, either.'

Irene rolls her eyes. 'Drink your water.'

'I'll be retiring in a couple of years.'

'Let's just enjoy the next few days. You've got dinner at Helen's to get through yet. Best behaviour tonight.'

Max grins and salutes her with his free hand.

The clan gathers at Helen and Pete's in the evening. Pete roasts a lamb leg with all the trimmings and Helen has made pavlova. Irene is surprised Max manages to fit in another large meal this soon after lunch. However, she doesn't do a bad job herself.

Much to Irene's relief, Max fits right in. Poppy is ecstatic at seeing him again and chatters incessantly. Caleb invites him for a tour of the farm the following day. By the end of the evening he has nursed three-year-old Tobias and been witness to Sing's announcement that she and Caleb are having another baby. The evening concludes with everyone in a celebratory mood and Irene breathes a sigh of relief.

Max takes Irene home in the rental car and sees her to the door.

'Well, cheerio,' he says.

She wonders if he's going to try and kiss her, but he doesn't. She stands at the door and watches as he slides his hands in his pockets and walks backwards down the driveway towards the car, grinning at her.

As he puts his hand on the door handle, he says, 'Your family is wonderful. The kind of family a man might like to adopt.'

Before Irene can reply, he hops in the car, calls out, 'See you tomorrow morning,' and closes the door.

Over the following few days, Irene shows Max around Durrunby and Crayfish Cove. He is captivated by the shop and buys one of Sing's ladies for his daughter. Caleb gives him a tour of the farm. They eat in Irene's favourite cafés. They take a rowboat out on the cove, climb to Madding Hill Lookout and go for numerous walks on the beach.

Irene admits to herself she enjoys this man's company. He's fun, he's open, she can tell him anything and know she will receive respect in return. None of her family members offer advice. They are respecting her and allowing her to find her own way without trying to influence her.

On the evening before Max is to return to Sydney, they walk along the river bank, talking about youthful dreams and how they compare to their current lives.

'Are you happy?' Max asks.

Irene stops to watch some ducks flapping under the willows. 'I am.'

'No regrets?'

'Everyone has regrets, don't they?'

'True.' Max runs his hand over his head. It reminds her of his nephew, Gregory, who Irene remembers had a similar mannerism. 'I do wonder sometimes if I've missed something I was meant to do. Do you ever feel like that?'

Irene puts her hands in her pockets and pulls her coat tight about herself. A dragonfly hovers on the surface of the water and darts away. 'It's funny,' she says. 'I always had this thought there was something big I was meant to do. Some significant, momentous thing I would achieve before I die. But it's not like that, is it?'

When she turns back to Max, she finds him watching her, his eyes taking her in.

'It's all the little things that are important,' she says. 'Every meaning-ful, intentional act. Life itself is the big thing.'

They resume walking and Irene leads him to the place where it is believed the platypus lives. She tells him about their weekly cleanup along the riverbank. 'When we were young, we didn't think about how our choices affected the environment. The rubbish pouring into the rivers and the sea—it's terrible. Do you know, on that cruise, I think I saw a plastic bag fly off the ship into the ocean.'

Max nods. 'Young people are more aware than we were.'

'I hope we haven't left it too late. Here's a bench, shall we sit?'

Max lifts his trousers at the knees as he lowers himself onto the seat. 'You're very caring, Irene,' he says.

'Well, I try.'

'Thing is—' Max sniffs and clears his throat. 'Well, I'd like to take care of you.'

'Max—'

'I know, you don't need taking care of. How about, be your companion? Ugh, that sounds awful. How about this—I think we have something special, I really do.'

Irene nods. 'Yes, we do.'

'Well—?'

'I have thought about it. You're wonderful, Max. Kind and lovely. I enjoy being with you.'

'Think about it, then. There's no rush.'

Irene smiles at his earnest face. 'I will.'

They watch the shadows stealing down from the high banks and clustering amongst the willows, as they amble back along the river in the glow of the sunset. Max takes Irene's hand and she enjoys the warmth emanating from his skin to hers. It's a safe, comfortable warmth. She hasn't felt like this about a man for a very long time.

Max leaves in the rental car, saying he'll be back to see her in the morning before he goes to the airport. Irene sits in her living room under a blanket and gazes out at the dimming sky through her window.

What does her future look like? She tries to imagine living somewhere different. Sydney? She doesn't like noisy places, or pollution, or any place where you can't see the stars. Imagine not being able to see the stars.

No, when Irene thinks of the future, she sees herself here. The shop. Her flat. The river. Caring for her people. Helping at the community centre. Friday night sleepovers with Poppy and Saturday breakfasts with Zoe and Milo. Regular catch-ups with Maggie in town. And her monthly support meetings.

How does Max fit into the picture? She tries to envision him in her world and finds it difficult. Her life is like a river set on a particular course and she's happy with the way it flows.

When Max returns the following morning, she takes him out to the deck to see the way the sunlight is bending itself through the willows and skipping across the surface of the water.

'You can almost hear it laughing,' she says as they lean on the railing, looking out.

When they turn to each other, Max's eyes search Irene's. She sees the cloud of disappointment cross his features and knows he has read her face. He knows her decision. They both turn back to the river.

'I'm sorry,' Irene says.

'It's alright. I understand.'

'Do you?'

'You belong here. Your family is here. My family's dispersed but I've made my home in Sydney. I guess there comes a time when you're too old to shift.'

'Are you calling me old?'

Max lets out a half laugh in a puff of air. 'I guess I'm saying we're both a little set in our ways?'

Irene holds out her arms and they hug.

'Goodbye, sweet Irene.'

A hollow space inside Irene fills with sadness. But when Max leaves, the sadness dissipates and she is surprised to find the greater feeling to be relief.

IRENE 2017

As soon as Max leaves, it starts to pour. It's as if the heavens were holding on, waiting for his departure—or for Irene's decision—before breaking open and letting loose a deluge. Irene is coming out of the supermarket when she feels the first raindrops fall—splat—on her head. Thinking she'll have time to reach the gift shop before the real rain starts, she hurries along the street, keeping to the side of the footpath close to the buildings.

The splats turn into a downpour and she jogs the rest of the way, turning into Maple Lane as Sing is hurrying up to the door. She opens it for Irene and they tumble inside.

Zoe looks up from her sewing table. 'Woah, you look like two drowned rats.'

'I feel like a drowned rat,' Irene says, taking off her jacket.

Sing shakes herself off and flops down on the two-seater sofa, fluffing up her hair with her hands. 'That was wild. We might be here for a while.'

The rain slants against the window and pours down the glass.

'It's cosy in here, anyway,' Irene says. 'Look, the windows are fogging up.' She sits down next to Sing and adds, 'Max must have taken the nice weather away with him.' She smiles and waits for the barrage of questions. She may as well get the interrogation over with.

Right on cue, Sing says, 'Is Max coming back soon? Or are you going to visit him? Do you have any plans? Whoops, I'm asking too many questions, aren't I?'

Zoe rolls her chair along the floor with her feet until she's next to the others, and says, 'I'm all ears.'

Irene says, 'It's like this. Max and I are friends. Good friends. That's all there is and ever will be.'

'Oh.' Zoe looks disappointed.

Sing pats her on the knee. 'I'll be honest, I thought you might go and live in Sydney and I wasn't looking forward to it. I'm happy you're staying.'

'I think if we'd become an item, I would have insisted Max move to Tassie.'

'Do you think he would've?' Zoe asked.

'He did mention it.'

Sing lets out an exaggerated sigh. 'Poor Max. He really loves you.'

Irene narrows her eyes at Sing, who bursts out laughing.

'Sorry. I just like to see people happy.'

Zoe stands and says, 'I've got something to show you.' She goes to the storage room and comes back with a box. 'I was at the Crayfish Cove op shop yesterday and Bea gave me these. She's been saving kids' shirts for us that need sprucing up.'

'That was nice of her,' Sing says as she inspects the clothes.

'Yeah, she's been great.'

'Did Bea say anything about me and Max, by any chance?' Irene asks.

'No, why?'

'Oh.' Irene is surprised. 'She saw us having lunch at a restaurant in Rosemere. I thought she may have mentioned it.'

'No, she just asked about the business. She wanted to know if there was anything else we'd like her to keep an eye out for.'

They talk some more about business and the afternoon wears on. Customers are few, likely kept away by the rain which slows to a constant drizzle.

Later, as Irene is reorganising a box of soap on the counter, she looks up to see a woman outside the shop, pressed up against the window under the eaves. She shakes off an umbrella, props it against the wall outside, and enters the shop.

As Irene greets her, the woman's gaze flies upward to the shelves where Sing's ladies pose, and she opens her mouth as if in amazement. She looks to be in her thirties, wearing wide-leg jeans with braces and a checked beret Irene can't help but admire. She turns herself about, taking in the rest of the shop.

'Wow, just wow. Of course, I'm generally more eloquent than that. May I?' She points to a row of tiny denim jackets.

'Of course,' Irene says. 'Feel free to browse.'

The woman lifts a hanger with one hand and strokes the embroidery on the shirt collar with the other. She shakes her head. 'Nicer even than I imagined.'

Zoe spins her chair around to watch the woman. She meets Irene's eye and flicks her eyebrows up. Sing comes out of the store room at that moment and sees the woman admiring the shirt. She stops short. 'Oh. Is that—are you—'

The woman looks up and smiles. 'Daisy Rayne at your service.'

'Oh my goodness.' Sing moves towards her, dropping the box she's carrying onto the counter as she goes. 'Daisy Rayne. Welcome to Maple Lane Gifts. I'm Sing.'

Daisy replaces the shirt and comes around to the other side of the clothes rack. She holds out her hand to Sing. 'Pleased to meet you. You're the designer of the ladies.'

'I am. And this is Irene, and Zoe who creates the upcycled children's clothes.'

'I know, I've been admiring your online shop.'

'You guys, this is Daisy Rayne.' When neither Irene nor Zoe say anything, she adds, 'She's an influencer. You haven't heard of her? She's famous.'

Daisy laughs. 'Not exactly famous.'

'What brings you to Durrunby?' Irene asks.

'Your shop, actually. I had to see it in person.'

Sing clasps her hands together under her chin. 'Daisy makes videos about Tasmanian experiences and posts them on social media. People actually take notice of what she says when they're coming to Tassie.'

Daisy puts her hands in her pockets and looks around the room. 'I was wondering how you'd feel about me featuring your shop on my channel. It would mean doing some filming and maybe one or all of you could explain what you do. It'd be done very professionally. I have my own camera person and everything.'

'Oh yes,' Sing says. 'Oops, sorry. I'm getting ahead of myself.' She turns to Irene with a sheepish expression.

Daisy laughs. 'I'm staying overnight at a chalet in Crayfish Cove. You should have a chat about it first. Is it alright if I pop back in tomorrow?'

'Of course,' Irene says. 'Anyway, I trust Sing. I'm sure the decision will be in the affirmative.'

'Good for business, I reckon,' Zoe adds.

'Oh yes.' Daisy smiles them. 'I promise you, it will be very good for business. Is it alright if I have a look around?'

When Daisy has left, Sing grabs her phone. 'Here, you have to see her. This is her channel. She's got... wow, over seventy thousand sub-scribers. And her videos have hundreds of thousands of views.'

Irene is stunned. 'Really? I didn't know this was a thing.'

Zoe's face lights up. 'Will we be able to keep up with stock when we go live?'

Irene pats her on the shoulder. 'Zoe, we can always employ someone to help if we need to.'

'True.' Zoe goes back to her work table. 'Well, I'd better get moving. Work to do, a living to make.'

Sing sighs happily. 'We're on the up.'

The sewing class Irene runs at the community centre is due to start soon so she leaves Zoe and Sing to their work. Outside, the rain has stopped and a fine mist hangs in the air, its tiny droplets catching Irene's face like a silken spider web. She walks up to the main road and finds it slick and clean, the surface of the road glinting as if sprinkled with gems.

She stands at the corner of Main Street and Maple Lane, watching the street resume its bustle with shoppers emerging from buildings and eaves. The air is warm and humid, and Irene's shirt sticks to her. It feels like she's in the tropics—heat rising up from the pavement, sweet smells hanging in the damp air. If she lived in a city, this is the place she'd like to come for a holiday. How blessed she is to live here.

Irene returns to Maple Lane and the entrance to the community centre. As she enters the building, voices call out— 'Here's Irene' ... 'G'day Irene' ... 'Oh yay, she's here' —and a band of helpers bustle about, moving tables and chairs and sewing machines. Getting ready to sew and learn and chatter and laugh.

Irene can't imagine wanting to be anywhere else in the world.

HELEN 2024

Helen's meeting with Claire has stirred up memories. She pulls out the boxes containing her mother's photo albums and piles them onto the dining table. Once settled with a cup of tea, she flips through the older albums containing pictures of Irene as a young woman, before she met Helen's father. Some photos feature Claire and some other of her friends. Helen doesn't recognise the others. Perhaps they didn't keep in touch.

In the later albums, Bill features a lot—on a tractor, at a table in a restaurant, walking through the botanical gardens, posing with a Tasmanian devil at a wildlife park. Irene was obviously the keener photographer.

Helen looks through the albums from all the decades. Helen and Caleb growing up. Poppy growing up. Irene's other grandchildren, Tobias and his sister, Eleni. The photos of the business with Sing and Zoe.

There's one dedicated entirely to the river, taken from the deck of the flat at different times of the day throughout the seasons. From crisp, sunny days to hazy scenes where mist rolls along the surface of the water. She recognises some of them as ones Irene emailed to the family during Covid when they were in lock down.

Helen finds the album for 2020. What a year that was. In January they were joking about it being the year of 20/20 vision, and by March, they were all in isolation. Irene's album is filled with photos they shared with each other online as a way of connecting. Pete in his 'hazmat' gear at the hospital. Irene at the community centre wearing a mask and helping dish up meals for people doing it tough. There's even a nice picture of Max and his new wife at their wedding. Helen thinks Irene might have felt a bit sad about it at the time. Not that she would ever have admitted it.

In some ways, 2020 was a good year. Sing and Zoe kept creating and their online shop took off, helped along by the influencer, Daisy's, videos and posts. After that, it grew into something bigger than they ever imagined and they had to hire an extra shop assistant.

Helen flips through more albums, year by year, until she comes to the photo book Irene made of Poppy's Leavers' formal at the end of her final year of high school. Poppy having her hair done at Zola's, getting ready at home, standing on the stage with her classmates. Next are the professional photographs that were taken on the day. They're beautifully done but lack the spontaneity of Irene's, which Helen loves best.

That was the day life went awry for Irene. She didn't make any more albums afterwards.

Helen closes the book. She still cries sometimes. Perhaps she always will.

IRENE 2023

Irene is getting old. She'll be seventy next month. How on earth did she get here? Helen's been coming into the shop, saying, 'Shouldn't you be at home with your feet up knitting socks by now?'

Irene keeps telling her, 'I'll never get old.'

Helen replies, 'No, I don't believe you will.'

But Irene has been feeling it over the past few months. Arthritis here. Shortness of breath there. Aches and pains she hasn't had before. Everything takes longer to do than it used to and she's had to cut down on her time in the shop.

She has been doing some knitting. Not socks, though. Mostly jumpers for Tobias and Eleni, scarves and beanies for Poppy and Milo. She tried to knit Poppy a pair of mittens but ended up with something that would barely fit a Muppet.

Irene curls up on the sofa and pulls her crocheted blanket around herself. The sun is going down and it's getting cold. Zoe and Milo will be down in the shop, checking on the builders' progress. They do this every afternoon when Milo comes home from school. Milo is tall now—fourteen and towering over his mother. Once the renovations are done, they'll be able to move into the back of the shop where Milo will have a good-sized bedroom instead of the poky one in the flat.

Irene is so proud of Zoe. What a hard-working woman she is. Irene knew it as soon as she met her, the day she backed her old station wagon into the fence. As soon as Irene set eyes on that well-cared for little boy, she knew she had a couple of gems living next door.

Oh, why this terrible tiredness? Seventy is the new sixty, so Helen tells her. She should have plenty of get-up-and-go, yet all her energy seems to have dissipated. It's still inside her somewhere, stored in her cells, potential energy for reuse—she remembers this from science classes over fifty years ago. Something to do with the conservation of energy. Perhaps it has moved to her brain which seems to be galloping at a frenetic pace. Grappling with questions about life and death and hope and forgiveness. What will happen to her energy when she dies? It must go somewhere.

All this thinking exhausts her. She will rest for the afternoon; they don't need her in the shop today. She must gather her strength for Poppy's Leavers' formal tomorrow. Her granddaughter's final year of high school and next year off to college in the city. Helen is beside herself with worry already, of course. Poppy is sensible. She'll be alright.

Irene pulls the blanket up to her chin and closes her eyes. It sure is cold in here.

Poppy beams from the stage in the school auditorium. She stands with her classmates, all done out in their fancy gear—pretty dresses, suits and ties. Poppy wears a red dress with a sash, sewn from scratch by Irene and Zoe. Irene secretly thinks it's the best looking frock of the lot. At least it has been hemmed properly.

Irene sits on a hard plastic seat alongside the rest of Poppy's family—Helen and Pete, Caleb and Sing with the children, and Zoe and

Milo. The principal is giving a final speech but Irene can't concentrate on it. She's too busy gazing at Poppy.

Helen grabs Irene's hand and whispers, 'My baby's all grown up.' Her eyes are misty.

'Not yet, she isn't. She's only sixteen,' Irene whispers back.

Sing, on the other side of Irene, leans into her ear and says, 'She looks like you.'

'You think?' Irene turns her eyes back to the stage. To the pretty girl with her hair in an up-do and poky-out ears, smiling self-consciously.

'I see you in her profile, so graceful. And she has such a kind face, don't you think?'

Irene feels her own eyes misting.

The principal finishes her speech and the room is invited to stand and clap the graduating class of 2023. While the students are having professional photos taken, families are asked to wait outside. Irene and her clan make their way to the doors, stopping to snap photos of the class with their phones. They follow the other families down to the main school gates where a bus waits to take the students to a local restaurant for dinner.

Irene's back aches from the hard seats. She leans against the fence and says to Helen, 'Maybe this is your time to move up.'

'What do you mean?' Helen stoops to pick up her crumpled tissue from the ground, and puts it in the pocket of her jeans.

'You've talked about moving up career-wise. With Poppy in town—very capable of looking after herself, I might add—you have time to plan for it. You'd make a good Assistant Principal. Dan's set to retire in another year, I hear.'

'You keep your ear to the wall, don't you? Been hanging out in the op shop with Bea?'

'She's alright,' Irene says, and feels a sliver of shame. She never did hear any gossip about herself and Max in the restaurant all those years ago. It seems Bea kept her mouth shut after all. Irene wishes she hadn't spoken cruelly about her to Max.

'I have thought about it,' Helen says, 'but I don't know if I'm brave enough.'

Before Irene can reply, Poppy emerges from the auditorium, arm-in-arm with a friend. When she sees them waiting by the gate, she slips her arm from her friend's and rushes over. There's a mad flurry of hugs and kisses, and Helen holds onto her for so long that the others make a show of tapping their feet impatiently.

Poppy gives Irene a tight hug and says, 'Thank you for everything, Reenie.'

'My pleasure, monkey.' Irene lifts a stray wisp of Poppy's hair and puts it behind her ear.

There's barely time to wish her a good evening before she's pulled away and hustled onto the waiting bus. Irene watches her going up the steps, her red dress with its perfect hem mingling with the other fancy fabrics, stockings and polished shoes.

As Irene watches, the dresses blur together. The scene swings before her eyes, the colours shifting and muddling into a dull grey that hurts her chest and sucks the breath out of her. She grabs for the fence and misses, realising too late that the muddle of grey is the ground that has come up to meet her.

'Mum!' Helen is beside her, pulling her upwards. Caleb has his arms around her too.

'Let's get you to the car,' Caleb says.

She finds herself being lifted and carried along, held between Caleb and Pete. They help her into the back seat where she closes her eyes with relief.

Voices buzz, decisions being made. Helen's perfume wafts pleasantly over her and she feels her daughter's body shifting against her side.

'I'm taking you to the hospital,' Pete's voice says. 'The others will meet us there.'

'I'm alright. I just had a dizzy turn.'

'It's best to be sure.'

Irene gives in to the decisions being made around her. Wherever her energy has gone, it seems to have deserted her this time. Perhaps it has hopped over to Helen who is arranging a blanket over Irene's legs. Or to the others, who are closing the car doors and calling messages to each other. Pete starts the engine and the car moves.

Irene keeps her eyes closed. A dull ache in her chest floods her with memories of Bill grasping at his shirt collar and falling to the ground.

Not that, she thinks. I don't want to go like that.

But Irene has her family around her. She feels Helen's hand gently squeezing her own, and is deeply grateful.

Irene sits in the waiting room of the district hospital in Crayfish Cove. Her doctor is apparently rearranging her afternoon to see Irene straight away. Irene has ordered Pete and Caleb to go home. She doesn't want them here looking hawk-eyed at her. Helen is all Irene can cope with right now.

'Are you feeling any worse?' Helen is on the edge of her seat, squinting into Irene's face.

'You've asked me already.'

'Well, I'm just making sure.' There's a hint of offence in Helen's tone.

'Sorry, no. I feel alright. Like I said, it was a dizzy turn.'

'Are you eating alright?'

Irene forces herself not to huff. 'Always.'

When the doctor calls her into her consulting room, Helen wants to go too. Irene gives her a look and Helen stays put.

'Irene. I hear you had a fall. Sit down and tell me about it.'

She doesn't beat about the bush, Irene thinks. 'I was dizzy and fell. That's all. And I have a pain in the chest.'

'Anything else out of the ordinary?'

Irene is compelled to be truthful. 'Sometimes short of breath. And lacking in energy. Headaches now and then. Back aches too. That's about getting old though, isn't it?'

'Considering your history, we should be thorough. I'll give you a general health check and we'll have some tests done and go from there. How does that sound?'

When Irene goes out to Helen in the waiting room, she plasters on a big smile. 'Just a dizzy spell,' she says.

Helen springs to her feet. 'But—'

'Relax, I'm getting some tests.' Irene holds up the pathology and radiology request forms.

'Oh. Good then.'

Irene has the blood test straight away. The x-rays she must come back for in the morning.

Helen drives her home. As Irene unlocks the front door, Helen takes her arm and tries to help her in. Irene shakes her off and points to the floor as they step in. 'Look, no lip. No tripping hazards. Perfectly accessible, this place.'

Helen purses her lips and sees Irene to her living room. 'You alright, then?'

'Yes, you can go now.'

That evening, Irene drops a glass on the floor that shatters into a thousand tiny shards. She leaves it on the floor and goes to bed, because she can't find the energy to sweep it up.

IRENE 2023

The results of Irene's blood tests and x-rays have warranted a referral to see the oncologist. Irene sits on the edge of the moulded plastic seat in Anya Chen's consulting room, nodding as if this is a regular medical appointment. As if she is receiving a routine test result and is impatient to be on her way.

Irene drove to the city by herself today, telling Helen it was one of those routine checkups they give former cancer patients periodically. She didn't want anyone with her if the news was bad. She would need time to process it which would be impossible with Helen distraught beside her.

There was always a chance the news wouldn't be too bad. A fixable glitch. However, it turns out Irene's suspicions were correct. And she has had her suspicions, ever since Poppy's Leavers' formal. The fall had clinched it. There'd been a familiarity about it. Even as she was crashing to the ground, her body recognised it, responding with waves of grief that had shuddered through her.

'Alright,' Irene says to the doctor, and stands to leave.

Doctor Chen asks her to sit back down to discuss the matter further. Irene sits obediently but is struggling to take in the words dropping from the doctor's mouth. She nods and squeezes her hands together in her lap.

The doctor asks Irene to wait and leaves the room. Irene scans the posters stuck to the wall. They're mostly pink breast-cancer care posters. How to look for and recognise symptoms. It's been many years since Irene has had to think about cancer.

The oncologist has explained everything and given Irene a lot of information. Too much for Irene to take in all at once. It bobs around Irene's head trying to penetrate the bubble she has enclosed herself in.

When the doctor returns, she has more glossy pamphlets in her hand which she hands to Irene. One of them is a brochure about palliative care. A stone pitches in Irene's chest. Oh, the cold hard weight of it.

Doctor Chen asks Irene if she'd like to phone someone. Her daughter, perhaps? Irene says no and says she wants to leave.

She finds a coffee shop, orders a double-shot cappuccino, changes her mind and requests an orange juice. She'll have to give up coffee again, and wine. No, she won't. She apologises and re-orders the coffee. She doesn't have to give up anything. Life is giving her up, isn't it?

She sits outside in a courtyard area, its brick walls covered with a pink climbing rose. Such a beautiful flower. It's called a Shropshire Lad, or something like that, she thinks.

At a nearby table, a woman shushes a young child who is intent on shouting about something. He's happy, that's the main thing. The woman shushes him again and looks nervously at Irene.

Irene says, 'Let him shout. Don't rein him in, life's too short. Let him bellow, I love to hear him.'

The woman gives her a tentative smile. She may have pegged Irene as a nutter, which Irene possibly is. She's been turning into an eccentric old lady of late. Silly how it takes you nearly a lifetime to figure out the things that matter.

Life. It's a tenuous thread. Irene has had seventy years of it, a lot more than many get. She's grateful, she really is. So very grateful. As her eyes start to prick, the waitress brings out Irene's coffee. As she sets the cup down, she raises her eyebrows at Irene in a conspiratorial manner and makes a face in the direction of the child who is bellowing again.

'Wonderful, isn't he?' Irene says, and the waitress hurries away.

Irene sips her coffee. The woman and the child finish whatever they're eating and, as they are leaving, the woman casts a genuine smile in Irene's direction.

Helen isn't the person Irene wants to phone. Nor Caleb, nor Sing. She takes out her mobile and calls Maggie. 'Any chance you have time to meet?' she asks.

Maggie, who lives in the city, comes straight to the coffee shop. Irene hasn't even finished her drink before Maggie comes bustling across the courtyard in the big faux fur coat she's worn for years, even though it's at least twenty degrees. Perhaps Irene isn't the only eccentric old woman about. Not that Maggie's old, she's a good ten years younger than Irene. Maybe she has just figured out earlier in life how to be herself.

Maggie asks Irene if she wants another coffee and Irene declines. Maggie takes off again to order a drink and comes back with a tall iced coffee. She flops herself, her coat and her drink down opposite Irene and says, 'I'm all yours.'

To her friend, Irene repeats the words she can remember that popped like bullets from the lips of the oncologist. The scary words—metastasis, terminal prognosis, chemotherapy, palliative care.

Maggie listens, nods, says none of the things people say when they're horrified and don't know what to say. The kinds of words Irene expects

Helen will say. Helen will want her to go through chemo again. Will cry and not know how to handle her own grief.

When Irene runs out of words, she stares at her empty coffee cup, twirling it round and round in the saucer.

Maggie says, 'Whatever you choose, I'll support you. And whenever you want to talk, my ears are yours.'

Irene lifts her eyes to the sky and blinks. She's not going to cry.

'Feel like going for a walk through the park?' Maggie says. 'I came through earlier and the lavender is so deliciously thick, you wouldn't believe. We can bury our faces in it.'

As they walk along the footpath together, Irene says, 'You know, I really love your coat. On you, I mean. It suits you.'

Maggie flashes a big, coral-lipped smile. 'I found it in Vinnies and thought, that is *me*.'

'It is,' Irene says. 'It really is you. I used to have a red wig. I loved that wig. I might ask Zola to colour my hair red.'

'Do it.'

Irene swings her arms as she walks, and gives a little skip. 'You know, I think I will.'

IRENE 2023

T here's no easy way to tell someone you're dying. Best to come straight out with it. Irene looks at the faces turned to her expectantly and has no idea what to say.

They're at Helen and Pete's for a pre-Christmas do—Caleb and Sing with the children and Poppy down from the city. Pete's been trying out his new barbecue and they've eaten only half of the mountain of meat he's cooked. They're sitting on the verandah, relaxing in the sun. It's very peaceful with their tummies gorged and everyone in a good mood. Even Tobias and Eleni are getting along, playing with a tub of Lego on the floor. Irene hates to spoil it. But what can you do?

'Is this about your oncology appointment, Mum?' Helen asks. She's scraping leftovers from a plate into a bin next to the barbecue.

Irene nods. 'It's not good, I'm afraid.'

There is silence for a moment. Helen's face pales. She sits down, grips the arm of her chair and stares at Irene.

'It's a recurrent metastatic breast cancer. It's in my lungs. And... other places.'

Poppy, sitting next to her, puts her hand on top of Irene's and squeezes. 'I'm sorry, Reenie,' she says.

Helen stands, wrings her hands and sits back down. 'Is that bad? How bad is that?'

Caleb drags a chair up next to Irene's. 'How are you feeling about it, Mum?'

Irene looks into his eyes and sees such tenderness there, she has to look away. 'Fine, actually.'

'You can have chemo again, right?' Helen says.

Irene smiles in her direction. 'I'm discussing all that with the oncologist.' Her reply seems to appease Helen for the moment.

Pete, on the edge of his seat, leans towards her. 'Anything we can do, I mean anything. Don't hesitate.'

'I know, thanks Pete. Sorry to drop the bombshell but I wanted to say it once, while everyone's here, so I don't have to keep repeating myself. I'll keep you posted.'

No one appears to know what to say.

Irene stands and heads for the sliding door. 'Well, I don't know about anyone else, but I'm ready for dessert.'

'Right.' Sing jumps up from her seat. 'If you can do it, so can I.'

The air is suddenly lighter, like it has been injected with bubbles. Irene could hug Sing.

On the way to the kitchen, Sing gives Irene's back a brief rub and says, 'With you all the way, Mum. Whatever.'

And Irene believes her. There'll be no expectations from Sing. Whatever Irene decides, Sing will simply be there.

Helen is angry with Irene and has gone off in a huff.

Irene sits outside The River Café, nibbling on her muffin. She understands, of course. Helen is frightened. She doesn't want to lose her mother. And Irene doesn't want to go. Trouble is, the choice has been made for her. She is leaving this life whether she likes it or not, either sooner or later. Helen wants it to be later.

What Irene has tried to make her understand is chemotherapy will only delay the inevitable for a short time. Not enough to warrant going through it again. Not in Irene's opinion, anyway. Clinging to a little scrap of time while vomiting her insides out. She shudders at the thought. It puts her in mind of the widow who clung too long to her husband's tombstone.

'If I have to go, I'm going with all my hair,' Irene had said to Helen. It was meant as a joke. She was trying to lighten the mood a bit, but Helen took offense.

'Hair!' She almost shouted the word, burst into tears and ran off.

Later in the afternoon, Helen comes to Irene's flat and apologises. Her eyes are red and swollen. There's grief in the lines of her face, but resolve too. 'I'm just not ready for you to go. But I won't ever be. So you should do what you need to.'

'Come outside for some fresh air.' Irene opens the door to the deck, goes back to the kitchen to pour glasses of water, and brings them and a packet of biscuits out to Helen.

'Don't even think of going to one of those palliative care places,' Helen says.

'Eh?'

'Sorry.' Helen's face reddens. 'I told myself not to do that.'

'What?'

'Tell you what to do.'

Irene laughs.

'Pete and I would like you to come and stay with us. You can have hospital care at home, did you know?'

'I did.'

'Well, will you?' Helen looks at Irene while biting her bottom lip.

'Yes. I would like that.'

Helen takes a big breath, lets it out noisily and smiles. 'That's settled then.'

'We should have some fun together,' Irene says. 'You're on holidays soon. How about we hang out.'

'That'd be nice.'

'I might opt out of doing any Christmas cooking this time though.'

Helen makes a 'pfft' sound and says, 'I was going to wake you up early to do the prep work in the kitchen.'

'Ha. I could try, but I don't think I'd last long.'

Helen takes a sip of her water and stretches her legs. 'How about you sit back on the day and let us wait on you.'

'It's a deal.'

Helen grins at Irene and says, 'Thanks, by the way.'

'What for?'

'Being such a good mum. I never did figure out how to please Dad. I could never really tell if he was proud of me or not.'

'He was proud of you.'

'Maybe he just wasn't good at showing it. It always felt like he was keeping me guessing.' She shrugs her shoulders. 'Anyway, it doesn't matter now.'

'We have always been proud of you.' Irene leans over to take the biscuit packet and holds it out to Helen.

Helen takes a bite and mumbles through the mouthful, 'Mm, these are good. Did you make them?'

Irene chuckles at the joke. 'Yep, they're called Tim Tams. Want the recipe?'

'Yes please. I could catch a man with these.'

'Another man, isn't one enough?'

'Yeah, I reckon.'

'They don't get much better than Pete. Hang onto him.'

'I intend to. I thought for a while you and Max might end up together.'

'I did too, for one fleeting moment. Until I came to my senses.'

Helen grins. 'He seems happy.'

Irene nods and watches the water. When she sees movement at the river bank, she shoots forward in her seat. 'Look at that.'

'What?'

'There.' Irene points.

They both watch as the platypus clambers up onto the rock, followed by two smaller brown, furry bodies.

'Babies!' Helen clasps her hands together.

'Well, I never. What a wonderful gift.'

They tiptoe quietly up to the deck rail and look down.

'Wait till I tell Poppy,' Helen says.

'I'll see if she wants to come and stay with me for a weekend. Like old times.'

There are many things Irene wants to do before she goes. She'll have to make a list. It won't be a long one as there's not much time left before she'll be too sick to do much.

'Helen?'

'Yes?'

'Want to go for a walk on the beach?'

'I'd love to.'

And in Irene's mind, she ticks one small thing off her bucket list.

HELEN 2024

Helen rifles through her clothes in the walk-in-robe, looking for something to wear to Zoe's house warming. She takes a favourite skirt, looks it over and puts it back. Must be time to buy some new clothes; she always ends up wearing the same ones.

When Helen's parents lived here, this space was filled with clothes and shoes and accessories. All those shirts of her father's. The boxes they'd filled with them after his death. Her mother's dresses had hung here too—a whole wall of them, in colour co-ordinating order like a fashion store. Most of them were gifts from Helen's father.

Helen makes a decision and chooses an outfit she hasn't worn for a while. As she's checking herself in the mirror, Pete comes in wearing jeans and a checked shirt. She says a silent hooray that he hasn't decided to go out in his ancient tracksuit.

'Wowee, you look amazing,' Pete says.

'Are you kidding?' Helen looks down at the blue spotty dress she's had for a hundred years.

'Have I seen that dress?'

'No, it's new.'

Pete beams. 'I knew it.'

Helen rolls her eyes. 'Joking. I've had it since I was thirty.'

'Well, it looks new on you.'

Helen shakes her head at him. Where would she be without Pete?

They meet Poppy in the kitchen, who is wearing jeans and a T-shirt and looks lovely no matter what she's wearing.

'A whole Saturday off to spend with the fam,' Pete says, and does a silly dance.

'Yeah, and it's about time, Dad.' Poppy leans down to pick up her jacket from the sofa. 'Can we go? Milo's waiting to show me the new budgie.'

They drive into Durrunby and park down the street from the shop in Maple Lane. Several cars are parked outside the building already. They walk down to the new entrance at the back via the driveway where fourteen-year-old Milo appears to be waiting for them.

'Hey,' he says as he opens the door to let them in.

Pete shakes his hand. 'You're nearly as tall as me, mate.'

Milo grins self-consciously and asks Poppy if she wants to check out his new pet bird.

They walk into a freshly painted living area. Natural light floods in through the back windows and a glass sliding door opens onto the yard. About fifteen guests are mingling. Helen recognises some as business people from the Durrunby hub. She spies Zoe's boyfriend chatting in a corner. Sam—a nice guy. The poor fellow has already been interrogated and watched carefully by everyone to make sure he's alright.

Helen sees Zoe next to a table laid out with plates of afternoon tea. As Pete stops to talk to someone, Helen takes her platter of scones over. Zoe's face lights up as Helen approaches.

'All finished.' She indicates the space around them with a wave of her hand. 'Well, except for a few bits of furniture I need. Obviously.' Her eyes dart to the centre of the room where one small couch sits by itself. The walls are lined with folding chairs. 'I borrowed some chairs from the community centre.'

'It looks wonderful,' Helen says. 'I haven't seen it since the final coat of paint.'

'Want to see the bedrooms?'

It's a modest build-on. Two doors from the main living area lead to the bedrooms. Milo has the larger one which is neatly set up with his bedroom furniture and a desk. A cricket bat leans against the wall in a corner. The room has its own sliding door out to the back yard.

'I want to build a deck out there eventually,' Zoe says. 'And renovate the kitchen and bathroom of course. I haven't done anything with those yet.'

'You'll get there.'

'I'm so happy, Helen. Our own place.'

Helen gives her a brief shoulder hug and says, 'You both deserve it.'

As they exit Milo's room, Zoe asks Helen to follow her outside. They stand together on the small back lawn next to a partly-dug garden bed. Helen assumes Zoe is about to tell her what she's planning for the garden.

Instead, Zoe squeezes her hands together and says, 'I need to tell you. Irene helped me with the reno.'

Helen smiles. 'I know.'

'First off—like, way back—she helped me work out a plan to save for a deposit. I didn't know what I was going to buy yet, but by the time this building came up for sale, I'd saved enough. I was able to start the renovation as well.'

'You've done well for someone your age.'

'Yeah, but I was a bit short and your mum helped me with the rest. The plan was to pay her back but she died before I could. I've got the full amount saved up now and I just need to know where to deposit it.'

'Didn't she tell you?'

Zoe frowns. 'What?'

'She wanted you to have the money as a gift. She made sure I knew about it.'

Zoe's face is a blaze of red. 'Really?' She blinks into the distance. 'Gosh. Maybe she did tell me but I didn't understand.'

'She wasn't very coherent at the end.' Helen looks down at the little garden bed, neatly shaped and dug over. 'She thought very highly of you. We all do. You and Milo will always be part of our family.'

Zoe swallows and looks at her feet. 'Thanks. I miss her so much.'

Helen feels the familiar rattling in her own spirit. 'She sure was something.'

As they walk back to the house, Zoe says, 'I guess I can afford to buy some furniture now.'

Helen grins. 'You could use some.'

As they go back inside, Caleb and Sing arrive through the side door. Sing rushes over to Zoe and gives her a hug and Helen leaves them to catch up. She piles some food on a plate and sits on a fold-up chair.

In the corner of the room, Milo and Poppy are standing near the bird cage which used to house Poppy's budgerigar. Milo has hand-reared the blue budgie that sits on his arm pecking his sleeve. Poppy puts her finger out and snatches it away as the bird goes to peck it.

At least Banjo's cage is getting some use. Helen thinks of the day she buried Banjo in the garden. The grief that had burst its way up from inside her. Too many deaths. How do you accept death as a part of life when you're so close to a person, your lives are like roots tangled up together? The separation like a ripping apart that tears pieces away from you. Helen still feels raw from the ripping, but she is healing, slowly and painfully. Grief moulds you into something new, she thinks. The roots drawing essence from other things, other people. Don't we all change, over time? Become something different?

As the side door opens, Comet the budgie is startled and flies to the top of a curtain rail. Milo coaxes him down and puts him back in his cage. Joss, the owner of The River Café, arrives with a plate of pastries. Helen goes to the table to snaffle one before they disappear. While moving around the room, talking to various people, she surreptitiously manages to eat four of them.

It's a lovely gathering of people. The shop has brought many visitors to Maple Lane and the two businesses on the opposite side of the road—antiques and woodcraft—have also reaped the benefits of the gift shop's success. Helen is glad to see those owners here also, celebrating Zoe and Milo's new home.

Later, as they're about to leave, Zoe comes up to Helen and says, 'I forgot to show you.' She gestures for Helen to follow her to a back window, and points to one side of the frame.

In a small section of the inside of the window frame, etched into the wood in cursive lettering, is the name—Irene.

'Your mum did it. I filled it in with a dark stain and re-sanded to make it stand out.'

Helen runs her fingers over the name. 'Wow, it's beautiful. She's left her mark here. A little piece of Irene on your window frame.'

'She said it was to remember her by. As if I would ever forget her.'

Helen shakes her head. 'No, she's not someone who could be easily forgotten.'

IRENE 2023

B ucket lists are supposed to be wild and adventurous, aren't they? Skydiving and bungee jumping, travelling to exotic places, climbing mountains, hot air ballooning...

Or there's learning another language, writing a book, learning an instrument, adopting a rescue pet...

Irene has been researching bucket lists on the internet. She actually takes a pen and paper and starts writing her own list, and it's none of those things. She doesn't have much time left, anyway. It'll be hard to fit in even these few small activities before she'll be restricted to a bed and a drip.

She's writing down *make appointment with Zola for a red rinse* when her mobile rings. When she sees it's Maggie, she gets up from her seat and heads out to the deck while swiping the screen.

'Maggie. Hello my friend.'

'You sound cheerful.'

'I'm writing my bucket list.'

There's a pause for a moment, and Maggie guffaws. 'What timing. You wouldn't believe it but I just had an idea for your bucket list.'

'What's that?'

'You don't have to give me an answer straight away, alright? Give it some thought and get back to me.'

'What is it?'

'I've been laying awake half the night thinking about it.'

'Spit it out then.'

'Why don't we go on a road trip? You and me.'

There's silence both ends before Maggie says, 'Like I said, no pressure.'

'Wait. I'm thinking on it.' Irene plonks down on a seat.

'You probably have a lot of other things you want to do. With your family and—'

'Hush, Maggie. Let me think.' Road trips came up quite a lot in Irene's online bucket list research. She just hadn't considered the idea for herself.

'It can be a short one. Say, two or three days?' Maggie says.

'And if I say yes?'

'Is there somewhere in Tassie you've never visited, that you'd like to?'

'Do you know, I've never been to the Nut.'

'You're kidding, that's hilarious. You did say you're Tasmanian, right?'

'Born and bred.'

'And you've never been to the Nut?'

'No need to rub it in.'

'Well then. How would you like to take a road trip with me to Stanley to see the Nut?'

'I'd love to.'

'Really?'

'Yes, I'd love to.'

Maggie lets out a noisy breath. 'Wonderful. Give me a date.'

'It'll have to be soon.'

Maggie says quietly, 'Of course.'

'And if I conk out early, you'll have to get me home.'

'You can count on me.'

'Looks like we're going on a road trip.'

The moment the call ends, Irene starts packing her overnight case. What an adventure. The more she thinks about it, the more energetic she feels. Her body has gone back into buzz mode. As if it is well and able to function like a normal person.

As if she doesn't have cancer and a rather short time left to live.

'What friend?' Helen asks as she peels potatoes in her kitchen.

Irene sits on a barstool with her elbows on the bench. 'You don't know her.'

'Someone you used to know?'

Irene nods. 'From years ago.' (Not a lie. After all, she met Maggie seven years ago.) 'I'll only be gone for a couple of days. Maybe three.'

Helen starts chopping. Irene is glad to see her using her own knives and not those sharp ones that used to hang on the wall. Irene made sure they were sold in the garage sale.

'What if something happens?'

'And by something…?'

'You're not strong, Mum.'

'Fiddlesticks. I'm alright for a while and the doctor gave me the all clear to go.'

'I suppose I can't argue with the doctor.'

'That's right.'

'Who is she again?'

'You don't know her. Her name's Eloise.' Irene was surprised to discover Maggie often changes her name for new people. *Tell them my name's Eloise,* she said. *It's safer if no one knows my real name.* Who was Irene to judge? She didn't know what it was like to have someone trying to track you down all over the country so you didn't feel safe.

'We'll leave Friday. Be back Sunday, all going well.'

Helen looks up. 'This Friday?'

'Yep.'

'I suppose you should do it as soon as possible.' She blushes. 'Oh! Sorry, I didn't mean that.'

'Why? I'd rather you came out and said it. We're going now because I'm going to die soon.'

Helen thumps the knife down on the bench. 'Why do you have to do that?'

'Do what—state the obvious? I'd rather be upfront. It makes it easier for me.'

'Not for me.' Helen blinks and takes up her knife again. She makes a few chops into the carrots, places the knife back on the bench and turns away. She takes a tea towel and puts it to her eyes.

'Sorry, love.' Irene gets up from her stool and goes into the living area. She stands at the window and watches the grass growing for a while. When she goes back to the kitchen, Helen is chopping beans.

'Dinner smells good.'

'I'm making your favourite Italian Lamb.' Helen smiles.

And Irene sees in her eyes the love and the pain, mixed together in a complicated slurry.

Irene catches a coach to Hobart on Friday morning and Maggie meets her at the station. She grabs Irene's overnight case and trundles it to her vehicle in the adjacent carpark.

'I like your car,' Irene says, admiring the late model Subaru.

'When it comes to driving, comfort is paramount,' Maggie says as she puts Irene's case in the boot. She takes off her fur coat and tosses it on the back seat. She's wearing cotton pants and a flowing top and Irene tells her she looks lovely. Irene's own wardrobe has been gradually diminished to a couple of pairs of pants and a few comfortable men's shirts. To think, she used to care about clothes. These days, she can't be bothered.

'Want the seat warmer on?' Maggie says as she hops into the driver's seat. They both laugh. It's twenty-four degrees today. 'Who says we can't have seat warmers and air-con on at the same time, eh?'

'I'll tell you a secret,' Irene says. 'At home in winter, I have the window open and my electric blanket on.'

'Ha. Well, you tell me what you need.'

'Just some fresh air will be nice, thanks.'

Maggie pulls out of the carpark and manoeuvres onto the main road. The city is hectic as usual and Irene thinks, not for the first time, how glad she is to live where she does.

'Once we're off this highway, it'll be plain sailing,' Maggie says.

'It was a good idea to take in some of the east coast as well.'

Maggie nods. 'Thought we could use some sea air.'

It isn't long before the busy streets and traffic lights give way to hills and green paddocks. An advantage of living on an island—you don't have to drive far to find open spaces or sea.

'Now for the fresh air.' Maggie opens all the windows. 'Smell that.'

'Eucalyptus. I love it.'

The smells of gum leaves, grass and summer blow all around them. Irene savours the air in her lungs and the breeze in her hair. The stresses of the past few weeks seem to gather up their skirts and flee, blowing away behind them as they drive.

'What do you want from this trip, Irene?'

'I want to have fun.'

'Fun, we will have. And no talk of men, if that's alright.'

'Fine by me. I don't want to talk about cancer either.'

'No mention of men or cancer—perfect. Now that we've laid the ground rules, let's have us some fun.'

Irene lets out a hoot.

They chat light-heartedly about what they see out the windows as they wind through hills and valleys, past fruit farms and paddocks of grazing sheep and cattle. As they pass some galahs pecking by the side of the road, Maggie says, 'You see that a lot. It's what you call living life on the edge.'

'They're very brave,' Irene agrees.

'Look out, turbo chooks!' Maggie slows down as a bunch of native hens scoot across the road in front of the car. 'The wildlife's out today.'

'Look at that place, not much left of it.' Irene points to the remains of a stone cottage—three walls and a fireplace.

'Gutted by fire,' Maggie says.

'We lived in an old place like that, the original farmhouse on our property where Caleb and Sing live now.'

'I hope it has a roof.'

'When we were there, it had a woodstove and all. The best bread I've ever made was baked in that thing.'

'Do you miss it?'

'I have fond memories of the place, but you move on, don't you?'

Maggie agrees.

'Helen goes on about me not cooking anymore. I did love cooking, but I like other things now. I don't have time to do everything.'

'Well, we won't be doing any cooking on this trip. No siree.'

Irene chuckles. 'You know what I feel like?'

'What do you feel like?'

'Hot chips and ice cream.'

'I know just the place.'

They stop beside a beach park to stretch and use the restrooms, and Maggie leads them to a corner takeaway.

'It doesn't look like much,' she says, 'but the fish and chips are to die for.' She slaps her hand to her mouth. 'Gosh, that was a bad choice of words, wasn't it?'

Irene laughs heartily and loops her arm in Maggie's as they cross the street.

They sit outside at a wooden table on the edge of the beach, where the grass meets the sand, each with their own meal in a cardboard box. It's so delicious, Irene scoffs the lot, leaving nothing for the seagulls hanging around expectantly. She feels a slight guilty pang which vanishes when she realises not one of those birds appears undernourished.

The beach is busy. Families and lots of children. Teenagers strutting about in their flimsy swimwear. Irene laughs inwardly. Perhaps it'll take them a lifetime too, to figure out what's important.

'I've booked us into a gem of a place,' Maggie says. 'We should be there in an hour and we can rest.'

Irene finds she needs to rest more these days. Sometimes she conks out early in the afternoon and can't get moving until the next morning. For that reason, they've decided on a stayover before they continue to their destination in the morning.

'It's got a pool and spa. And a five-star restaurant.'

'Have you been there?'

'No, I found it online. Surprisingly affordable. Are you ready for ice cream?'

After they've demolished their ice cream cones, Maggie types the address of their accommodation into the navigation system in her car and they head off. Irene is feeling tired already and starts to doze off. When she opens her eyes, it's to the sound of the engine cutting off and an expletive from Maggie.

'Huh, what's up?'

They've pulled over on the side of the road and Maggie is looking out Irene's side window and frowning. 'That's not the hotel I booked.'

Irene turns and looks at the sign—Farley Street Motel—and the two rows of units behind it. 'The hotel will be here somewhere,' she assures Maggie.

Maggie grabs her mobile and starts jabbing it with her finger. Staring at the screen, she moans, 'Nooo. Please show me I booked Fairshaw Hotel and not this place.' She swears again. 'I'm sorry, I can't believe I did that. I called the wrong number when I booked. They were both next to each other.'

She pokes at her phone a few more times and holds it up to her ear, saying, 'I'll sort it out.'

Irene hears the sound of ringing and a voice as the call is answered. Maggie asks about the booking and, by the faces she pulls, is obviously being told no such reservation has been made. Sweat beads have gathered above her top lip.

'Could I please book rooms for tonight then? What— are you sure, can you double check? Alright. Thank you, anyway.' Maggie turns to Irene with a face like a half-deflated balloon. 'Holiday season. No rooms left.'

Irene and Maggie both turn to peer at the two rows of conjoined units with the cracked red-brick façade. They meet each other's eyes and burst out laughing.

'Let's make the most of it,' Irene says. 'Come on. We said we wanted an adventure.'

Maggie switches the motor on and pulls into the drive and up to reception. She tells Irene to stay put while she goes inside for the key. When she comes out, she says, 'Apparently I'm not the only one to make that mistake.'

'Really?'

'The woman was very nice. She gave us complimentary vouchers for a drink at the pub next door.'

'There's a pub next door?'

Maggie grimaces. 'We may as well have that free drink later, anyway.'

They crawl the car down the centre drive between the units. There doesn't appear to be much happening, despite the fact of it being holiday season. There are a couple of cars and not a body in sight.

'Maybe everyone's out doing touristy things,' Maggie says. 'At least it's quiet. You'll be able to have a decent rest.'

They unlock the door to their unit and trundle their cases inside.

Irene stops and screws up her nose. 'Ugh, I hate the smell of cheap air freshener.' She lifts the venetian blinds and opens the window.

They have a look around the unit and Maggie says, 'At least we have two bedrooms, even if they are the size of broom cupboards. To think, I thought I'd booked a plush room with two bedrooms in a fancy hotel. No wonder it was cheap.'

Irene says, 'It looks comfortable enough. Clean too.'

Maggie slumps down on the sofa. 'You're generous. Anyway, we're staying at a lovely bed-and-breakfast in Stanley. I didn't get that wrong.'

Irene sits next to Maggie and picks up the TV remote from a scuffed wood-veneer coffee table. 'Shall we see what's on?'

They spend the next while drinking tea and flicking channels, before Irene goes to her room for a rest. The bed isn't too bad and the sheets are crisp. She slips between them and relaxes into the soft mattress.

When she wakes, it's to the sound of the unit door closing. She struggles out of bed, scrubs her face with her hands and wanders out to the living area.

'You're up,' Maggie says. 'I tried to be quiet.'

Irene sniffs the air. 'Something smells good. What time is it?'

'Ten past six.'

'Gosh, did I sleep that long?'

'I found a Chinese restaurant and bought us some takeaway. I hope that's alright.'

'Perfect. I'm starved.'

After their meal, they spend a couple of hours watching comedy shows on the TV. As they start watching a movie, the TV is drowned out by noises from outside—car engines, voices and music starting up from the pub next door.

Maggie huffs, 'A band at this time of night?' She gets up to investigate, pushing down one of the venetian blind slats with her finger and peering into the twilight. 'There are a lot of cars over there.'

Irene turns up the volume on the TV and they try for a while to watch the movie, but the music from next door is too loud and Irene turns it off.

Maggie grimaces. 'Is it my imagination, or is the singer really bad?'

Irene stands by the window, listening. 'Hm, my musical ear isn't spectacular, but that woman is definitely out of tune.'

The song finishes and another starts. This time it's a different singer and the quality of their voice is as bad as, if not worse than, the last.

'Ha.' Maggie's face lights up. 'It's karaoke.'

'So it is.'

Maggie grins. 'Hey, how tired are you?'

'Are you thinking what I'm thinking?'

'Let's do it. I'll spruce myself up and put some lippy on.'

Maggie changes into a sparkly top. Irene brushes her teeth and figures she'll do as she is.

By the time they enter the pub, the place is packed and rocking. Most of the tables are taken so Maggie and Irene stand by the bar. The stage is set up with microphones and coloured lights. As they watch, two young women in tight outfits take the microphones and give a truly horrible rendition of ABBA's *Mamma Mia*. The crowd claps to the music and sings along.

'This is great.' Maggie starts clapping too.

A voice—raised above the music—says, 'What can I get you ladies?'

They turn around to find the bartender, a bald fellow maybe in his forties, leaning over the bar.

Maggie hands over their drink vouchers. 'Two lemonades, please.'

'Two lemonades coming up. Where do you hail from?'

'Down south,' Irene half-shouts. 'We're on our way to Stanley.'

'The Nut?'

They nod.

He hands them their drinks and says, 'You have a nice time. See Pauline over there if you want to have a go on stage.'

Maggie laughs and shakes her head. They seat themselves on barstools and watch as a middle-aged couple goes onstage and sings *Ain't No Mountain High Enough.*

'They're pretty good,' Irene says.

'What?' Maggie cups her ear with her hand.

Irene shouts, 'They're *good.*'

'They are,' Maggie shouts back. 'Oh look.'

As the song finishes, the man takes the woman by the waist and dips her, planting a kiss on her lips. The audience claps and cheers.

As Maggie and Irene hoot with the rest of the audience, a man staggers past them, knocking into other patrons as he goes. He stops, turns and starts shuffling back. The noise dies down as the couple exit the stage, and in the quiet interim, the man plants himself right in front of Irene and Maggie, and drawls, 'What have we here?' He's obviously drunk.

Maggie smiles tightly and says, 'What have we *here*?'

The man looks Maggie up and down and pulls a face. 'You ain't from round here, that's fer sure.' His words slur together and his body tilts as he tries to stay upright. He rights himself by planting his feet far apart, shoves his hands in his pockets and stares at Maggie.

'Bazza!' Irene sees the bartender approaching. He gives a nod to someone by the door and a burly bloke in black appears. The bouncer, saying nothing, takes Bazza by the shirt collar.

Bazza squeals. 'Get the— Get off me.' As he's dragged away, he yells some offensive words back at Maggie. He squeaks as the bouncer lifts him off the floor by his shirt, opens the door with his free hand and shoves him outside. The room has hushed with the commotion and the women find many eyes turned towards them.

The bartender says, 'I'm sorry about that. In this town, we don't stand for that kind of behaviour. Drinks on the house for both of you. Are you sure you won't have something stronger?'

'Thank you,' Irene says. 'Lemonade's fine for me.'

'Orange juice, thanks,' Maggie says. She presses her lips together and lifts her chin in what Irene thinks is a determined display of composure.

Two young women approach Irene and Maggie. The one with spiky white-blonde hair says, 'We wondered if you'd like to come and sit at our table. We've got spare seats.'

They find themselves hustled to a table near the stage where a group of women of various ages sit. They're immediately welcomed by Glenda the local vet, Granny Sue and Florist Sue, and Anna and Melody from the IGA.

'You all live locally?' Irene asks.

'Yeah, everyone knows everyone in this town,' spiky-haired Melody says.

'We're a good lot, mostly,' Granny Sue says.

The karaoke continues and Irene and Maggie join in clapping and singing. The bartender keeps bringing free drinks to the table and Irene complains to Maggie that the sugar will keep her awake.

Maggie hisses in her ear, 'Apologies in advance, I'll be running to the loo all night.'

Glenda the vet suggests they go up and do a group number together. Before Irene can protest her own involvement, the song is chosen and she's being pulled onto the stage by Granny Sue and the others and a microphone is placed in her hand. Her knees start to wobble as she stands there looking out at the sea of faces. She turns to Maggie, who gives her a wink. Maggie looks confident anyway. As do the other five women. Oh well, what's the worst that can happen?

The song is one by Joan Jett & the Blackhearts. Irene hasn't heard them in years, but as soon as the heavy guitar and rhythmic drumbeat start up, she recognises the song—*I Love Rock and Roll.* Maybe this one is played here regularly, because the audience immediately starts clapping in time and singing along.

Irene follows the lead of the others, watching the lyrics on the screen carefully and keeping up as best she can. The audience is so caught up in it, Irene starts enjoying herself and does a little sideways jig as she sings. Someone's voice in the group is amazing, and Irene looks around to see if she can figure out who.

As she glances at Maggie, she forgets to sing for a moment. Maggie is the one with the extraordinary voice, and not only that. She's moving along the stage, holding the microphone like she's done this before and belting out the song like a pro. Next, she moves forward to the edge of the stage, screams 'owww' and starts strutting from one side of the stage to the other.

The audience goes wild, punching the air and shouting out the chorus. Some have leapt to their feet and are dancing at their tables. Maggie plays to the audience, gesturing with her hand for them to sing up. She raises her arms in the air and claps her hands above her head, and all over the room, people spring to their feet and do the same. At the chorus, everyone shouts the lyrics. They love it. They love her. As the song finishes, the whole room erupts with hooting and banging on tables.

Back at their table, the women flop into their seats, out of breath and laughing.

'I haven't had this much fun in a long time!' Granny Sue shouts.

'You were amazing, Maggie,' Glenda the vet says.

Maggie wipes the sweat from her face with her sleeve. 'Can't believe I did that.'

'Really?' Irene grins at her.

'Oh alright, I've done it before. I'm a rocker from way back.'

'I can tell.'

A young woman takes the stage and this time, gentle music plays. The room hushes. She appears self-conscious as she takes the microphone. Voices call out, 'Go Selina,' and 'Smash it, Selina.'

Selina sings Cyndi Lauper's *True Colors* so beautifully, Irene finds tears forming. She looks to the ceiling and blinks them back. The whole room appears mesmerised and when Selina finishes the song, there is an explosion of cheers.

Maggie grins at the women sitting around the table. 'What a nice town. You're all lovely.'

'We're not bad,' Glenda the vet says.

Granny Sue pats her arm. 'You two make sure to come back, won't you?'

Irene and Maggie glance at each other. Irene knows she won't be back.

Maggie says, 'You look sleepy,' and Irene nods. 'We'd best be off,' Maggie says to the others. 'Need our beauty sleep.'

They rise to leave and the other women give them hugs goodbye. They wave to the bartender on their way past the bar and head for the door. The bouncer, standing solemnly by the exit with his arms crossed, nods as they go out.

They walk arm-in-arm across the carpark, laughing. Irene feels both exhilarated and exhausted, her insides heaving with complicated feelings of happiness and grief. What a wonderful world this is. So much yet to learn. Experiences to be had. What has she missed out on? Has she done enough?

As they're passing a tree by the road, a figure emerges from behind it, dark and menacing. It happens so fast. One moment, someone is lunging at Maggie, and the next, Maggie has the person in a throttle hold, her arm around their neck. Bazza, the weaselly drunk from the pub, squeaks out an expletive and scrabbles at Maggie's arm with his fingers. She lets him go, pushing him away. He lands on his knees on the ground, stumbles to his feet and tails it out of the carpark.

Maggie slaps her hands together and says, 'He won't be back.'

'You're full of surprises,' Irene says. She tries to laugh but doesn't quite manage it. There's pain on Maggie's face.

'Are you alright?'

'Yes, he missed me.'

'That's not what I meant.'

Maggie shrugs. 'I'm fine.'

Inside the unit, Maggie is quiet. She says she's sleepy and goes to bed. As Irene lies in her own bed trying to sleep, she pushes away the image of the drunken Bazza. Instead, she pictures Maggie up there on the stage. Her wild joyfulness. The way she held the room in her hands.

She thinks of the first time she and Maggie went out for coffee together after their support group session, and how their friendship has grown over time. Even after Irene stopped going regularly, she and Maggie kept meeting. All those afternoons in the city—lunches, movies, art shows.

Maggie has continued with the group, supporting Laurel with the facilitation. There's so much empathy underneath that big fur coat. Irene would love to introduce her to her family, however, she has honoured Maggie's wish to remain anonymous.

Irene's thoughts swing back to tonight and Maggie on stage—big smile, hands in the air, her glitter top sparkling under the stage lights. They've had some fun over the years, but nothing like this performance which is like seeing further into the soul of her friend. Being given the opportunity to peek under another layer.

Oh, how sad Irene feels all of a sudden. To think she'll be saying goodbye soon to a friend she realises she is only just getting to know.

IRENE 2023

A ding from Irene's mobile phone wakes her in the morning. She finds missed calls from Helen from the night before, and two text messages. She texts Helen back to assure her she's feeling fine and having a great time. A message comes immediately back asking why she didn't answer last night, to which Irene replies she was at karaoke and didn't hear her phone. There, that should appease Helen for a while. She puts her phone in her handbag and wanders out to the kitchen.

Maggie seems to have recovered her good spirits. She has already set places at the small Formica table and is making toast. She looks up and smiles. 'Sit down madam, breakfast is served.'

Irene takes her seat. 'Something fancy I hope?'

In a posh voice, Maggie says, 'Toast and tea, darling. Unless you'd prefer instant coffee.'

Irene pulls a face.

Maggie sets the toast on the table, sits opposite Irene and peels the foil away from a marmalade sachet. 'Have you noticed they always have marmalade in these places? It's got so I crave marmalade every time I'm in a motel. I never eat it otherwise.'

'I can't go past Vegemite.'

'We're the best motel room buddies then. No fighting over the condiments.' Maggie stirs sugar into her tea. Glancing up at Irene, she adds, 'Don't you worry about me. I don't dwell on people like Bazza. I feel sorry for them. Imagine being him.'

'I daresay he doesn't have many friends,' Irene says. 'Anyway, Maggie, you were incredible on stage last night.'

'I'm not bad.' Maggie takes a bite of her marmalade toast and winks.

The drive to Stanley takes a couple of hours through picturesque countryside. Irene leans back in the plush seat and watches the hills and paddocks roll by. Maggie hasn't played any music in the car during their trip and Irene wonders if she's keeping the atmosphere quiet for her sake.

As they draw near to Stanley, Irene says, 'Is that it?' She recognises the Nut from pictures she's seen on the internet—a long flat hill looking as if it's rising from the sea.

'Yep.'

'Doesn't look much like a nut.'

'I don't think that's why it's called that. It's supposed to come from an Aboriginal name for the place. Moo-Nut-Re-Ker.'

'Ah, yep. I remember reading it. It's a volcanic plug.' Irene has been reading up on the internet about volcanic plugs which form when molten rock hardens inside the vent of an active volcano.

'Apparently,' Maggie says, 'we've got lots of ancient volcanoes in Tassie, but none that are active.'

'Well, good. I hope they stay that way.'

They drive into the historic village and Maggie says, 'Here we are. Named after Lord Edward-Smith Stanley, former Prime Minister of the UK.'

Maggie drives them around to look at some of the historic buildings built in the 1800s and beautifully preserved. Some elegant and elaborate, some humble. They pull up outside a tiny weatherboard house, reminiscent of a child's drawing with two windows, a door and a pointed roof with a chimney.

'Lyons Cottage,' she says. 'The house where Tasmania's first and only Prime Minister, Joseph Lyons, was born.'

'It's lovely,' Irene says. 'I can't imagine it would get much light though.'

'Are you ready to ascend the Nut?'

'Let's do it.'

They find their way to the carpark near the walking track. Despite the morning being summery warm, it's chillier here and they grab their coats.

'Are we doing the 152 metre climb?' Maggie says.

Irene shrugs her shoulders. 'Sure, why not.'

They both giggle and Maggie takes Irene's arm. 'Come on, we'll get the chair lift.'

A couple returning from the top call out, 'You'll need your coats. It's blowing a gale up there.'

They find the entrance to the chair lift and a young woman shows them where to stand to wait for the chair.

'Over here, dear,' she says to Irene, leading her gently by the elbow to the correct spot.

When the chair arrives, they hop quickly into the wobbly metal seat and the woman pulls the safety bar down over their laps. She pats Maggie on the arm and says, 'Have a lovely ride.'

The chair trundles through the shed with a metallic hum. As it moves out into the open, Irene leans into Maggie's ear and says, 'She called me "dear."'

'Did you see the way she patted my arm?' Maggie says.

Irene snorts. 'Young people look at us and see old people.'

Maggie swings her feet back and forth playfully. 'They don't realise we're just young people trapped in old people's bodies.'

'They'll find out.'

'Yes, when they're getting patted on the arm and called "dear."'

Suddenly the ground falls away beneath them.

'Whoa,' Irene grabs the safety bar.

'Are you alright?' Maggie reaches for Irene's arm.

Irene's heart clatters against her chest. She holds her breath and squeaks out the words, 'Fine. I'm fine.'

'Don't tell me you're afraid of heights.'

Irene grins sheepishly.

'Why didn't you say?'

'Last time I went in one of these, I kept my eyes shut all the way.'

'You've got them open now.'

Irene nods. 'I'm being brave this time.'

Maggie guffaws. 'My goodness, Irene. You're really pushing your own boundaries, aren't you? Karaoke. Chair lifts. What's next?'

'Facing death, I guess.'

Maggie takes Irene's hand and squeezes. They rise up and up, and Irene breathes deeply. She forces herself not to think about the drop beneath them and what would happen if the cable snapped. Instead, she looks out at the town, the fields, the beaches and the ocean in the distance. It's stunning. Even so, she will forget what it all looked like. If she takes anything with her into the next life, it won't be this view. It'll be the memory of the friend beside her.

The wind picks up and the chair wobbles. Irene's insides wobble with it.

'Hang on, we're nearly there,' Maggie says.

By the time they're out of their seats at the top, Irene feels like she's faced a terrible fear and won. Can she keep facing fear and winning? That's the question.

The wind at the top is stiff. Irene holds her jacket tight to her body and Maggie struggles with her buttons as her fur coat blows about. With their hair and clothes being blown every which way, they hold onto each other and start doing the circuit. It isn't long before Irene feels the strain on her body and she sits for a while on a bench seat while Maggie takes photographs.

'Can I take some of you, for your family?' Maggie asks.

Irene poses on the seat, then at the wooden rail with the ocean behind her. As Maggie holds her phone up to snap Irene, her buttons undo, her coat flies out either side of her and her hair blows up above her head. She's such a comical sight, Irene bursts out laughing.

'Oh, what a good one,' Maggie shouts. She goes to Irene and shows her the screen and the photo she has taken of Irene laughing.

'That *is* good,' Irene says.

'I'm sorry I don't allow photos of myself.'

Irene puts her hand over her heart and says, 'That's alright. I've got you in here.'

This is as far as Irene can go, and they turn back towards the chair lift. Irene peers down at the cemetery beneath them. 'Lovely view of the dead centre,' she says drolly.

Maggie laughs and shakes her head. 'Come on. Time for lunch, I think. My belly's starting to rumble.'

The bed and breakfast Maggie booked is comfort itself. Plush carpets, leather furniture, high-end everything in the kitchen.

'Have you seen the loo?' Irene says. 'It's got a gold seat.'

They've eaten their takeaway lunch on the patio overlooking a beautifully tended garden. The sun beams down on them as they lie back in the loungers.

'Thanks for organising all this, Maggie. I didn't realise how nice it is up here.'

'It is lovely. The last time I came here was with—oh.'

'What?'

'We weren't going to talk about men.'

Irene chuckles. 'Nope. No men allowed.'

'The bartender was nice last night, though.'

'The bartender *was* nice.'

Maggie nods. 'And the bouncer.'

'The bouncer was very nice.'

'I haven't met a lot of nice men.'

Irene bats a fly away with her hand. 'You'd like my friend, Andrew.'

'He's the minister?'

'That's right.'

Maggie shakes her head. 'Church people don't seem to like me much. I tried it once.'

'Going to a service?'

'They tried to cast demons out of me.'

Irene gasps. 'Oh, Maggie. They didn't.'

'I nearly gave up that night. It was close.'

'Maggie.'

Maggie sniffs and smooths her pant leg with one hand. 'A friend rang me up and we had a talk. I'm really grateful for that friend.'

'I'm grateful for that friend, too,' Irene says quietly. 'Anyway, Andrew's different.'

Maggie screws up her nose. 'Are you sure?'

'Oh yes. He spends a lot of time at the community centre and we get all sorts in there. He genuinely enjoys getting to know people, and he doesn't try to change them.'

'Really?'

'People don't need fixing, he says. And even if they did, he reckons he's not the one qualified to do it.'

'He said that?'

Irene nods.

'He sounds like a goodun.'

'You should talk to him.'

'Maybe I will.'

'Oh, look.' A magpie has flapped down to the lawn and another joins it as they watch. 'A baby,' Irene says. 'You can tell by the brown feathers.'

'They hang around their parents for a long time, don't they?' Maggie says.

'A bit like some humans.'

Maggie tosses a piece of leftover hamburger to the birds. 'Speaking of children, have you decided whether to tell yours yet?'

Irene takes a deep breath and lets it out slowly. 'What would I say, anyway? Parts of my life are a strange blur, you know.'

'Why do you still doubt yourself?'

Irene shakes her head. 'I don't, really. I've accepted what happened, though it took me a while. It's there in code, you know. In my notebooks. Well, not all of it.'

'Would anyone be able to decipher it?'

'Not likely. Although, if I do decide not to tell, I should get rid of the books.'

'Yes, you should do that.' Maggie gets up and starts stacking their lunch plates.

Irene stands and stretches. 'Must be time for dessert, I think.'

Maggie picks up the plates and heads for the door into the house. 'I'll get the triple-choc-ripple ice cream out, shall I?'

Irene sends Helen another text in the evening—*Having a great time. Feeling fine. Don't worry. Eloise dropping me home tomorrow.* Afterwards, she realises she shouldn't have said not to worry, as the message is certain to have the opposite effect.

She snuggles into her bed, savouring the soft feel of the sheets which must be made of a super expensive cotton. She imagines this is what floating on a cloud must feel like. Which is silly, of course, because clouds are wet and cold. And anyway, you'd fall straight through them. Her strange thoughts slide about, disconnect and shatter into fragments.

She wakes with an ache in her back and turns over to relieve it. She wakes again with a knife in her head, slicing down into her neck. She rubs her neck with her hand. The next time she wakes she is aching all over. She lies on her back for a while, doing her deep breathing exercises. When she hears Maggie in the kitchen, she slips out of bed, straight onto the floor. Not sure how that happened. She pulls herself up by holding onto the side of the bed and wobbles as she stands. After washing her face in the bathroom, she feels better, and goes out to meet Maggie.

'Good morning, my friend,' Maggie says. As she looks up, her smile vanishes. 'Are you alright?'

'Why, don't I look alright?'

'You look tired. How did you sleep?'

'Not too bad. A few aches and pains. What do you think of those sheets, are they glorious or what?'

'They are good. We could pinch them.'

'What's for breakfast?'

'Cinnamon scrolls from the bakery. I popped out early.'

'Gosh, what time is it?'

'Eight.'

'Well.' Irene sits down gingerly on the edge of the chair. 'Too many aches this morning. I might have to take one of my over-the-top painkillers. Apologies in advance if it knocks me out for the day.'

'No problem. You can recline the car seat and have a sleep. I'll even put the seat warmer on, if you like.'

They pack the car and stand at the gate one more time, looking down on the Nut and the surrounding sea.

'You did well to find this place,' Irene says. 'Mind you, the motel ended up being a hoot, didn't it?'

Maggie grins. 'We got you some fun. That was the plan.'

They settle in for the drive and Irene reclines her seat so she can rest. As they wind their way down onto the highway, she asks, 'How many times have you changed your name? You don't need to tell me any of them.'

'Oh... maybe six. The first name I chose for myself is the one I think of as my real name. I feel sad sometimes that I can't use it.'

'I'm sorry. Maggie suits you, though.'

'I think so.'

'I like my name. It means peace, you know.'

'Does it? That suits you very well.'

Irene's eyelids droop and she closes them, thinking to have a short rest. When she opens them again, she's surprised to find they're only an hour away from Durrunby.

Irene glances at the clock on the dashboard. 'Gosh, did I sleep that long?'

'Hello, sleepyhead.' Maggie grins at Irene. 'You're awake just in time. I'm pulling up for petrol.'

As Irene is getting out of the car to stretch her legs, she pauses with one foot in the car and one on the ground. She grabs the door and closes her eyes as a wave of pain shoots up her back.

Maggie rushes around to Irene's side and takes her arm. 'Are you okay?'

Irene tries to laugh. 'Must have got a crick in my back.'

Maggie holds onto her as she removes her other leg from the car, and says, 'I'll never forgive myself if I've damaged you.'

This time, Irene does laugh. 'This was always going to happen, Maggie. I'm dying. My biggest wish is to have fun while I'm doing it.'

'Well, you'll be home soon and you can enjoy some time with your family.'

'Yes, I guess it's time. The big roll-up to the end.'

Irene's oncologist could only give her an estimate of the time she has left, but Irene's body is telling her it won't be long. Time to tick off the few items left on her bucket list.

When they arrive at Irene's flat, Maggie helps her inside and sets her up on the sofa with a blanket, her phone and a glass of water.

'Do you need anything else?' she asks, tucking the blanket around Irene's body.

Irene shakes her head. 'Zoe's next door, I'll give her a call shortly.'

'You're sure you're alright?'

'Fit as a fiddle.'

When Maggie leaves, Irene lies her head on the cushion and closes her eyes. She'll have a little rest first. Because, right now, she doesn't have the energy to reach over and pick up her phone.

HELEN 2024

Helen decides to make one last attempt to decipher the messages in her mother's notebooks. If she enlists Caleb's help, between them they may be able to crack it.

Poppy is home for the weekend and they're seated around Caleb and Sing's table, finishing a meal. Helen takes one of the notebooks she's brought with her and pushes it across the dining table in Caleb's direction.

'See for yourself, tell me what you think.' She ignores Pete's pointed look. He's tired of hearing about it, but Helen doesn't like unsolved mysteries. She likes to know exactly how things are. Black and white, that's her.

Caleb frowns at the page Helen points to. 'Gosh, I don't know. I'm sure it's nothing. Didn't Mum used to like doing puzzles? Maybe they were her workings-out.'

'Hmm.' Helen hadn't thought of that.

'And the lists of drawer and cupboard items are probably exactly what you said. Mum testing her memory.'

'Or making up games for herself,' Pete adds.

'Sing, any thoughts?' Helen looks up at her sister-in-law who is stacking dishes in the sink with her back to them.

Sing turns, draws her lips in and leans back against the bench. 'I don't think it's anything to worry about.'

Helen shakes her head. 'I'm not worried. I can't help being curious, though.'

'Obsessed, don't you mean?' Pete says. He puts up his hands in mock surrender when Helen glares at him.

Sing pulls her chair out and sits back at the table, clasping her hands on the tabletop. 'Your mum is gone. Whatever the meaning of her notes, she's taken it with her. They were *her* notes, written for herself, not meant for anyone else.'

Helen huffs. What Sing says is true, yet she doesn't want to give up. She turns to Poppy and finds her studying a page of another of the books, her brow furrowed.

'What've you found, Poppy?' Helen asks.

Poppy flips back to another page, keeping her finger in the place of the first. 'These pictures remind me of something. I don't know what though.'

'Well, keep thinking,' Helen says. She smiles at everyone. 'Maybe Poppy'll crack the code.'

Sing rises from her seat and asks who wants tea or coffee. Caleb ushers everyone into the lounge room. Helen sits next to Pete on the sofa and Poppy curls up in a corner chair under a lamp with her nose in her grandmother's notebook.

While they're immersed in general chatter, Poppy straightens in her seat and says, 'I've got it.'

Helen leans forward. 'What? What have you got?'

'I know what these drawings remind me of. Remember that game Milo and I used to play with Reenie? The door knob one.'

'That memory game,' Helen says.

Poppy holds the book up for everyone to see the page, and points. 'See the circle and the arrow? It looks like one of the door knobs on the game. You had to remember which way the knobs and handles turned.'

'Show me.' Helen takes the book and studies the picture. She flips back to other pages containing similar circles and arrows, sometimes pointing in one direction, sometimes in another.

'There you are,' Pete says happily. 'Puzzle solved. Your mum was playing the door knob game by herself.'

Helen rolls her eyes. 'Doesn't make sense. Anyway, they weren't all knobs. Some were handles.'

'Do you have a better explanation?'

Helen admits defeat. 'Alright. Maybe it was that. Or some other game she was playing.' It seems unlikely, but what other explanation is there?

'What are you going to do with the books?' Sing asks.

'I guess I'll dispose of them. Unless anyone else wants them?' There is a general shaking of heads. 'I will keep the one from their overseas holiday, though. You can really hear Mum in her words. You should read it, Caleb.'

'I'd like to,' Caleb says. He sighs and adds, 'Gosh, I miss her.'

IRENE 2023

Irene had hoped she would have more time. But if these pains are anything to go by, time is something she's almost out of. She keeps these thoughts to herself. She doesn't want people moping around her. She wants to enjoy the bit she has left.

She and Helen do a lot of 'hanging out' together, ticking off Irene's bucket list. Irene can't venture far anymore, but she explores parts of Crayfish Cove and surrounds that she hasn't seen in a long time. The house she grew up in as a child has been renovated almost beyond recognition but she knows the family who live there and they are glad to have Irene visit. At the back of the house, the small room which was Irene's bedroom is almost unchanged and Irene sits in there for a while remembering, while Helen has a cup of tea with the owner.

She spends days on the Crayfish Cove beach, paddling in the water. She sits on the jetty, watching the fishing boats come in. One day, she has a hankering to make toffees like her mother used to make when Irene was a child, so she and Helen set about making two dozen toffees in paper cases.

'What on earth will we do with all these?' Helen says.

Irene shrugs one shoulder and says, 'Eat them?'

So they sit in front of the TV for the afternoon, sucking on toffees until they feel sick.

Some of Irene's fun includes helping Zoe and Milo sand the window frames in their new extension. It's going to be beautiful. Zoe won't ever have to worry about not having a roof over her and Milo's heads. Unlike so many families.

Irene doesn't drive anymore. She has sold her BMW to Poppy for a dollar and either walks slowly to wherever she wants to go, or catches lifts with people. Today she walks down Main Street, heading for Pyre Lane to attend her final Christmas service.

The streets are quiet for a change. The businesses are closed and the usual crowd reduced to a few folk wandering through the park. A chip wrapper blows across the pavement and Irene stoops to pick it up and put it in a bin.

Andrew meets her at the gate and she takes his arm as they go into the building.

'There aren't many here,' she says.

'A lot are already at the community centre, setting up.'

Irene finds herself surrounded by some of the dear folk she has come to know over the past years. They help her into a seat at the front with cushions. Once, she would have balked at the attention, but today she soaks up their kindness.

'Are you coming to the lunch?' Jean asks her.

'Of course,' Irene says. 'Wouldn't miss it.'

In fact, Irene's whole family is coming to help out at the free community lunch. Irene hadn't expected it, but when she told them of her intentions, they decided unanimously to join her, even though Helen has had her menu planned two months in advance. That's alright, she'd said, they'll do their family lunch on a different day. Even Helen can flex a bit when put to it.

Irene won't be physically helping, of course. She'll sit and chat with people. It'll be her last opportunity to spend time with most of them. Apparently, there's a crowd coming—people with no family, families with no money, a few homeless people currently living in tents in Durrunby Park. And others who are tired of trying to live up to Christmas Day expectations.

Irene wishes she'd thought more about how those expectations alienate people. The impossible picture for many, of families gathered around tinselled trees, opening expensive gifts, eating copious amounts of food. Well, Irene's flat will be available soon. Irene hopes it will be a source of relief for someone who needs it. And that they will find peace by the river, as she has.

As Irene nestles amongst her cushions in the pew, more people come over to greet her. She's kissed, hugged and patted on the arm by the folk who have become like family to her.

Human connection, how crucial it is. She finds her mind slipping back to her support group. A similarly caring bunch of people, sharing their vulnerability, opening their hearts to dark and broken places they couldn't reveal to anyone else. The trust that enabled them to forge bonds which helped them grow stronger. She thinks of Bob, Ginny and Laurel. The woman with the scarf she met the first day. Irene wonders where she is and if she's alright.

The sun is shining through one of the stained glass windows and the colours shimmer on Irene's lap. The window itself appears as a picture of Jesus with children gathered around him. On Irene's lap, it becomes disjointed fragments of colour, the picture unrecognisable. And yet, how beautiful it is. A glimmering mystery.

Irene holds her hand where it catches the light, and her skin glows with spots of red and gold. At this moment, the most important thing in the world is to admire them. Everything else fades into the background. If six-year-old Eleni were here, she would be mesmerised. Children are good at discerning what's important and ignoring what isn't.

Irene feels she may be reverting to childhood. Everything vital is becoming distinct again, the lines much clearer. The unnecessary things are blowing away in the wind. Things that—she now sees—were all the time made of straw.

The music starts.

Jean is playing the organ this morning. She's not very good at it, and Irene smiles to herself as she recognises the perfect beauty in that.

Irene stays seated, nestled against her cushions, closes her eyes and sings.

HELEN 2024

As school finishes on Monday afternoon, Helen ducks out to the carpark, narrowly missing Briony Haslett's mother who appears to be hurrying in the direction of Helen's classroom block. She slips into her car, looks about and drives away when she's sure the woman is out of eyeshot.

Once home, she goes out to the verandah with a drink and her mother's mobile phone. She's been putting this off. If she does it now she can enjoy the relief she'll feel afterwards.

She runs through the contact list again. Ginny, Laurel, Maggie. No listing for the friend she went away with on the road trip she took before she died—Eloise. Helen never did get to the bottom of that.

She finds the listing for *Support Group* in her mother's phone contacts and punches the numbers into her own mobile. As it rings, she leans back in her chair, watching a sparrow pecking at the lawn.

A young female voice answers. 'Good afternoon. Wesley Road Community House. This is Brooke speaking.'

'Hello Brooke. My name's Helen. Did you say you're a community house?'

'That's right. Wesley Road Community House in Hobart. What can I do for you?'

'I was wondering if I could talk to someone about a cancer support group you run there?'

There's a pause on the other end. 'You said, cancer support group, is that correct?'

'Yes.'

'Um—I don't think there is one. Sorry, I'm new here. Can I put you on hold for a moment?'

Helen listens to elevator-type music as she waits. The sparrow has pulled something tasty from the ground and flies off with it. Eventually, the music cuts out and Brooke says, 'Are you there, Helen?'

'Yes.'

'I'm afraid there are no cancer support groups held here. I believe there is one at—'

'It's alright, I don't actually need one. It's—well—I have your phone number listed as a contact number for a support group.'

'There is a group that meets here, but that one is for domestic abuse support— Oh, one moment—'

Helen hears someone speak in the background the moment before she is put on hold again. When Brooke returns, she says, 'Sorry, that one is a private group. Can I help you with anything else?'

Helen sighs. 'Listen, I should tell you why I'm calling. My mother has your phone number listed in her mobile under *Support Group*. She died recently and I wanted to let her friends and acquaintances know of her death. If she was a member of a group, I'm sure she would want those people to know.'

'Oh, I'm sorry to hear that.' Brooke's tone is sympathetic now. 'I'm not sure I can help you though. Unless you think this group might be the one your mother was attending? I could give you Laurel's number.'

'Who did you say?'

'Laurel. We don't give out surnames. She's the facilitator of the domestic abuse group. Perhaps you could call her and ask if that was the one your mother was attending?'

Helen's mind spins.

'Hello?'

'Yes please, that would be helpful.' Helen quickly scrolls up to find the contact in her mother's phone listed as *Laurel*. It can't be a coincidence. As Brooke reads out the phone number, Helen matches it with the one in her mother's contact list.

Brooke says goodbye with another outpouring of sympathy and Helen slaps the phone down on the table. Her mother, the dark horse, was becoming darker still.

Well, Helen may as well keep going. She picks up her mother's mobile again and scrolls to the number for Laurel. As she types it into her own phone, she plans how she can word her enquiry in order to gather more information.

A soft, cultivated voice answers. 'Good afternoon, Laurel speaking.'

Helen says good afternoon in a professional tone and gives her name. 'I was given your number by Wesley Road Community House. I believe you run a domestic abuse support group?'

'That's right. I facilitate a monthly group for adults who are experiencing, or have experienced, any level of domestic violence or coercive control. Are you enquiring for yourself or another person?'

'Actually, no. My reason for phoning is because my mother was attending the group. Irene Blackford. She died recently, January actually, and I've only recently discovered she was attending your group. I'm sure she would have wanted me to pass on the news of her death. I was hoping you would be able to do that.'

There's a pause and Helen wonders briefly if she's been cut off.

'I'm sorry, Helen. The group has a strict confidentiality policy. I'm unable to speak to the circumstances you've mentioned.'

'But can you at least pass on the message?'

'I'm not at liberty to disclose whether there was a person by that name attending the group.'

Helen sighs. 'How can I get the message to them, then?'

'I do apologise that I'm unable to help you. Please be assured, if there was a person by that name attending the group, your message would be passed on. Have a good afternoon.'

As the call is disconnected, Helen lets out a noise like something between a scream and a growl. She leaps to her feet, bursting with anger-fuelled energy. What was her mother doing? What was so confidential she couldn't share it with her own daughter? Helen thinks she's never been as furious with her mother as she is right now.

IRENE 2024

Irene speaks to Max via the app on her phone. His hair is quite grey now, the skin around his eyes criss-crossed with lines. Still handsome.

'How are you feeling?' Max asks.

That question again. Everyone starts with it. 'Terrible. How's Sandra?'

'Good. She puts up with me.'

'I'm glad.'

'I see you have red hair today.'

'My hairdresser has fun with me.'

'It's nice. So, you're at Helen's now?'

'They've got me set up in a bed by the living room window. I can see a bit of the cove from here.'

'You must miss the river.'

'Not as much as I thought I would. I grew up near the cove so it's special too. It was a good life there. I've had several good lives.'

'That's an interesting way of thinking about it.'

'I had a good life on the farm too. A good life by the river. A good life—' There's a memory slipping away. Irene wants to tell Max about it, but it has blown away like a leaf on the wind. How does one chase a memory when it blows away like that?

'Irene?'

'Did I ever tell you about my friend, Claire? We had a flat in Hobart next door to a drug dealer. They were fun times.'

Max chuckles. 'I'll bet.'

'That was another good life.'

'What do you get up to in your bed by the window?'

'Oh, listen to audio books. I can't focus on a real book, something going on with my eyes. I look at photos. Talk to everyone—they're always here, won't leave me alone. And I look at the little patch of sea out there.'

'Sounds nice.'

'You think?'

'Gotta get what you can out of life, eh?'

'True.' Irene sighs. 'Life's a messy beast, Max.'

'Isn't it just.'

'Do you think that? Life's a messy beast?'

'Life's a messy beast alright, Irene.'

'Max?'

'Yes, Irene.'

'You're a sweet, sweet man. Did I ever tell you that?'

'Irene?'

'Yes, Max.'

'I think the drugs are doing their thing.'

'They are doing a thing. Shoulda took them years ago. Life would be a dream, sha-boom.'

'Would you like me to read to you?'

'Please. What have you got?'

'How about some poetry this time?'

'Sure. Do you know the one about the goblet?'

'Which one is that?'

'Who is it? Longfellow.'

'I don't think I have that.'

'Longfellow?'

'No.'

'Lovely man, have you met him?'

Irene smells Helen's perfume. She opens her eyes to find Helen's face close to hers.

'What happened?' Irene asks.

'Mum, you have a visitor.'

'What happened to Max?'

'You fell asleep while you were talking to him.'

'I did? How embarrassing.' Irene hopes she didn't start snoring.

'He said to say cheerio and he'll call back tomorrow.'

'Did you say there's a visitor?' Irene tries to pull herself up to a sitting position.

'Stay there. I'll fix your pillows.'

Helen adjusts Irene's pillows and helps her sit up.

'Who's come?' Irene asks.

'It's your friend, Star.'

'Star?'

From behind Helen, a woman in a large, faux fur coat appears. While Helen isn't looking, she grins at Irene, puts her finger to her lips and winks.

Irene chuckles. 'My friend. Good to see you.'

'Would you like a drink, Star? Tea, coffee?' Helen asks.

'I'm fine, thank you.'

'I'll leave you two to catch up, then.'

When Helen leaves the room, Irene lifts her eyebrows. 'Star?'

Maggie grins. 'Today I'm Star. Tomorrow... who knows?'

'It suits you.' Irene nods and the effort sends a pain through her head.

'I'm not going to ask how you're feeling, because that's obvious. I've come to sit and talk or watch the cows grazing or whatever you like.'

'Good to see you. Let me touch your coat.'

Maggie lays her arm next to Irene, who pats the fur with her fingers. 'I don't have strength for big things so I'm appreciating the little ones.'

'We should all of us appreciate those.' Maggie blinks and looks away, her forehead creasing up as if in pain.

'What's the matter?'

Maggie licks her lips. 'I don't know how to say this, but you should know. It's Ginny.'

Irene's mind conjures a vivid image of Ginny from the last support group meeting Irene attended—hunched in a corner of the couch, eyes dull, her usually frizzy red hair lank and lifeless.

'She's in hospital. It's not looking good.'

'Her partner?'

Maggie nods.

Irene quivers with the wave of grief that courses through her body. She closes her eyes, glad that Maggie chooses not to elaborate. They sit quietly for a few moments, each in their own thoughts.

Maggie takes Irene's hand, stroking the back of it with her thumb. 'I like your hair.'

Irene tries to laugh but the sound comes out as a short wheeze. 'I said I'd do it, didn't I? It's just a rinse.'

'It's lovely. I should visit your hairdresser.'

The women reminisce for a short while, until Irene feels the weight of exhaustion and pain bearing down on her.

'I'm sorry,' she croaks.

'It's alright, my friend. I'll leave you to rest.' Maggie picks up her handbag and swings it over her shoulder. 'You'll never guess where I'm off to next.'

'Where?'

'To visit your friend, Andrew.'

'Ha. You'll like him.'

'I hope so.'

'Maggie? Before you go—'

'Yes, sweetheart.'

'Afterwards—'

Maggie nods and sits back down.

'Promise me.'

'Anything.'

'You won't tell my family. Even if they ask. They don't need to know the truth about—you know.'

Maggie reaches out to smooth the hair on Irene's forehead. 'Irene, they already have all the truth they need.'

Irene lets out another wheeze.

Maggie tells her she'll come back and visit soon, but Irene knows this is the last time she'll see her.

'Before I go, I want to give you a gift.'

'What?' Irene croaks.

'I want to tell you my real name. I don't get to use it much.'

'I'd love to know it.'

Maggie leans down so close, her lips brush Irene's ear, and whispers. 'Lisa.'

Irene touches Maggie's hand and whispers back, 'Thank you.'

Helen is sitting on the verandah, scrolling through her mother's mobile phone contact list once more. After opening the contacts for Ginny and Maggie, she's discovered they're both members of her mother's support group. Well. Helen has an obligation to these people. If Laurel won't tell them, Helen will.

She takes a deep breath, wriggles in her chair to make herself comfortable and punches in Ginny's number. She hears a click before an automated message. *The number you have called is not connected. Please check the number and try again.*

Okay, she has fulfilled her obligation by trying. One to go. Another deep breath, and she enters Maggie's number. The call is answered and there's a pause before a voice says, 'Hello.'

'Hello, my name's Helen. I'm calling because your number is listed in my mother's phone contacts under Maggie? My mother's name is Irene Blackford.'

Helen waits for the person to speak. She's about to ask if they're still there, when the voice says, 'Yes, I know Irene.'

'Um, are you Maggie?'

'I am.'

'I—uh—don't know if you know this or not. My mother died in January. I didn't have her phone, therefore I wasn't able to contact everyone she knew. I'm really sorry to deliver the news like this and a bit late.'

The woman on the other end breathes noisily through her nose.

'Are you okay?'

'It's alright, Helen,' the woman says. 'I did know.'

'Okay, good. I mean—' Helen shakes her head and takes another breath to ease her nerves. 'I noticed she listed you as someone she was attending a support group with?'

'Yes.'

Something about the woman's voice—deep and warm—encourages Helen to delve further. 'I've learned it was a domestic abuse support group my mother was attending. Can you please confirm she was attending the group?' Helen tries to keep her voice calm but it quivers, betraying the state of her emotions.

The woman says nothing, still breathing heavily through her nose.

Helen rolls on. 'I realise the group is private and confidential. I have spoken briefly to the facilitator, Laurel, but she wouldn't disclose any-thing. I wanted to ensure the members were informed about Mum's death.'

'I see. Thank you.'

'I um—the thing is, I'm a little confused. You see, there was no violence in our family. I mean, *none*. So I don't understand why she was at the group. Sorry, I guess I was hoping someone could shed some light on the situation for me.'

Maggie sighs into the phone. 'I can answer your questions.'

'Thank you.'

The woman clears her throat. 'Irene was my support person. She came along to the group to support me. To hold my hand, if you like.'

'Oh.' A wave of relief washes through Helen's body. 'That makes sense.'

'She didn't tell you because we have a strict confidentiality policy. Some of our members are in potentially dangerous situations.'

'I'm sorry. No wonder you were hesitant to talk to me.'

Maggie lets out a deep chuckle. 'It's alright. Irene told me about you, Helen, so I'm quite sure you are who you say you are, and not someone my ex-partner has sent to find me. I did inform the group of your mother's death. Please know, everyone was deeply saddened. If we'd been any other sort of group, we would have rallied round and helped to send her off. But unfortunately, it wasn't possible.'

'Of course. Thank you, Maggie.'

'You're most welcome.'

'Before you go, do you mind telling me how you met Mum?'

'Not at all. We met on some steps one day, in Hobart. We got talking, you know, and just hit it off.'

'That sounds like Mum.'

'She was a lovely person, Helen.'

There's a hitch in Maggie's voice which spurs Helen to ask the next question.

'Do you mind telling me, were you close?'

'Yes. We were close.'

And Helen thinks she hears a swallowed sob as Maggie says goodbye.

PART TWO

IRENE – 13th January 2014

As soon as he enters the room behind her, Irene knows he's there. It's the click of his hip, a sound he doesn't know he makes. Irene has heard it so many times, her brain usually tunes it out. Except today, when she hears it.

Irene is dusting the yellow room, rubbing wood polish over the antique dresser with a soft cloth. She wears her usual cleaning attire—fleecy track pants, T-shirt, long hair hoisted up in a bun and held together with a scrunchie. The wires from her earphones snake their way down from her head into her back pocket where she's tucked Helen's old iPod.

She hears the hip-click because it happens that a song on the iPod has finished, and one of her earphones has slipped. The click is evidence of his presence, neatly sandwiched between two songs. She doesn't turn around, but instead, hums along to Annie Lennox, pretending she doesn't know he's there.

Irene polishes the dresser, round in circles and down the front of the drawers. She takes her time, poking the corner of the cloth around the fancy handles. Next, she moves around the perimeter of the room to the sliding door where she makes a show of inspecting the glass. At her sewing table, she rubs the duster over the top before squatting on the floor to clean the front. She hums along to the music, careful not to turn her head, giving him time to exit.

Finally, Irene stands and moves around the bed, almost afraid to look at the door. When she finally turns, he is gone.

She knows in her bones she will find something altered. And there it is. Near the door, the chair that sits across the corner where two walls meet now juts up flush against the wall. She didn't leave it that way.

Things have been moving around again lately, starting around the time she joined the church group in Rosemere. She would come home to find a shelf subtly rearranged or a door handle turning in a different direction. It was her imagination, she was told. Then her car refused to start so she couldn't drive to Rosemere.

The vanishing of her amethyst earrings was the catalyst. Claire gave her those earrings back when they were friends—a long time ago. He didn't know she had taken them in her hand that very morning, sat them in a specific place and decided to wear them in the evening to dinner at Helen's. That was when she leaned into her suspicions. Refused to be duped.

And now she knows.

Irene feels strangely calm. She takes the iPod from her pocket, pulls the earphones from her ears and sets them on the chair. Down the hallway she walks, and through the kitchen door.

Bill looks up from the table where he sits with the newspaper.

'Oh, you're home,' Irene says.

'Hello love. How was your day?' He beams at her and Irene almost doubts herself.

She forces a smile. 'I had a productive day.'

'I'm glad.' He nods and goes back to reading his paper.

Irene grabs a glass from a cupboard in the kitchen and fills it with water. She stands at the bench, takes a sip and says, 'Bill, were you in the yellow room a moment ago?'

Bill's forehead crinkles. 'No, why?'

'You didn't go in there at all? You didn't move a chair?'

Bill gives a little chuckle. 'No, of course not. Is the furniture moving around by itself?'

Irene consciously arranges her face into what she hopes resembles confusion. She slumps her shoulders slightly and blinks. 'Oh, I dusted the chair and thought I'd set it one way. I don't know, I must have shoved it against the wall instead. I don't remember doing it, that's all.'

She looks up to study Bill's face. He appears concerned—eyebrows pulled slightly together, a soft expression, lips turning slightly up in a half-smile.

He does it so well.

Irene's husband pushes his chair out, moves towards her and reaches out his hand. His smile verges on an expression of pity. 'How about I make you a cuppa, love. You look a bit frazzled.'

Irene lets him pull her into a hug. Lets him caress her back with his hands. But all the while, she wants to run to the bathroom and vomit.

She has him. Finally, Irene knows for sure.

Irene has read somewhere that the time during which a woman plans to leave an abusive partner is the most dangerous. That woman must be on her guard. From the moment Bill denied having entered the yellow room to move the chair, Irene has known she will leave.

She lies in bed, feigning sleep, her husband beside her. Is Bill dangerous? He has never laid a violent hand on her physically. On the contrary, she's been showered with expensive gifts, wined and dined in the best restaurants, taken on an extravagant holiday across Europe.

She's seen sights rarely seen by most people. Had opportunities other people only dream about. She has never wanted for any material thing. But she is afraid.

Irene wants to believe she *had* moved the chair herself to clean behind it, and absent-mindedly set it against the wall. But hasn't she always done that? —scrabbled for logical explanations, made excuses, chosen to believe whatever Bill tells her. She understands it's her brain trying to make everything appear right. Like pulling a sheet tight across a bed, smoothing over the bumps and creases, straightening the fabric. She has always done this so she can keep going and remain happy. But how can she go on now, knowing the truth?

She could choose to believe she moved the chair. It would be easy. But did she rearrange the order of the kitchen drawers too? And alter the direction the bathroom door knob turned—clockwise one day, anti-clockwise the next? The proof is in her own notebooks—her drawings of the handles and the arrows indicating which way they turned, and how the direction kept changing. At least she knows now that it wasn't a trick of her imagination. She is sane. She isn't losing her mind.

Irene wants to turn over onto her other side but forces herself to remain motionless. She doesn't want to disturb Bill. Her body zings with so much anger she wonders that he doesn't feel it vibrating through the bed sheets.

How many friendships has she missed out on? How many adventures? She thinks of all the times her car broke down as she was about to go somewhere or do something new. The art classes she enrolled in and never started, the book club she joined a couple of times, her attempt to start volunteering at the op shop. What else? She looks back and can't help but imagine a plethora of paths she could have taken but didn't. Opportunities snatched away the moment she tried to grab hold of them.

As quickly as the anger took hold of her, it vanishes. How numb she is. As if she floats outside her body, not quite connected to herself. She is aware of a terrible ache inside but to connect properly with that ache, to allow herself to feel… she's not sure she'll be able to survive it.

IRENE14th January 2014

I rene wakes to the tickle of Bill's lips on her ear. He's already showered and smelling of aftershave. He strokes her hair. 'I have to take off shortly, love. I'll pop the coffee on.'

Irene murmurs 'alright' and pulls the covers up to her face.

'Did you want me to take you anywhere today?' he asks.

'No, thank you. When's my car being fixed?'

'I booked it into Batty's for next week.'

'Where are you going now?'

'Into Durrunby. Send me a text if you think of anything you want me to pick up.'

Irene keeps her eyes closed and nods. She doesn't want to look at him. If she does, she's afraid of what he'll see on her face.

She stays in bed. Hears him stirring his coffee, moving about the house, grabbing his keys. Pretends to have gone back to sleep when he comes to say goodbye. She waits until she hears the ute drive away before sliding out of bed.

Now what? She stands on the plush carpet, soft on her toes. She has always liked this carpet. Bill had chosen a grey one and they almost bought it, but Irene had fallen in love with the pink. It was one of the few times she stood firm.

Irene must leave but has no idea how. She should move fast, not knowing how long Bill will be out, but she seems to be frozen. Her body clamps itself together, like an unoiled spring, coiled and taut.

She forces herself to dress, pulling on a pair of trackpants and a T-shirt. Washes her face and brushes her teeth. In the kitchen, she pours the coffee from the pot down the sink. Her stomach is churning too much to eat or drink.

A bag. That's the first thing. She goes to the yellow room and finds a travel bag in the cupboard. What does one pack into an escape bag? Irene hasn't thought about it before. A couple of changes of clothes, toiletries, medication. She packs these in first.

She'll need legal documents—birth certificate, passport, marriage certificate. She goes into Bill's office and pulls on the filing cabinet drawer but it won't budge. Where would Bill keep the key? Without the energy to look, she slumps against the desk, her legs like lead.

Those items can wait. Instead, she slides her laptop into the bag, padding it between layers of clothing. She adds her laptop charger and Helen's old iPod for company. Next, she hurries out to the living room and picks up her favourite photo album—all the best shots of Caleb and Helen growing up. She takes it back to the bedroom and tucks it into the zippered side compartment.

She retrieves her handbag from the walk-in-robe and rifles through it. It contains her purse, some cash, her phone, a keycard for their joint bank account, driver's licence. She stares into it for a few moments, shoves it into the travel bag and slumps onto the bed.

Reality sinks in. She has nothing to call her own. No bank account. No car to drive away in. She can't even open the filing cabinet to retrieve her own documents. How did she let this happen? Even if she could drive away, where would she go? She has no real friends, no one she can confide in. Bill has seen to that.

She clenches her teeth against the rage bubbling up inside her. All the lost time. Missed opportunities for friendships. She even lost the one real friend she did have, because of Bill. That horrible dinner party with Claire and her partner. Bill's reference to Irene's business— *Irene does a bit of sewing.* And Claire's retort—*Your wife's a designer, Bill. And a successful business woman.* The flash in Bill's eyes—how dare she correct him in front of other people.

That was the night the sharp German knife found its way into the sink and Irene gashed her hand which needed stitches. It was Bill who put the knife there, not Claire. Didn't she know deep down, even then, that Bill was lying when he blamed Claire? But her marriage was important to her and she had the children to care for. She chose to believe her husband. Because who would do that to their own wife?

Irene lies down on the bed and pulls her knees to her chest. All those years of being undermined. Of having her confidence scraped away little by little, leaving her befuddled, unsure of her own sanity. Had her cognitive function really been affected by the chemo, or was it Bill all along? Even if she does manage to leave, Bill will convince everyone she's losing her mind. After all, he's done it before.

The sound of an engine pulls her to her feet. How can Bill be home already? But she recognises the sound of the ute rumbling over the gravel and pulling up in the drive.

Irene grabs the travel bag and pulls it off the bed. She only has hold of one handle and it gapes open. Her handbag falls out onto the floor so she scoops it up and shoves it back into the bag. She hears Bill's footsteps nearing the house as she slips quickly into the yellow room and zips the bag closed. She kicks it under the bed with the camphor wood chest. All her secrets are hidden under that bed, she thinks.

As she exits the room, Bill comes through the front door and takes his boots off. He calls out, 'It's me, love.'

Irene has scurried into the kitchen. She calls, 'In here. You weren't gone long.' She forces a smile as he enters the room.

'I forgot, I arranged something with Caleb. I'll go into Durrunby later. Are you alright, you look a bit flushed?'

Irene puts the plug in the kitchen sink and turns on the tap. 'I was doing some tidying up and got a bit hot. Would you like a drink?'

'Yes, thank you.'

He sits at the table, pulls a handkerchief from his pocket and mops his forehead. 'I was thinking we might go out for some lunch later. I can call in and sort this thing with Caleb on the way.'

'I can wait for you to come back from Caleb's.'

'No, no. I'm sure Sing would like to see you.'

While Irene makes the tea, Bill gets up and phones Caleb from the living room. He stands with his legs wide apart, facing the windows. Irene watches him, the way he commands the space he inhabits. What else has she missed over the years?

She wonders about her scarf and her grandmother's ring. Items that had brought her some small happiness before they vanished. She thinks of Claire, her one true friend, and her throat tightens.

They take their tea to the living room and Irene sits in her favourite armchair, facing the window and the view she loves. When she turns to Bill, he's pulling at his collar, the capillaries in his cheeks standing out stark and red.

'Are you alright?' she asks.

'Huh? Yes, I'm fine.'

'I feel a bit peaky, myself,' Irene says. 'I think I'll stay home today.'

'Nonsense,' Bill says. 'We'll go to the café in Durrunby with the outdoor area. You know the one. It should be nice and quiet there. I'll pick up the few bits and pieces I need from the hardware store after we've eaten. It shouldn't take long.'

There's something different in the way Bill looks at her. Is he suspicious? Did he wonder, as he was driving along, about her behaviour this morning? Is that why he turned around and came back?

Irene smiles and says, 'Alright, that sounds nice.'

Bill's shoulders relax. He takes a sip of his tea and says, 'This retirement caper suits me very nicely. Helping Caleb out a bit but not having to overdo it.'

'Caleb's managing well with the farm,' Irene says. 'He learnt from the best.'

She watches Bill's chin come up. Yes, he enjoys praise. Complimenting him should keep his mind on himself while she plans her escape.

At eleven o'clock, she and Bill take the ute down the gravel drive that leads to the old farmhouse. Sing greets them at the door and offers to make tea.

'No need,' Bill says. 'I'm taking my beautiful wife out for lunch.'

'How lovely,' Sing says, and ushers them into the kitchen.

Caleb appears and the two men head off, talking loudly. Irene sits at the kitchen table and asks Sing what the men are doing.

'Didn't Bill tell you? Caleb's setting up a new water tank.'

Irene nods. She knew little about what went on at the farm. Was there a reason Bill didn't tell her much? 'How are you going with your ceramics?' she asks.

Sing's face lights up. 'Can I show you? I'm working on a new line.'

Irene follows her outside to a shed she and Caleb have fixed up for her to work in. It's a cosy space with shelves and work benches along each wall, and a potter's wheel at the centre. The shelves are mostly filled with handmade pots and tableware.

'Look.' Sing leads Irene to a shelf containing a different kind of creation. 'These are my ladies.'

Sing's 'ladies' are a row of ceramic women in various poses, most of them carrying objects. One woman in a long dress is leaning backwards and looking into a jar she holds in her hands. The line of her body and her subtle facial features suggest she is pondering the contents of the jar, or perhaps deciding what to put in it. The more Irene looks at it, the more possibilities she sees. Is the woman trying to decide on the jar's purpose?

Another woman carries a placard, her stance one of strength and determination. What could be written on the placard is left to the imagination.

The next woman holds a large round object to her abdomen, her own body seeming to merge with it as if it is becoming part of herself. Or is the object emerging *from* her body? Again, Irene realises there are multiple meanings that could be implied by these pieces, depending on the person looking at them.

Irene is stunned. 'These are beautiful. I mean, actually incredible.'

'Do you think so? Thank you,' Sing says quietly.

Irene moves along, taking in all the pieces. She's drawn to the image of a woman with a stooped back, bending over as if she has carried a load which has permanently altered the shape of her body. Or is she still carrying it—an invisible weight? Again, there are multiple interpretations of the piece. The woman, though apparently weighed down, lifts her head and looks skyward, as if to find hope there. The more Irene looks at it, the more it grows into her spirit, affecting her on some deep level. She reaches out to run her fingers over the woman's back.

'Oh, Sing.' Irene tries to find the words. 'How did you manage to—' Tears spring to her eyes and she has to turn away.

Sing either doesn't notice Irene's moist eyes, or pretends not to. 'I watch people,' she says. 'I find I can, I don't know, get a sense of people. More than just the outside of a person.'

Irene nods and looks at the other ladies. Sing's pots and tableware are wonderful, but these ladies are a cut above.

'How's your online shop going?'

'Really well, but I haven't put the ladies up yet. I'm trying to figure out how to package them for posting. They're a bit trickier than the pots.'

'Have you thought about asking at the craft shops in Durrunby? They might sell them on consignment for you.'

'Yes, I have thought about it. But I'm not sure I want to give my ladies to someone else to sell on to people. Does that sound silly?'

Irene turns to Sing. 'Not at all. They're very special.'

They return to the house and wait for the men in the lounge. Irene and Bill lived here once, sat in this same old lounge room with the too-small window, the shadowy corners and the musty smell emanating from the walls. Yet, Sing has made it cheerful with colour and obvious love.

Sing leans towards Irene, her head tilted. 'Mum, how are you?'

Yes, Irene's daughter-in-law did notice things. 'Well, alright,' Irene says. 'I might have a cold coming on.'

Sing nods and leans back. 'If you need anything, Caleb and I are here.' There is something pointed about the tone of Sing's voice, and Irene thinks it's more than a mere casual comment.

Irene imagines telling Sing what is going on up in the big house. Sing would believe her. Irene could tell Sing how afraid she is. How she needs to leave Bill and has nowhere to go. She thinks about the ceramic lady with her bent back and the hope in her features. For a moment, Irene feels hopeful.

The back door bangs open and the moment is gone. The voices of the men fill the kitchen and the women stand. Irene gives Sing a hug and is surprised by the strength in the arms of the tiny woman.

They say goodbye and Bill and Irene walk to the car. As Irene hops into the ute she looks back and Sing nods to her from the door. There's a message in the nod, Irene is sure of it. She holds onto it as Bill starts up the engine. But as they drive away and Bill chats about water tanks and rust and other things, the message becomes what it most likely is. A simple nod goodbye.

As they drive into Durrunby, it starts to drizzle. When they arrive at the café, the back courtyard is too wet to sit in. They find a table in a quiet corner and Bill orders their lunch. Though they have been married for thirty-four years and Irene knows her husband, she watches him today through a new lens. She recognises his subtle manipulation of her menu choices. The sense of entitlement in the way he speaks to the wait staff. The large tip he leaves them afterwards, what Irene once regarded as generosity. He likes to be seen, admired, respected.

Even the way he places his hand on her back as they leave the café, she receives in a more sinister light. Of course, she could be exaggerating its significance. It may simply be his way of being loving.

But love doesn't manipulate. Doesn't lie. Does not do harm and point the finger at someone else. Bill does not love Irene.

In the afternoon, Irene busies herself in the kitchen. She bakes muffins and a loaf of bread. Spends time over an involved marinade for a leg of lamb. Cuts up the vegetables with slow and meticulous care.

Bill is tinkering in the garage. Irene quietly opens the front door and hears him out there. She closes the door and goes back to making dinner. She still hasn't come up with a plan.

When Bill comes in he says, 'Looks like you're cooking for an army. We should invite family over.'

But Irene says, 'I feel like I'm coming down with something. I'd rather rest tonight.'

If her car was running, she'd leave immediately. She'd grab her handbag and say she was going to the shops. Drive to Hobart, withdraw a heap of cash and book herself into a motel.

A stupid idea, of course.

They eat dinner, watch television, go to bed. Much the same as any other evening during the past thirty-four years. And Irene lies in bed, trying to figure out how to leave. Because it has to happen tomorrow. She won't spend another night in this house with Bill.

IRENE15th January 2014

Irene rises early, before Bill has stirred. She showers, dresses and makes coffee. By the time Bill is awake, she has cooked porridge.

'There you are, my sweet,' she says, placing a steaming bowl at his place on the dining table.

Bill smiles as she sets the milk, sugar and a pot of coffee before him. She sits down with a bowl of porridge for herself and inclines her head towards the windows. 'It looks like a reasonable day out there. What are you up to?'

Bill mixes a spoon of brown sugar into his breakfast. 'I'll help Caleb for a bit. What about yourself?'

'I might spend some time with Sing. She's made some beautiful ceramic pieces. She showed me yesterday. She's very talented.'

Bill nods absently, his mind evidently on Caleb and the farm. He swallows, puts his hand to his chest and grimaces.

'A bit hot?' Irene asks.

'Mm, a little.' He clears his throat and continues to eat.

Helen shows up mid-morning and asks Irene if she wants to go with her into Durrunby. 'I probably should have rung first, but I was out in the car anyway dropping Poppy at a birthday party.'

While Helen is talking to her father, Irene slips into the yellow room to retrieve her handbag from the travel bag under the bed. As she has her arm and half her head under the bed, she hears footsteps coming up the hall. She yanks the handbag out quickly and stands. Helen looks in and says, 'There you are. Let's go.'

The streets of Durrunby sparkle with the rain that has fallen during the night. The road looks like it has been sprinkled with tiny gemstones and Irene feels her heart lighten, until reality hits her again and her gut churns.

They buy pastries from the bakery and walk by the river. Irene forces herself to concentrate on the water and the life going on around it. When she does this, her stomach settles and she finds she can enjoy the taste of her food.

'How cute are these ducks?' Helen says, throwing them pieces of her pastry. 'This is the perfect place for us to do our mindfulness exercise, Mum.'

Irene licks the last of the pastry from her fingers and shoves her hands in her pockets. She doubts any mindfulness exercise could help her right now.

'Come on.' Helen gestures for Irene to move up beside her at the river's edge. 'Close your eyes. What do you hear?'

'Ducks.'

'What else? Be quiet for a few moments and really listen.'

Irene sighs inwardly. Her brain is on buzz-mode, but she tries to concentrate. 'The river. I can hear it trickling.'

'Good,' Helen says. 'Now open your eyes and look around. Find something nice to focus on. I'm looking at the willows on the other side, how the tips of some of the branches are touching the water.'

Irene looks at the grass at her feet. Gosh, she could do with a new pair of boots. The toe is coming out of this one.

'Now sniff,' Helen continued. 'What can you smell?'

'Dog poo?'

'Gosh, Mum.' Helen shakes her head. 'Next you're meant to find something to touch and something to taste. I suggest your coffee as the taste one.' She sighs. 'But I can tell you're not into this.'

'Sorry. I'm trying.'

'Never mind, another time.'

They resume their walk along the edge of the river.

'You look nice today,' Irene says. 'You've done something to your hair.'

Helen shrugs her shoulders. 'I used a curling brush.' She smiles brightly and Irene thinks she looks younger than her years today.

'The school holidays suit you,' Irene says.

'I do feel pretty good. Let's take a selfie.' Helen takes her phone from her pocket. They squish up together with the river behind them, and Helen holds up her phone and clicks. 'I'll text it to you,' she says, and fiddles with the phone as they walk.

'Come and sit down for a bit,' Irene says. She wipes a bench seat with her sleeve and Helen sits beside her, still fiddling with her mobile.

'I didn't hear your phone go off,' Helen says.

Irene rummages through her bag. 'It's not here. I must have left it at home.'

'Oh well, I've sent you the photo.'

They sit for a while and soak up the sun. Helen chats about school. She does love teaching the students, she says, but not the politics of the place.

'You're a good teacher,' Irene says.

'How would you know?'

'People talk. You're known as a teacher who really cares about the kids. And I see it, anyway, in your passion.'

Helen does a rare thing. She leans her head on Irene's shoulder and says, 'Thanks, Mum.' Irene kisses her on the top of her head like she used to when Helen was a child.

Back at the car, as Irene is getting in, Helen retrieves her mobile from her pocket again. As Irene is clipping her seatbelt on, Helen pokes her head through the door and looks about.

'What are you doing?' Irene asks.

'Shh, can you hear anything?'

'What am I listening for?'

But Helen hushes her and says, 'I'll try again.' She pokes her finger at her phone while sliding into the car seat and tilts her head, as if listening. 'I think it was that man's phone I heard,' she says. She jerks her head in the direction of a man standing next to his car, who also holds a phone in his hand.

'But what are you doing?' Irene asks.

'Calling your mobile. I thought you might have dropped it in here somewhere. I can't hear it though.'

Irene looks at the glowing red spot on Helen's phone that means it is dialling a number. Her stomach lurches. 'Stop!'

'What?'

'Stop dialling.'

Helen presses the red button and raises her eyebrows. 'Why?'

Irene has a sudden vision of her phone under the bed in the spare room. Did it fall out into the travel bag when she yanked her handbag from it? What if Bill hears it ringing and looks for it?

'Are you alright, Mum?'

'It's probably in the house and sometimes your father has a nap. I didn't want my ringing phone to wake him.'

'Oh, sorry.'

Irene shakes her head. 'It's alright. Can I buy you lunch? I don't feel like going home yet.'

Helen smiles. 'I won't pass up a free lunch. Even if I have just had morning tea.'

They climb back out of the car and go in search of food. Irene thinks she'd like to postpone going home for as long as possible. But she can't stay in Durrunby forever. She imagines telling Helen of her dilemma and shakes off the idea immediately. She doesn't think Helen would believe Irene about her father. Nor Caleb.

Sitting in a café with a pie in front of her, Irene finds she can't eat. She is so wound up she feels ill. 'Sorry, I seem to have lost my appetite.'

Helen shrugs one shoulder, takes a bite of her sausage roll and mumbles, 'Take it home with you.'

Irene takes small sips of her mineral water and pokes at her pie. When Helen finishes her lunch, Irene pushes her own plate towards her and says, 'Think you can fit in another?'

Helen demolishes the pie and laughs at herself. 'Amazing what I can squeeze in when I try.' She wipes her hands on a serviette and adds, 'I suppose I should go pick Poppy up now.'

'Do you think I could come with you? It feels nice to be out and about.'

'Oh, your car. I forgot about that, what a nuisance. When's it getting fixed?'

'Next week.'

'You've been waiting a while. Couldn't Don Batty fit it in?'

Irene shrugs. 'Maybe he's been busy.'

'Well, Poppy will be glad to see you. Are you ready to go?'

Irene knows the family where the birthday party is being held. As she and Helen go inside, Irene looks around at the other adults arriving to pick up children. Every face is familiar. However, there is no one here that she is close to. No one she can call a friend. She feels like such a fool. How could she have allowed Bill to control her all these years?

They wander into a large room where a table is laid out with the remains of a party feast. A mess of streamers and balloons is strewn over the floor. A couple of children are picking over the plates while the rest, as Irene can see through the open sliding door, are outside on the lawn playing a game with hoops.

'Irene, nice to see you.' Gretchen from the post office. Nice lady. She would have made a nice friend.

'You're picking up a grandchild too?' Irene says.

'Yes, our Lachy.' Gretchen looks to the window and waves. A boy in a pink party hat waves back.

'There's Poppy,' Helen says and goes to the sliding door to call her.

Irene watches the other adults waving to children, who come straggling in looking tired. At the door, the host parent gives out party bags and balloons attached to strings.

A child races towards her mother, a young woman named Emma. There'd been a story circulating about Emma and her estranged partner. Something about a restraining order. He was violent, so the story went, and Emma had fled. Irene watches as the young girl, grinning, opens her treat bag and offers it to her mother.

Emma was brave. She must have reported the partner at some stage. Did she have friends or family to help her at the time? Irene wants to take hold of this young woman's arm and ask her a dozen questions. Which, of course, she won't.

'Reenie.'

Poppy runs towards her, pulling along a green balloon whose string gets caught up on a chair.

'Hold on, I'll help you.' Irene untangles the string while Helen collects Poppy's jacket, and they go to the car.

'I guess we should take you home, Mum,' Helen says. 'We have guests coming for dinner and I need to sort the roast.'

'I'm sorry,' Irene says. 'I didn't mean to hold you up.'

'You haven't. It's been nice.' Helen turns the engine on and gives Irene such a genuine smile, Irene feels almost happy.

She can't stay out forever. Helen drops her back at the house and drives away. Irene watches the car rumble over the cattle grid and swing onto the main road, with a twist in her gut.

The house is quiet as she steps inside and she thinks she is alone. Until she enters the kitchen and sees Bill at the living end of the room, sitting in his armchair with a book.

He looks up. 'Hello love. Did you have a nice time with Helen?'

Irene goes into the kitchen and takes a glass from the cupboard. 'I did. How about you? How was Caleb?'

'We got the tank sorted. I'm having a gin and tonic. Would you like one?'

'No, not for me thanks.' She needs her wits about her. She pours water into her glass and takes a sip.

Bill lifts his glass and the ice clinks. 'Come and sit down. I have to go back out shortly. Thought we could have a drink together first.'

Irene takes her water into the living room and sits in her armchair. 'We went into Durrunby and had lunch in a café. And a walk along the river, it was lovely.' She looks out over the paddocks, sees the patch of sea in the distance, its surface ruffled.

'Sounds nice.' Bill smiles and takes a sip of his gin. His eyes are glassy and Irene wonders how many drinks he's had.

She holds her glass with both hands, running a thumb up the side to catch a drip of water. Her thoughts swing to the yellow room and her bag beneath the bed. She needs to check whether her phone is there. She silently prays it won't ring while she's sitting here with Bill.

Bill crosses one leg over the other and gazes out the window. 'My grandfather started this farm from scratch.'

'I know,' Irene says.

'Worked two jobs and saved every penny until he could buy the land. Then worked his guts out to make it viable.'

Irene's insides are pulled tight like a violin string. 'Yes, he was a hard-working man. All the Blackfords have been.'

Bill takes a gulp of his drink and nods. 'Did it all by himself until he had enough to support a wife and employ a few men.'

'Your grandmother worked hard too. They were a successful partnership.'

'Grandfather did the farm work.' He takes another sip and the muscles around his jaw tighten.

So that's how it is, Irene thinks. He's baiting her to challenge him. Irene keeps silent and watches waves kick up on the surface of the sliver of sea.

'Caleb's a hard worker, anyway,' he says.

Irene watches him until he meets her eye. 'So is Helen,' Irene says.

Bill smiles. What a handsome man he still is. From the moment he'd lifted his hat to her from the seat of a tractor thirty-six years ago, Irene has loved him. Unconditionally, whole-heartedly. Oh, how she hurts.

Bill takes one last sip, draining his glass, and rises. 'Anyway, I have something I need to do.'

'So soon?' Didn't he say he wanted her to sit with him?

'I'll see you later.' He rises, bends down to kiss her on the cheek and leaves the room, setting his glass in the kitchen sink on his way out.

Irene hears him leave the house. She waits in her seat in case he comes back but soon sees him through the window, walking down the hill towards the farmhouse. Off to help Caleb again, she guesses.

Once he's out of sight, she goes to the yellow room and reaches under the bed for the travel bag. Her hand flails about under the bed and finds the camphor wood chest, but nothing else. She bends down and squints into the shadows. The bag is gone.

She stands and closes her eyes. *Breathe in for four, hold for eight, let it out slowly. Repeat.*

Irene opens the cupboard in the yellow room where she'd initially found the travel bag, but it isn't there. She hurries to the main bedroom and looks under the bed. Not there either. When she opens the door of the walk-in-robe, there it is, sitting in the middle of the floor. She checks inside and finds it empty.

Bill knows.

Her heart is doing cartwheels so violently she feels giddy. She searches frantically through her drawers and finds the clothes she had packed into the escape bag, now neatly placed back where they belong. The photo album has been returned to the shelf in the living room. Looking out the window, she sees no sign of Bill. There's still time to leave.

Irene goes back to the bedroom. She leaves the travel bag in the walk-in-robe and grabs her handbag. She will escape. She will walk all the way to Helen's in Crayfish Cove proper. Now she will have to tell Helen, whether her daughter believes her or not. But she won't stay here another day with Bill.

Irene slings her bag over her shoulder and hurries to the front door. But when she turns the handle, the door doesn't open. Her heart pitches in her chest. She looks up and sees the keys are missing. She doesn't bother hunting around up there, she knows she won't find them. As she goes from room to room, trying the doors and the windows, she finds them locked. And all the keys are missing.

Every window, even the laundry one, is fashioned from polycarbonate—unbreakable glass. Now Irene wonders why Bill made that choice. There's no point trying to break them. She tried to do that before when Bill locked her in the house the first time, and later pretended she was losing her mind.

She forces herself to remain calm. All she needs to do is call Helen. Helen will come and get her. But when she searches for her phone, it is nowhere to be found. Not in any of the rooms, not under the bed in the yellow room, not anywhere.

Her computer. She could send private messages via her social media and hope someone is online. It's a good idea; she mentally pats herself on the back for thinking of it. But her laptop is also missing.

That's alright. Irene will wait for Bill to come back from the farm. He'll have to come back sometime. And when he does, he will unlock the door. And Irene will walk out the door and leave.

Irene pushes her favourite armchair over to the corner window and sits, watching the paddock. She keeps her handbag latched over her shoulder, even as she gets up to go to the bathroom. She will escape the moment she hears Bill return. Somehow.

As she sits there, she watches a magpie feeding its baby on the grass beside the verandah. So close, yet she can't reach them with the thick glass between them. The two birds fly off into the trees and Irene's heart longs to go with them.

After a while, dark clouds scud over from the cove and the sky turns from blue to mud-colour. In the distance, the waves toss up, their peaks foaming. And a small dot moves along the paddock, from the old farmhouse towards Irene.

Soon, she will be able to see Bill clearly as he comes across the paddock. But she doesn't want to watch him. The sight of him produces bile, rising in her gut and almost making her retch. She goes back to the bedroom to wait, passing the oven and its flashing clock—the power has been off again. She glances at her watch to check the time, but her mind has flown elsewhere, flapping its panicked wings. Bill will be here soon. She stands in the bedroom, her back against the wall, waiting. She will walk out as soon as he unlocks the door. Maybe she'll be able to slip out of the bedroom unnoticed and flee before he realises she's gone.

It occurs to her, as she stands there, that she can fit a change of clothes in her handbag. She takes a dress from the walk-in-robe and some underwear from a drawer, rolls them together and squeezes them into her bag. As she swings it back over her shoulder she catches a movement from the corner of her eye.

Bill is ambling across the paddock outside the bedroom window. He stops and stands with his hands in his pockets, staring out as if assessing the land. Irene doesn't know why he stops there, not far from the bedroom window where she stands watching him.

No doubt he knows by now that she has tried to escape the house and failed. Perhaps he's standing where she can see him for a reason. Taunting her? Reminding her of who holds the power? Irene watches, waiting for him to move back towards the house. She longs for the sound of the door being unlocked, and dreads it in equal measure.

As she stands at the back wall of the bedroom, watching Bill, he suddenly clutches at his chest with his hand. For a second, she thinks this is part of the show, until he slumps to his knees. His mouth twists into a grimace while both hands scrabble at his collar, and he falls to the ground.

Irene rushes to the window. Bill is lying on the grass, his hand pulling at the neck of his shirt. He turns his head to look towards the window with his face contorted in pain.

For a moment Irene is frozen. They lock eyes. She sees his fear.

Irene drops the bag from her shoulder and runs from the room. There must be a way out. She tries every door and every window again. She searches for something heavy and all she can find is a mop bucket. She has an idea that a smaller window will be easier to break. Is there any logic to it? Maybe not, but she throws the bucket against the bathroom window, over and over. Not even a scrape. She needs a hammer but a search of the laundry reveals nothing like one. Bill keeps all the tools in the shed.

She rushes from room to room, searching for something that might break a window. The heaviest item she can find is a metal ornament from one of Bill's collections. She's not even sure what it's supposed to be. It's huge. She lifts it with difficulty and carries it to the bathroom, held tightly against her chest. She tries to throw it at the window but it's too heavy and misses the mark, bouncing off the window ledge. A piece breaks away from it and flies into the bath.

Irene hurries back to the bedroom window and looks out. Bill is lying there, facing the window, his knees bent, hand on his chest. His eyes meet hers again and he lifts his hand a fraction. He sees her.

Irene puts her hand to the glass. This is your fault Bill, she thinks. You did this.

A shadow sweeps across the paddock and a spatter of rain comes down. It can't rain. Not while Bill is out there. Panic pushes against Irene's chest. She squeezes her fist tight and tries to breathe.

Breathe in for four …

The spatter turns to drizzle, the drizzle to a sudden pouring down. Bill lies motionless with the rain pummelling his pale cheeks and running down his neck into his collar which he has not been able to tear away from his throat. Irene bangs on the window with her fists as it soaks his chest and the fabric clings to him. A grey lick of hair slides down his face and over one eye.

He looks so small, so beaten.

The rain hurls itself at the bedroom window. A crashing torrent, pelting the glass and pouring down like waves. Irene doesn't know how long she stands there with her hand on the glass.

The rain stops as suddenly as it began. As the clouds crack apart and sunshine pours out, the water slips down the pane in fat runnels like a giant's tears.

Irene puts her eye to a clear spot amid the blurry glass and squints. Bill no longer has his face turned towards her. His head has flopped back. He appears to be staring at the sky, his eye sockets filled with rainwater.

Sing is the one who saves her. Her sweet head comes bobbing over the hill as Irene sits in the living room, staring out at the grey sky and the distant billowing waves of the cove. Irene watches Sing striding up the paddock, sees her stop and look over at the body on the wet grass, sees her run to Bill, drop to the ground and take his hand, her mouth opening and closing. Sees her touch his neck, pull her phone from her pocket and put it to her ear.

When Sing bangs on the door, Irene is waiting for her. 'Sing, I can't get out.'

'It's alright, Mum,' she says, and Irene wonders that there is no surprise in her voice. Irene hears her footsteps treading away towards the garage where the spare key is hidden. She returns and unlocks the door.

'The ambulance is on its way,' she says. 'I don't think there's anything we can do. Do you want to go to him?'

Irene takes a towel from the bathroom and they go out to Bill together. Kneeling beside him, Irene dries his face. Sing stands a few paces away, rubbing her upper arms and listening for the ambulance.

Irene can't bear the sight of him. She puts the towel to her own face and bursts into tears.

Sing is beside her in an instant. 'There, there. Let's go back inside.'

Irene follows her into the house where they wait in the living room, away from the window so Irene can't see Bill's body.

As Sing makes tea in the kitchen, there's a knock on the door. Irene springs from her seat but Sing is first to the door. Irene hears a male voice, then Sing saying, 'We just found him. Irene was asleep. She's in shock.'

Senior Constable Angus Marks meets Irene in the hallway. His eyes are gentle. 'Hello Irene. My presence here is just procedure. Go and sit down. I'll deal with the ambulance. It's on its way.'

Irene nods. She can't find any words and it doesn't seem to matter. Sing leads her into the living room and half closes the blinds so they don't have to see the officer out there with Bill's body. She supplies Irene with a cup of very sweet tea and turns the radio on to an easy-listening station.

'Do you want a couple of painkillers?' she asks. 'Something to make you a bit drowsy might help.'

Irene declines. Says she'll be fine. Angus will be back soon. He'll have questions, Irene is sure of it. Irene went to school with Angus. He was a quiet boy, shy, very smart. A strong sense of justice even then, Irene thinks.

It isn't long before they hear the ambulance arriving, voices, doors slamming and the ambulance driving away. Another knock on the door. Angus wants to speak to Irene alone. Sing says she's going back to her house for half an hour and will come back.

'Angus,' Irene says.

Angus sits on the edge of the sofa. 'Irene. I'm sorry. You know Bill's dead?'

'Yes.'

'I need to ask you some questions. Do you feel up to it?'

'I wasn't asleep.'

'Pardon?'

'Sing said I was asleep. I wasn't. I saw him fall down.'

A brief pause, barely perceptible. 'What time was that?'

'I don't know.' A memory... 'The oven clock was flashing. Three twos. That's why I remembered it. Because it was three twos flashing.' Irene slowly shakes her head. Is she making any sense? She hardly knows what she's saying.

'That's helpful, thanks.' He goes to the kitchen, Irene presumes to check the clock, and comes back.

'He locked me in,' Irene says.

Angus sits back down on the sofa and leans towards Irene. 'Start from the beginning. Tell me everything that happened today.'

His eyes peer into hers. Is he already figuring it out? Angus is still a smart lad. Lad?—he's Irene's age. Irene starts to shiver. Angus asks where the blankets are kept. He comes back with a quilt and lays it around her shoulders. He hands her the cup of sweet tea.

'Take your time,' he says.

Irene is so embarrassed she wants to curl up and cry. 'I was going to leave him. He found the bag I packed while I was out with Helen. When I came home, he went out. I tried to leave—I was going to walk to Helen's. But he'd taken the keys. And my phone. I can't find my laptop either. I couldn't contact anyone.'

'Did you try to break a window?'

'The windows won't break. I tried the bathroom.' She takes a sip of tea.

'I'll be back in a moment,' Angus says.

Of course he has to check her story. Irene understands that. But to have her classmate know this about her. It's past humiliation. She wants to die.

'Why do you think the window wouldn't break?' he asks when he returns. He would have seen the mess in the bathroom—the mop bucket, the broken ornament, chipped wood on the window ledge.

'They're all polycarbonate. Every single one.'

Angus nods. 'I'm sorry, Irene.'

He reaches into his pocket and takes out a handful of keys. 'These were in Bill's pocket. And is this your phone?'

Irene nods.

He sets the phone on the coffee table. 'I'm going around your house to put these back. Is that alright?'

Irene waits, her head in her hands as Angus tries the keys and hangs them back in their respective places.

He returns and says, 'When your daughter-in-law comes back, I'll check outside for your laptop.' He walks to the window and gazes out.

'Angus.'

He turns to look at her.

'They don't need to know, do they? About what Bill did.'

'Irene—'

'There's no point now. He's dead.'

He turns back to the window and puts his hands in his pockets. Irene realises she's at the mercy of this man. He can shatter her family with a few words and Irene will forever be trying to explain something she has no idea how to explain. She has so much unravelling of her own to do and no inkling of where to begin.

'Looks like she's coming up, I can see a car.' Angus turns and strides from the room. He disappears down the hall and Irene hears him banging around. When he returns to the living room he says, 'I've tidied up in the bathroom. I'll check outside for your computer. And Irene, you will need to come down to the station. Tomorrow will be fine. And please don't worry, it'll be alright.'

Irene hears an engine, car doors slamming and voices at the front door. Caleb rushes over, kneels on the floor beside her and wraps his arms around her. 'Oh, Mum,' he says, and she feels her son shake with grief.

'Helen's on her way,' Sing says. 'I'll make some tea.'

Irene falls into a fog. It's a soft place, a cotton-wool kind of place. Her feelings are there but somehow suspended, hanging out of reach like wet washing on a line, stretched out of proportion by their heaviness. She will feel them eventually and it won't be easy.

For now, she leans into small moments. Her laptop is found and returned to the house by Angus. Pizza appears. Helen is surprisingly calm and says she's staying over. Sing keeps making pot after pot of tea. Pete arrives with cheesecake which is such a surprise, they all laugh.

Irene gathers herself into a tight, numb space, with her family circled about her.

PART THREE

IRENE 2024

'I'm not finished yet.'

Irene lies on the bed in Helen and Pete's living room. The sliding door is open and a breeze wafts in. She can smell roses mingled with cow dung. What wonderful smells. Will she miss them in the afterlife?

Helen rushes over. Irene shouldn't have spoken out loud. Helen never rests.

'What did you say, Mum?'

Irene finds it difficult to talk sometimes. Her body has emptied itself of energy. She digs for some, finds a little.

'I'm not finished yet.'

'The doctor said you might sometimes find it difficult to accept what's happening—'

'No.' Irene tries to shake her head. The effort to speak is mammoth. 'I don't mean that. I'm alright with dying.'

Helen sits on the seat next to Irene's bed and takes her hand. 'What then, Mum?' she says gently.

'I mean, I don't feel finished. This isn't the end.'

Helen nods. 'The afterlife, you mean. I hope you're right.'

'Maybe we keep on learning.' Irene hears the rasp of her own breath as she struggles to take it in. 'That'd be something, wouldn't it?

'Have a rest. I'll rustle you up something to eat.'

Irene didn't think she'd like leaving the river. She has lived beside it for eight years. It has been more than a home. It's a song inside her. A burble of a song, interspersed with notes of platypus and children's laughter. A song housed in her soul which she'll take with her into the next life. A river song. Irene is a river full of platypus and laughter. What strange thoughts she is having.

'Did you say something, Mum?'

Helen again. What does she want?

Irene slips back into the river.

Irene wants to go through her box of photos. Helen puts it on the overbed table and lifts the lid. As Helen takes out each photo she hands it to Irene.

'Look Mum, there's Uncle Jed. Oh my goodness, was he a scream or what?... Oh, Nanna. What a sweetie.'

Irene watches her daughter's face light up, her cherub-lipped smile, the beauty of her precious face.

'Mum, here's one of you. How elegant you look.'

Bill and Irene's engagement party. Even through the faded colours, Bill's face stands out as handsome and strong. It's ten years since his death.

Each photo conjures up past years. Irene's history, contained in photographs and memories which will all, eventually, fade out. Irene ends up with piles of photos covering her bed and is having a wonderful time.

As Helen makes tea, a phone rings. 'It's yours, Mum,' she says, and brings it to Irene.

It's Max wishing her a happy day. He does this often. Irene thinks he does it to see if she's still alive. Oh well, that's alright. She doesn't mind why he does it. She enjoys hearing his voice, hearing his news. She even likes hearing about his wife, though he talks more about their rescue dog. And that's okay by Irene too. She loves Max and wouldn't want to change him for anything.

They say 'cheerio' to each other. A friendly goodbye that is not like a goodbye, but a wish for good cheer. At least, that's how Irene thinks of it.

Irene has had enough of the photos. She's getting tired. Helen is busy doing something so Irene starts lifting the piles of photos back into the box. She has done half of them when Helen rushes over and puts the rest in.

Helen takes the container off the overbed table to carry it back to the spare room. Irene straightens her bedclothes and the effort exhausts her. She pats around for her phone but she can't find it. She'll look for it later. She must rest now.

Outside the window, whisks of grass lift and flatten in the wind. Now up, now down. The rhythm drags Irene's eyelids closed and she fancies she hears the grass singing.

Blurry faces, voices, a touch on her hand. Irene grabs for them, tries to keep them with her. Are they recent or a distant memory? Irene can't keep track of them. How many days has she lain here? She hears Andrew laugh, his voice and Helen's mingling. Irene answers them but isn't sure if she has really spoken or if it's a dream. Andrew. Such a lovely man.

Poppy in a red dress. No, that's a memory.

Here's Poppy in jeans and a striped top. She's telling Irene about her friends and swimming at the beach. Irene hugs the stories to herself, tries to hold them in her head, but holes have appeared and everything is seeping out. The more medication, the more holes. Pain or cognition—it's a choice, but not a choice. The pain has become too intense. Her thoughts keep slipping through the holes. Poppy is a pirate, waving a silver sword... 'Aarrr, ahoy there'...

Zoe now... she talks of platypuses, her new home behind the shop, a man she's seeing. Sam. He's a goodun, she says. Where has Irene heard that before? Irene's people are all gooduns. Irene is a goodun.

Is she? Caleb's hand on her forehead, stroking her hair. His eyes so blue. Like the sea on a good day. A goodun. Caleb and Sing. Sing is a song. Sing has kept secrets for Irene.

Oh, terrible loss. All the years.

Caleb wipes tears from her cheeks. Or is it Sing? Life should be a dream.

What next? The river calls and she longs to slip into it. The water laps at her feet. Rises to her ankles. She could wade into it right now if she wanted. It would be easy.

God is there, she knows it. He waits for Irene. His peace fills the river.

Irene's name means *peace.* Her mother chose it. Did she know it was something Irene would seek her whole life? Helen's name means *light.* Oh, beautiful baby with the cherub lips, light to Irene's soul.

Is that the river lapping at Irene's chest? Filling her lungs. Squeezing out the air.

Voices pull Irene from shallow dreams. Here's the clan gathered about. Someone must be having a birthday.

Irene's head clears.

That's right, she's the reason. She's dying and no one wants to miss it. Irene almost giggles at the thought but doesn't, because laughing hurts her body. They want to make sure she doesn't die alone. Kind of them, but everyone dies alone, don't they? No one comes with you.

Irene is lying in the bed by the window, facing the room. There's food and Irene has been offered some, but it won't go down. She's given up eating now.

Sing brings Eleni over to say hello. The child complies, staying for a bare minute before running back to her Lego.

Sing sits on the chair beside Irene. 'How're you feeling?' she asks.

'Like crap.'

'That's good.' No one else gets their humour.

Sing leans in closer and strokes Irene's head. 'Mum? I want you to know. You don't need to worry about Caleb.'

Irene squints at her daughter-in-law.

'He's a good man,' she says.

Irene knows it. She has watched him to make sure.

She looks over at Helen and Pete. Pete grabs the back of the sofa and does a sideways jump right over it, landing himself in the seat next to Helen. Helen rolls her eyes at him and he puts his arm around her.

Dear Helen. She'll be alright. She and Pete have fused themselves together, super-glued. Irene's family is strong and good. When Irene goes, they'll continue to be strong.

Only Bill is missing. Irene sees an image of him and herself in a photograph on a shelf. Their wedding day—Bill in his wedding suit, Irene in a flouncy dress. Bill's father stands beside him. An unyielding man with a steel set to his features whose wife left him many years before and was never forgiven.

Irene has long forgiven Bill.

Suddenly, the notebooks pop into Irene's head. They're still in the camphor wood chest in the flat. They serve no purpose now. What if someone finds them and deciphers the cryptic messages she has hidden in them? Those notes were only ever meant for herself. To help her keep track of things when she thought she was losing her mind. Why on earth did she not destroy them?

Tobias calls to his mother and Sing goes to him. Irene calls Pete over. Her voice is a croak but he hears her and sits by her bed.

'How are you feeling?' he asks.

Irene wishes everyone wouldn't start with that. She doesn't have the strength to answer such a banal question. She opens her mouth but only a wheeze comes out.

'What was that?' Pete frowns and lowers his face towards hers.

'Notebooks,' Irene says. At least, that's what she meant to say, but the words come out slurred because of the drugs.

'Pardon?'

'Destroy—note—books.' Irene's head is pounding. She winces with the pain.

'What do you need, Irene?'

'Get rid—of them.' She lifts her heavy head from the pillow, strains her neck to make him hear her. 'My note—books.'

Pete nods. He smiles and pats her arm. He understands. Pete will do as she's asked and destroy the notebooks. Irene can relax. She lays her head back on the pillow.

She watches her people—Milo and Poppy in deep conversation about global warming or something, Helen and Zoe having a laugh on the sofa. Eleni starts singing a song about a frog and Caleb joins in. Sing hops along the floor, doing some funny thing with her hands. She doesn't look much like a frog in Irene's opinion.

They're a solid lot. Holding each other together like banked up earth. They don't need her anymore. There's an adventure waiting and Irene is acutely curious about it. She gives them one last look and closes her eyes.

The river calls. Must be about time to leave.

Epilogue

'Hello, Mum.'

Helen casts a quick glance around. In a far corner of the cemetery a woman is laying flowers. Nearby, an elderly couple walk around, holding hands as they read the gravestones. No one else is about. Helen turns back to her mother's grave.

'Well. I hope you're having a wild adventure, Mum. You did say you were planning to.'

Helen hovers for a moment, before kneeling on the ground next to the gravestone. She pours the water and old flowers from the jar and replaces them with daffodils from her garden.

'Pete and Poppy send their love. Poppy's enjoying school in the city and has made some nice friends. Did you worry about me this much when I was Poppy's age?'

Helen runs her hand through her hair as every kind of danger flashes into her mind.

The elderly couple pass behind her, heading towards the exit and Helen waits until she sees them turn through the cemetery gate.

'By the way, I saw your friend Andrew the other day. I was passing by the old church building and said hello and we got talking about you. He was very fond of you, did you know that? I'm going back on Sunday to hear him speak. Yes, I thought you'd like that. I can hear you chuckling from here.'

Helen herself starts to laugh, stops and looks around to check no one has heard her. She leans closer to the gravestone.

'He showed me the cemetery and told me a strange story about a flood and a young widow who was washed away, clinging to her husband's tombstone. I don't know why he told me. Maybe there's a lesson in it.

'Oh and by the way, I'm going to apply for the Assistant Principal position. You were right, it's time.'

Helen pulls a weed from a corner of the grave and tosses it away. As she does so, a movement catches her eye. The flower-laying woman has lifted her arms in the air and stands with her face turned up to the sky. It's a strangely beautiful sight and Helen finds herself smiling.

She sighs and returns to tidying the grave. There are so many things she wants to tell her mother.

'I finally went through your filing cabinet. It was mostly out-of-date receipts and stuff, and an old telephone. Some ancient paperwork from the farm too, which I gave to Caleb in case it's useful.

'There was something else though. A few things, actually, rattling around in a box. One was your butterfly scarf, remember that? You wore it a lot when you were having chemo. Your address book was in there too, and a pair of earrings. I don't remember the earrings, but I suppose they're yours. I expect you put them there absent-mindedly when you weren't well. Mystery solved, anyway.'

Helen takes a deep breath and pushes herself to her feet. She brushes the dirt from her knees.

'Well, I'll get going. I just wanted to talk to you for a bit. Not because I think you can hear me, because I know you can't. After all, you're off on that adventure. I'm doing it for me. I want to be brave, Mum, like you. It's never too late to start trying, is it?'

Helen pauses for a moment before squatting back down on the ground.

'One more thing,' she says. 'I love you, Mum.'

And without checking to see if anyone is about, she leans over and plants a kiss on the gravestone.

Right on top of her mother's name—Irene.

Author's Note

For those who are curious about the Tasmanian towns in the story – Crayfish Cove, Durrunby and Rosemere – they are all fictional places.

However, I have loosely based the topography of **Crayfish Cove** on the town where I was raised. Nubeena is a fishing and farming community on the Tasman Peninsula, named for an Aboriginal word meaning 'crayfish', which is how I came up with the name for Crayfish Cove. The cove in the story resembles Parsons Bay – a beautiful spot with sandstone cliffs and a view of the local jetty – where I have pleasant memories of rambling as a child.

If **Durrunby** is a place you'd like to visit, I suggest checking out the historic town of Richmond with its Georgian buildings, quaint shops and galleries, and famous stone bridge (the oldest bridge in Australia).

Rosemere is a place concocted in my imagination but it could resemble many small communities tucked away in the wilds of Tasmania. Perhaps you know of one?

Stanley and **The Nut** are real places and well worth a visit.

All the people and events in the story are fictional. Any resemblance of characters to real persons, living or dead, is entirely coincidental.

Acknowledgements

The other day as I set out to roast a leg of lamb, I absent-mindedly tossed a lump of beef (earmarked for a curry) in the oven. Even as I sliced the boneless piece of baked meat (which didn't look quite right) and even as I chewed it, I didn't realise my mistake. Because in my head, I was flinging my main character into a sticky predicament and planning how to rescue her, while in the real world I was cooking on autopilot. It was only when my husband said, "Are you sure this is lamb?" that I realised what I'd done.

So my first outpouring of gratitude must go to my husband, Doug, who keeps loving the woman who spends too much time staring into space and scribbles notes in the dark when she should be sleeping. Gardener extraordinaire, Doug has again answered my many questions about plants and saved the lavender from blooming in the wrong month. If any other flowers in the story appear in the wrong season, I am to blame.

My heartfelt thanks to all the other people who have helped bring this book into existence:

Lynne from Lloyd-Moss Editing, for again providing invaluable feedback and advice and alerting me to my bad habits (especially around the excessive and overabundant use of far too many words). Thanks to Lynne, the book is a few hundred words shorter than it might have been (which is a good thing).

Mum and Dad for their continual cheers and support. Special thanks to Mum for being my unofficial marketing manager and trekking around town telling everyone she meets about my books.

Jennifer Magno for the wonderful cover art, title pages and butterfly illustration which capture the essence of Irene's story beautifully.

Rose Ising, my eagle-eyed proofreader, who I turn to again and again to find those pesky slip-ups.

My online writing group – Barb, Dienece, Donna, Kel, Steph and Sue – for encouragement, honest feedback, helpful tips, knowledge sharing and plenty of laughs. I have learnt so much in this space.

My friend Christine (aka author Chrissy Garwood) and Ezra, for meeting me in cafés so we can write together, thus providing the perfect excuse to eat all those vanilla slices.

Janet Tiitinen for excellent feedback, friendship and being such an encourager.

Nissy Lukose for her in-depth answers to my medical and nursing questions. Any remaining errors in the book are mine.

And a special thank you to all the people from the "ninch" who have been reading my books. I hope you enjoy the rest of my Crayfish Cove stories.

PS. My husband knew the beef wasn't lamb. He was just too polite to say!

Book club questions / topics for discussion

1. Do you have a favourite character from the story, or one you identify with? Who is it and what do you like about them?

2. What are your thoughts about Irene's decision to leave everything behind and move into a tiny flat by the river? Have you ever had a similar urge? What adventures could you see yourself pursuing?

3. The book raises the heavy issue of coercive control, which is a form of domestic abuse. Did Irene's story influence your understanding of coercive control in any way?

4. Why do you think the abuse remained hidden from everyone, including Irene, for so many years?

5. Irene has battled cancer and undergone chemotherapy and breast surgery. How have these experiences added to her "complicated grief" over the death of her husband.

6. Discuss Irene's notebooks and her cryptic messages. Was there a point in the story where you began to suspect anyone of wrongdoing?

7. Why does Irene decide not to tell her family about what was going on? Do you think she did the right thing? What would you have done in Irene's situation?

8. Discuss Irene and Helen's relationship. How do their personality differences affect their ability to relate to each other?

9. Though Irene lost a good friend earlier in her life (Claire) she later meets and bonds with Maggie. Why do you think they are drawn to each other? What are your thoughts about Maggie?

10. Irene didn't believe death was the end, but rather the beginning of a new adventure. What are your thoughts about this?

About the author

Suzie Peace Pybus lives on a little fruit and vegetable farm in southern Tasmania with her husband and springer spaniel, Pepper.

Her first manuscript won the Omega Writers CALEB Award for unpublished fiction in 2022, which she later recrafted and published as *Paint the Walls Red*. Her debut novel, *When All the Birds Sing,* was a finalist in the 2025 ACFW Carol Awards.

Join her newsletter at: suziepeacepybus.com